CONFESSIONS OF A RAKEHELL

The Rakehells of Mayfair
Book 2

April Moran

Dragonblade Publishing, Inc. is an imprint of Kathryn Le Veque Novels, Inc.
P.O. Box 23
Moreno Valley, CA 92556
ceo@dragonbladepublishing.com

Produced in the United States of America

First Edition November 2025
Trade Paperback Edition

ARE YOU SIGNED UP FOR DRAGONBLADE'S BLOG?

You'll get the latest news and information on exclusive giveaways, exclusive excerpts, coming releases, sales, free books, cover reveals and more.

Check out our complete list of authors, too!

No spam, no junk. That's a promise!

Sign Up Here

www.dragonbladepublishing.com

Dearest Reader;

Thank you for your support of a small press. At Dragonblade Publishing, we strive to bring you the highest quality Historical Romance from some of the best authors in the business. Without your support, there is no 'us', so we sincerely hope you adore these stories and find some new favorite authors along the way.

Happy Reading!

CEO, Dragonblade Publishing

Additional Dragonblade books by Author April Moran

The Rakehells of Mayfair

Redemption of a Rakehell (Book 1)
Confessions of a Rakehell (Book 2)

PROLOGUE

Wylder St. Clair
Earl of Wyldewood, heir to the Duke of Claymore, and a few other soon-to-be worthless titles.

Mayfair, England
The Spring of 1816, Blackthorne Debutante Ball, and the beginning of a
dangerous attraction.

I T WAS AN unfortunate fact that Lady Emily Blackthorne was as clever as she was beautiful. Her antics proved especially problematic for Wylder St. Clair. He could not entirely ignore her as he wished. Being that she was the younger sister of his dearest friend created a hazardous situation, but she persisted in ignoring the peril.

"Lord Wyldewood... did you not hear me calling your name?"

The pressure of a delicate hand lightly gripping Wylder's forearm accompanied the breathless question. Courtesy dictated that he acknowledge the young lady, but his stomach clenched at the thought of staring into her sparkling blue eyes. A man such as himself only possessed so much restraint, and all of his usually evaporated into mist around Emily.

"Lord Wyldewood, isn't it all so very exciting?" Emily asked, her fingers clutching his coat sleeve as though well aware of his desire to bolt. "I've never seen Blackthorne Manor so full of people."

"It's quite the crush," Wylder gruffly agreed as Emily gazed up at him, an expectant look spreading across her features.

"Have you ever seen so many beautiful women in such lovely gowns as those here tonight?" Her tone had a lilting, musical quality, and despite having only recently turned eighteen, Wylder recognized the womanly challenge in her words. He knew very well she was hoping for a compliment, but there was danger even in that.

"Hmmm," he said while casually sipping from his glass of champagne.

"Cad," Emily accused in an affectionately exasperated tone. "I haven't the faintest idea why I thought you might bestow a compliment on my bewitching appearance. I mean, the gown on its own is worthy of some manner of praise. Mother nearly fainted when she received the dressmaker's bill. And then there is, of course, the girl currently wearing said gown." Emily glanced down at the dress and gently lifted the delicate bow gracing the center of the bodice. Her brow furrowed. "Mother believes my complexion is very suited for wearing white, but I think it is the most boring of all colors. I'd much rather wear a gorgeous shade of purple. Or even red, for that matter. Whenever I wear my scarlet riding habit, Father says it sets my eyes to dancing. Which I think is quite silly, don't you? How can eyes possibly dance if they lack legs and feet?" Her sapphire-hued gaze searched his. "Do you think that what Father says is true, Lord Wyldewood? That certain colors can make one's eyes more lively than others?"

"Perhaps." Wylder shifted his feet, his gaze flitting around the ballroom. He hoped to find Lady Emily's brother bearing down on them, but the earl was nowhere to be seen. He breathed a little easier as he allowed himself to take in Emily's appearance fully. "You are easily the most stunning woman in attendance tonight, Lady Emily. All other debutantes pale in comparison, and that is the truth."

Emily's face brightened with a grin. "Now, was that so diffi-cult to say aloud, Lord Wyldewood?" Her fingers loosened their grip on his coat and now rested almost caressingly on his forearm.

"I confess that when I put this gown on tonight, my greatest hope was that you would find it pleasing."

"Emily," he muttered with another sip of his wine. "I would have to be struck blind not to see how beautiful you are, but this is hardly an appropriate conversation. If your brother only knew…"

Leaning closer, Emily swatted his arm with her closed fan. "If only my brother could mind his own business, Lord Wyldewood. What harm is there in the two of us having a cordial conversation? After all, you and Simon have been friends since childhood, and you've known me practically my entire life. We are… what is the word I'm searching for? Oh, yes," she trilled. "We are intimately acquainted with one another."

Wylder nearly gaped at her before snapping his mouth shut and growling between clenched teeth, "You mustn't say such things aloud, especially words like that. Someone could mistake your meaning."

Emily released his arm and pulled a long curl of hair over her shoulder as she stared up at him. Letting the tendril wrap around her index finger, she regarded him with her head tilted slightly. "What meaning could one possibly attach to that? I mean that you know me almost as well as my own brother does. How is that scandalous, pray tell?"

"Do not toy with me, Emily," Wylder grumbled. "You've no idea the trouble you could get us both into."

Emily smiled. "Whatever do you mean, Lord Wyldewood?"

Wylder swallowed the remaining champagne in the glass. The little minx was deliberately trying to provoke him, and it was working. "You know very well that Simon would shoot me through the heart if there were even the slightest hint of inappropriate behavior when it comes to you."

A pout formed on Emily's lusciously plump, pink lips. "Is it inappropriate for one of my brother's best friends to dance with me? Surely he cannot object to that!"

Wylder's mouth twisted into a wry grin. "Do you wish to

visit my or Lucien's graveside if either one of us were to indulge you?"

For the first time, a whisper of uncertainty crossed Emily's features. From the corner where they stood, she perused Blackthorne Manor's elegant ballroom for a long moment. When she finally responded, it was in a tone that was carefully measured. "Do you think Simon would care that much, Wylder? After all, the whole point of this feminine display is to snare a husband. The problem is that there is not a single one of this season's eligible bachelors who is to my liking, with the exception of yourself. And I am of the opinion that you would make an excellent husband."

"You just turned eighteen, Emily. And I'm far too old for you," Wylder murmured, although he knew that particular argument was ridiculous. Barely seven years separated them, and marriage between young women and much older men was a common occurrence among the ton. "Certainly, you realize that. If you do not, you must try harder to recognize that you and I can never be together in the manner you wish. You are my best friend's sister and nothing more."

"Hmmm," she said, deliberately mimicking his earlier indifference. "What if someone like Lord Jenner should offer for me? Would you consider him to be too old? Or should I expect a proposal from a man closer to my age? Let's say, Sir Fieldstone? He recently celebrated his twentieth birthday and is a pleasant enough fellow."

Wylder's hand tightened around the empty glass. "I think you should follow the advice of your parents when it comes to choosing a husband. Even Simon will undoubtedly have some input on the matter." His eyes softened, recognizing that he was upsetting her with his steadfast refusal to acknowledge the attraction that had flared unbidden between them over the last year. But he'd been told Emily was not a woman even to consider pursuing. Simon's warning to keep his distance stung, but Wylder understood the reasoning behind it. Not only was he as depraved and debauched as the two men he considered brothers, he also teetered on the edge of bankruptcy thanks to his father's spendthrift ways—hardly an ideal candidate for marriage, even with the threat of lost fortunes still a closely held secret.

Emily stomped her foot. "This is very unfair."

"Yes. It is," Wylder said. "But this is how things must be. Simon trusts that I will not pursue his sister. I'll not betray him."

"Even at the cost of your own heart's desires?" Emily questioned in a voice full of resentment and hurt.

Wylder took her gloved hand within his, lifting it to his lips and brushing a slight kiss across it. "Yes. Even then."

Emily closed her fingers around his when he tried to release her hand. The spark of determination in her eyes made Wylder nervous, but he did not resist when she tugged him deeper into the alcove's shadows. With a bit more privacy but still within eyesight of any number of people milling about, Emily gripped his arm again.

"I've loved you since the day I met you, Wylder St. Clair. I was five years old, and you tied my braids together on a dare from my brother. When I cried, you kissed my forehead and apologized even while Simon mocked you for it." Her smile was pensive, her eyes searching his. "The times I've caught you staring at me this past year speak volumes. You may be able to hide it from Simon and the rest of the world, but you cannot hide it from me. We both know you do not view me as a child anymore."

"Emily, Simon will never—"

"It's not up to Simon," she interrupted him. "This is about you and me." She took a deep breath and met his gaze, her beautiful features earnest and hopeful. "If you believe I am worth fighting for, you will meet me in the west garden gazebo in half an hour." She squeezed his arm, desperation lacing her tone. "Please... meet me there, Wylder."

"You know that's impossible," Wylder hissed, his jaw clenching tight when he recognized the stubborn glint of rebellion in her eyes. "Don't you *dare* go to that gazebo, Emily."

"Or what?" she asked, one dark eyebrow arching high as she taunted him. "What will you do if I disobey you? What if I go there and, because you refused me, another gentleman takes your place? What shall you do about that?"

"Brattish behavior deserves punishment, minx."

The moment the words flew out, Wylder regretted it. Emily's eyes widened with confusion before dangerous curiosity blazed like a flame in the pretty blue depths. Gritting his teeth, his gaze raked over her form, lingering for a brief moment on the bodice of her gown. The twin globes of creamy flesh swelling above the exquisitely embroidered trim made his mouth water. Damn her for provoking him. "That was an ill-advised thing for me to say aloud, Lady Emily. Forgive me."

"Of course, I don't understand it, but if you meet me in the gazebo, I'm sure you will explain it, Lord Wyldewood."

And with a challenging smirk, Emily smoothed her hands down the front of her dress, dipped a slight curtsey, and floated out of his reach.

EMILY BIT THE inside of her cheek to keep her frustration hidden from the other guests.

"Lord, but he is a stubborn man," she muttered beneath her breath. Weaving through the crush of people, she made her way to a small group of debutantes huddled near the refreshment tables. One girl broke from the group, meeting Emily halfway with a shy smile.

"You spoke with him," Miss Penelope True said in a low voice full of awe, linking her arm with Emily's. "I don't know how you do it, Emily. How you carry on a conversation as though his scowls do not frighten you half to death."

A little shiver passed through Emily, but she laughed at the woman's obvious concern. "I am occasionally made somewhat nervous by his surliness, but Lord Wyldewood would never intentionally harm me." She truly believed that, but still, his tone when speaking of punishments made her pulse race a bit faster. For some unknown reason, a sudden image of her upended over Wylder's lap flashed in her brain. She swallowed hard as another delicious and completely mysterious shiver tickled her insides. What might it feel like? To be so helpless in his grasp? To submit to the darkness of his desires and discover the shadows that existed within herself?

Penelope's gaze drifted to where the three most eligible and carefree bachelors in all of London now stood before one of the many terrace doors. The men were the center of attention, targeted by many marriage-minded mamas despite their rakehell reputations. "Your brother... when he is displeased, it's like a thunderstorm gathering overhead. It's dark and silent and quite threatening." She let out a tiny huff of laughter, her cheeks turning bright pink. "I imagine you've seen that many times over the years and are used to it, but truthfully, I find it terrifying."

Emily hugged the other girl. Penelope True, with her soft, chestnut-brown curls and heavily lashed green eyes, was one of the loveliest girls in this year's crop of debutantes, but she was also painfully shy. Easily overlooked at the social events they'd attended since being presented to the Queen, she tended to melt into the background and seemed content to be there. But Emily formed an instant liking for the girl, appreciating her quick, quiet wit and the elegant manner in which she rose above her family's unfortunate reputation. Lady Camden, Emily's mother, graciously agreed to sponsor the girl, allowing her to have a season, although on a limited budget.

"Simon's not all that bad. Truly, he's not."

Penelope's mossy-green eyes narrowed with doubt, but she tactfully changed the subject. "Lord Wyldewood agreed to your request?"

Emily nodded, her gaze finding Wylder across the crowded

ballroom. "He did. Remember, if anyone asks about my whereabouts, I've gone upstairs to find a new fan as I set mine down somewhere and lost track of it. This will not surprise my mother in the least, and she will not press you on it."

"What if..." Penelope chewed her bottom lip, then blurted out in a worried tone, "What if it is Lord Camden who comes searching for you?"

"He won't," Emily said confidently. "My brother signed Lady Raiborne's dance card for the first waltz, God help him. That woman will monopolize his evening until he manages to slip away for the games of chance my father arranged. Do not worry overmuch about him."

Penelope did not seem convinced, but she smiled when Emily hugged her again. "Thank you, Pen. And please do not fret. I'll be fine."

As the half hour ticked by, Emily found herself so apprehensive that her palms were sweating. Thankfully, her gloves hid the condition from others, and if anyone noticed how tense her smile was, they had the good grace not to mention it aloud. It was with a sigh of relief that she slipped away from the loud, overly crowded ballroom. Hurrying down the path toward the gazebo deep within the west gardens, she frequently checked over her shoulder to ensure no one else followed.

The gazebo was empty, lit by the glow of a full moon and the faint illumination cast by the terrace lanterns, which were some distance away. The steady chirp of crickets blended with the lilting strains of the music drifting out of the ballroom's open doors. Leaning against the railing and staring out into the shadowy depths of the garden, Emily breathed deeply of the night air scented by roses surrounding the base of the gazebo and the blooming jasmine that twined around the structure's frame.

Was she doing the right thing? Forcing Wylder's hand in such a way? Indecision now plagued Emily, now that she was alone with her thoughts. Wylder was not happy about the challenge she'd thrown him, but what else could she do? This was the only option available. Drastic, yes, but she never believed it would be this difficult to make this dark and moody earl see that they were meant to be together. Why he fought so hard against it was a perplexing mystery. All that noble talk of remaining loyal to Simon did not explain it, and Emily was determined to discover the truth.

"I should have known you would choose to act foolhardy." Wylder's voice was low and rough, coming unexpectedly from the gazebo steps behind her.

Emily cried out in surprise, whirling to see the earl standing on the last riser. He had approached the gazebo like a true predator, his footsteps on the gravel silent.

"You-you startled me," she exclaimed with a small laugh, her hand over her heart to steady its galloping beat. "I did not hear your approach…"

"If you are startled now, then you best prepare yourself for what is coming next," Wylder replied with a heavy sigh. Slowly, deliberately, he stalked toward her until Emily stood trapped against the gazebo's railing. "You are the most reckless, foolish, stubborn female I know, Emily Blackthorne." A whisper of reluctant pride laced his words, and Emily basked in it.

"I don't mean to be, Wylder," she said honestly. "But you refuse to acknowledge—"

"I keep my distance to keep you safe, Emily. Why can't you understand that?"

He stood so close she could smell his cologne. It was a masculine scent, reminiscent of sandalwood and cloves. Sharp and yet enveloping. It was perfect for him, and it melted Emily's insides.

"Keep me safe?" she scoffed even as she swallowed past a lump of apprehension. "From whom? My own brother?"

Wylder gripped Emily's elbow, jerking her closer. "From me, Emily. You must be protected from me."

"That's ridiculous… I trust you with my life, Wylder," she asserted with far more conviction than she felt in that moment.

Wylder glared down at her, frustration rolling from him. "If you had any idea what I wished to do to you right now, you would run screaming." His mouth tightened into a thin line. "But I fear action is the only way to truly dissuade you from this course you've set. I must show you so that you completely understand."

Emily's knees nearly buckled with shock. Was Wylder about to kiss her at last? Her limbs turned to jelly, her head falling back as she licked her lips in anticipation. He loomed over her. Dangerous energy, hot and molten, crackled in the air between them.

"Wylder…" she murmured, her voice breaking with the power he held over her. She would do anything for him. Go anywhere. Submit fully to him. If only he would admit that he wanted her with similar desperation.

"Emily," he rasped, the words a husky growl of warning, his gray eyes glittering in the shadows of the gazebo. "Remember, you provoked me to this."

The next instant, Wylder's mouth descended upon her own in a quicksilver moment of heated passion and frustration. His lips were a burning brand of wickedness and brandy and honey-sweet temptation. Emily moaned in surprise, melting against him, but as quickly as the kiss began, it ended, leaving her adrift and wanting something she could not name.

Ignoring her gasp, Wylder abruptly spun her away from the railing, plopped down on one of the gazebo's benches, and hauled her across his lap. With the striking quickness of a tiger, one large hand secured her wrists in the small of her back.

"What on earth are you doing?" Emily let out a muted screech even as her nerve endings abruptly exploded into brilliant, almost painful awareness. "Wylder, what's gotten into you?"

"I warned you, Emily. Warned you of the danger in pushing me to the breaking point. It is a pity your father has failed to enforce any semblance of discipline. I personally believe you would benefit greatly from such attention."

"That-that is none of your business!" Emily choked out. Embarrassment stabbed her with merciless, needle-like pinpoints because while her body definitely agreed with the way it was being handled, her mind was arguing that she should not enjoy being held across Wylder's very firm and muscular lap.

"At this particular moment, you've made it my business, minx. Now, you must endure the consequences of your own stubbornness."

There was a moment when it felt as though all the air surrounding them was suddenly sucked into a deep, black void. Emily's senses grew sharper, almost to the point of agony, her skin stretching tight across her bones, her heart thudding so hard she could hardly hear anything other than its slow, muffled beat.

Then Wylder's palm connected with her bottom, and a surprising burst of sensations left her breathless and frozen with shock.

"That is for defying me." His words were calm and almost detached. He swatted her rear again, the strange ache pronounced despite the layers of silk and muslin separating her bare flesh from his hand. "That is for provoking me into this."

Emily tried wiggling off his lap, but Wylder held firm, his grip loose enough to avoid leaving bruises on her wrists but impossible to break. Beneath her stomach, his thighs clenched with the effort to keep her positioned where he wanted her. The heat from his body seeped through her gown, igniting tiny flames in places she'd never paid much attention to before this moment. Her nipples tingled with excruciating awareness as they rubbed against the half-stays, and she squeezed her legs together against a confusing surge of pleasure.

Another strike, and Emily squealed as desire flamed into astonishing life. She sagged helplessly into him, speechless at the strength of the sensations coursing through her body. *What on earth is happening to me?*

"That's for ignoring the danger in meeting a man like me in a place like this," he explained in a deadly calm manner, apparently unaware of the turmoil that roiled within Emily. "Do you know how easily I could take advantage of you and with no one the wiser for it? One can only hope you learn a lesson here tonight and remember it well."

Emily whimpered then caught herself, swallowing the tiny noise with an inaudible gulp. If Wylder believed her to be weak while enduring what he called punishment, then he would consider the lesson a success. She was made of stronger stuff than the women who usually fluttered about the earl. She would not dissolve into tears or even entertain the idea of female hysterics. Oh, no. She knew what she wanted most in this world, and that was the gentleman currently holding her hostage across his lap. Her chin lifted, a particularly difficult action as her head hung toward the ground in a position that left her slightly dizzy. Somehow, she managed to twist her body enough so that she could look at him over her shoulder. One slim eyebrow rose high with a well-practiced impertinence as Wylder met her gaze. Something crackled between them as they regarded one another in silence—something hot and dangerous and fraught with bewildering possibilities.

Then, a slow, teasing smile lifted the corners of Emily's mouth.

"I'm unsure of the lesson you are attempting to teach me," she challenged in the most provoking manner she could manage. Experimentally, she wiggled again and was rewarded by Wylder's strangled groan. "Should you perhaps try it again?"

"*Wyldewood!* What in the *bloody hell* are you doing to my sister?"

Simon Blackthorne's fury-filled voice fractured the night air, and the ensuing silence was only accentuated by the raspy sounds of Emily's jagged breaths.

Wylder paused, his hand tightening reflexively around her wrists. And for the first time, true panic raced through Emily.

Oh, no. No. No. No. This was going to be very bad.

"What does it look like I'm doing, Simon?" Wylder's tone was as unaffected as if he'd been interrupted while reading the morning papers. There was no hint of shame or even irritation. Just a straightforward answer delivered with no inflection of anger. "I'm in the process of teaching your sister a much-deserved lesson."

"Have you gone absolutely *mad*? Get your hands off her. Let her up right now before I smash your goddamn face in," Simon hissed, and when Emily twisted her head back around, she saw her older brother standing on the steps of the gazebo. His fists were clenched into twin balls, his face darkened with rage.

Wylder slowly released Emily's wrists. With impassive silence, he shoved her upright, then rose from the bench like a giant tiger stretching its body. With subtle determination, he moved until he stood in front of her, effectively shielding her from the earl and his obvious anger.

"Come here, Emily," Simon barked, reaching out a hand toward her and beckoning impatiently.

Wylder slowly shook his head at his friend. "Do not take your anger out on her, Simon. While it's true that her actions led to this, I won't have her blamed for it. Besides, this is a personal matter between Emily and me—one that I hope you can understand and accept."

"The hell it is!" Simon raked a hand through his thick, dark hair, glaring at his friend. "I'd be well within my rights to shoot you on the spot, and no one would blink twice. I've warned you repeatedly to keep your distance from her. To not infect her with your depravity and yet, given the first opportunity to ruin her, you snatch it up with both hands."

"Simon, you don't know what you are saying," Emily said in a whisper while inside she was reeling from Simon's accusations. *He warned Wylder to stay away from me? But why?* "This-this was a simple misunderstanding. And I'm hardly ruined despite what you think happened..."

"You would be far beyond ruin if anyone discovered this incident had occurred. Irrevocably. And if I managed to keep from killing my best friend, you would find yourself married before the week was out. But *that* won't happen."

"Of course, it won't because I would not marry her. You know that, Simon," Wylder interjected. His tone was so cold, so impersonal, that he might have been a stranger discussing something as innocuous as the weather. "This was nothing more than your sister paying a price for brattish behavior. You should be grateful that I am the one meeting her in this gazebo. Anyone else would have taken full advantage of her recklessness."

"Do you really mean that, Wylder? You-you would not marry me if necessary?" Emily asked haltingly. Her lower lip trembled as she gripped his muscled forearm, silently demanding that he look at her.

"No, I would not. I don't care for you in that manner," Wylder answered, his attention remaining centered on Simon, who practically vibrated with rage. "Return to the ball, Emily. Your brother and I must reach an agreement before bloodshed becomes the only solution."

"And I have no say in the matter? Is that it? You decide for me, and I must accept it?" Emily dug her nails into the wool of his coat, trying to hurt him as she was hurting. She wanted to beat his chest with her fists but restrained herself with difficulty. "I won't leave...not when you are both hungry for a fight. I won't let you kill each other over something like this. And I'm not a child to be sent away."

"Your behavior suggests otherwise," Wylder snapped, prying her hand off his arm with a low growl. "Now, will you do as I say, or must your brother drag you away from me?"

Emily stiffened, her heart freezing within the cage of her chest. She could not believe Wylder was speaking to her like this. As if she meant nothing to him... as if he truly regarded her as little more than a distraction to be eliminated. "Why are you doing this?" she bit out in cold, clipped words. "Don't you realize you are breaking my heart? Can you not see that?"

Wylder finally glanced down at her. A spark of sympathy lit the cool gray depths of his eyes before it was banked behind a curtain of careful indifference. "Of course, Emily. I know exactly what I am doing, and the reasons for it matter more than you know. Believe me, this is for the best."

CHAPTER ONE

Wylder

Three years later
Mayfair, England
September 1819

WYLDER WATCHED IN silence as his best friend scrubbed his jaw and blew out a heavy sigh of frustration.

Simon leaned forward in his chair and leveled a glare at Wylder. White's, the premier gentlemen's club in London, was bursting at the seams tonight. The elegant rooms swarmed with other men much like the two of them. Men searching for distractions from the endless round of balls, parties, and musicales of London society.

"It's not the same without him, Wylder, and you know it." Simon's voice vibrated with aggravation. "We're like a statue that's suddenly missing a leg. It still stands, but it's certainly not the same."

Wylder suppressed his own irritation with the subject matter. It was something the two of them had discussed to excess following the Earl of Ashcroft's recent wedding.

"I've never seen someone so in love as Lucien is with Charlotte. He fucking adores her," Wylder said glumly, recognizing the source of Simon's current state. Young, entitled, and selfish was the blueprint for men who grew up being indulged and catered to. To have circumstances spiral out of their control was something no one had anticipated. "It's quite depressing."

"I know. However, this only means we must remain diligent if we are serious about retaining our status. All of the women coming out of the woodwork of late, believing we shall fall in the same manner as Lucien, is astounding. It's become a hazardous activity just attending a simple ball. Even my own sister has stars in her eyes when it comes to seeing me married off. She's convinced she must pair me with one of her simpering, vapid friends."

Wylder studied the brandy in his glass, his gray eyes darkening at the mention of Simon's younger sister. Steeling his jaw, he reminded himself that any hint of interest in Emily Blackthorne must remain buried. He'd done a fair job of it thus far. Over the last three years, he and Emily shared only benign pleasantries in passing. Wylder became so adept at ignoring the girl when others were around that no one had any idea he secretly kept track of her activities and the gentlemen pursuing her.

"Maybe we should—" Wylder began, only to have Simon cut him off.

"Don't even think it, Wylder. There may only be two of us left, but the Rakehells of Mayfair shall not go down in flames. We owe it to ourselves and to Lucien to continue doing the things we thoroughly enjoy." Simon's eyes sparked like blue flames.

"I was only about to suggest a new gambling den I thought we might try. We could go tonight." Wylder shrugged his broad shoulders in an attempt at placation. "They have comfort women there as well. Perhaps a new place, new experiences, will bring us out of the doldrums we find ourselves in since Lucien and Charlotte married."

Wylder knew that Simon's father had threatened to banish his only son to one of their numerous country estates, convinced that such a move would result in a blissful union similar to Lucien and Charlotte's. The threat had definitely rattled Simon, and his anger was understandable, although it differed from Wylder's situation. His frustration with his own father stemmed from the financial ruin their family teetered upon. Indeed, marriage to a woman blessed with a large fortune would be a heaven-sent answer to his own prayers. While he'd been busy rebuilding his personal fortune with Simon's expert guidance, his father, the Duke of Claymore, was rapidly depleting the family's inheritance at an alarming rate.

"That's an excellent idea," Simon replied enthusiastically. Raising his glass, he leaned toward his friend with a conspiratorial grin. "So, are you ready to show our fathers and all of London that the Rakehells cannot be controlled or ruled?"

Loyalty to his friend demanded Wylder's participation, of course. Continuing on the path of a rakehell also kept Emily safely out of his reach. That was a relationship Simon would never allow, considering Wylder's sexual proclivities and sordid reputation. And had he possessed a sister, Wylder knew he would likely feel the same way.

The subject of the event at the Blackthorne Ball never came up in conversation between the two men. As agreed upon that night, the matter was handled to the satisfaction of both men. A short-lived fist fight and the unexpected intervention by Lucien, Earl of Ashcroft and leader of the Mayfair Rakehells, had resolved things rather quickly. Simon would provide financial advice to rebuild the Wyldewood coffers, and Wylder would ignore and suppress any interest he had in Simon's younger sister.

Regardless of how terribly it wrecked him, this was a devil's bargain Wylder would abide by. For Emily's sake. And his own.

Wylder clinked his glass to Simon's, tossing back the drink with a slight grimace of resignation skillfully hidden from his best friend. Pushing aside any lingering thoughts of Emily Blackthorne, he smiled at the man. "I cannot wait. Let us do our worst."

FEW VEHICLES TRAVERSED the dark and narrow streets at this

hour, and those people moving about in the misty shadows consisted of bakery carts and a couple of flower vendors sleepily setting up their wares. The occasional light-skirt trudged by, exhausted by the toils of the previous night and now seeking a doss to sleep a few hours away before starting back up again for the evening.

"Will you be traveling to your personal residence, milord?" the coachman asked from his perch as the sleepy-eyed groom riding at the back of the vehicle opened the door for Wylder.

Wylder frowned at the thought. Making the trip to his town-home on Davis Street meant additional time spent on the rough, cobblestone streets of London. Based on his current location outside of The Grinning Cockrel, it was far more convenient to go instead to his family's manor near Hyde Park. However, just the thought of seeing his parents made his stomach tighten with dread. He wasn't sure he was prepared to face the two of them once they discovered his impromptu visit. In particular, the duke would annoy him with inquiries relating to the search for a wealthy bride worthy of replenishing the ducal coffers.

"Yes, if you please, Robert." Wylder made his decision then slumped against the plush squabs of the coach seat, rubbing his eyes as his lungs adjusted to the somewhat fresher air of London. A fallacy when one compared it to the smoky, alcohol-infused interior of the gambling den he had just departed.

"Very good, milord. St. Clair Manor, it is."

For the next ten minutes, Wylder dozed as the coach wound its way along the roads now dimly lit by the glow of a rising sun. The streets of London would come alive in a different manner over the next few hours, a different sort of energy holding sway during the daylight hours when compared to the debauchery of the night. It was relatively quiet until a commotion outside the coach—a noise somewhere between the sharpness of a cry and the strident exclamation of outrage—disturbed Wylder enough to furrow his brow.

"Let go this instance, sir! Oh! You cretin! How dare you…!"

The feminine voice sounded close by but muffled. It was likely coming from one of the narrow alleys that formed a spider-web-like network off the main thoroughfare.

Wylder bolted upright, all his senses immediately alert. He rapped the roof of the coach, which immediately halted the clip-clop of the matched bays.

"Milord?" Robert called down from his perch. "Is there something amiss?"

Swinging the door open, Wylder leaped down from the coach and stumbled on the uneven cobblestones. "Wait here, Robert." Staring in the direction they'd just come from, he saw a flash of a dark-blue pelisse in the darkened entrance of an alleyway. Another feminine squeal of anger rang out, and Wylder clenched his fists as a feeling of dread washed over him.

It cannot be… it cannot. What the hell is she doing this far from home? This early in the morning?

Wylder sprinted toward the lyrical voice, reaching the alley just in time to witness Lady Emily Blackthorne furiously punching the arm of a scrawny, older boy with a ragged mop of dirty blond hair. The street urchin couldn't be more than thirteen years of age, and he currently had a grip on Emily's reticule, his grubby fingers clutching the silk cord with a desperation born of necessity. Her bonnet was askew, her shoes scuffed, and the blue pelisse was unbuttoned, revealing the thin material of an icy-blue ballgown.

"You think that because I am a woman, you have a right to accost my person? To steal my reticule?" Emily accused him breathlessly, ripping the item away from the boy's hand. She let out a victorious cry and proceeded to strike him repeatedly with the small, intricately beaded bag while he tried shielding his head.

"Lud, miss! Stop hittin' me! It 'urts, it does!"

"Of course it hurts, you imbecile! And it will hurt a lot worse when the bobbies throw you into Newgate for thievery!" Emily threatened, stopping for a moment only to land one more blow to the boy's midsection. "Say that you are sorry and that you will never do this again, and I'll consider letting you go…"

"Emily!" Wylder's voice rang out like a pistol shot in the small, dank space.

Emily whirled around, her blue eyes wide with surprise. They widened more as Wylder stalked toward her, and she stumbled back a few steps when he finally reached the pair.

"Lord Wyldewood… what are you doing here?" Emily's words trailed off as Wylder clamped a hand around the back of the boy's neck and practically lifted him off his feet.

"I'm sorry, guvnor! Sorry!" the boy screeched, his legs flailing as he tried escaping Wylder's ironlike grip. "I wasn't gonna harm her! I swear I wasn't!"

"Silence," Wylder instructed the lad, his tone deadly calm.

"Lord Wyldewood… stop!" Emily cried, grabbing Wylder's arm. "You're hurting him and—"

"Step aside, Emily," he snarled, giving the boy a rough shake. "I will handle this matter, and once I'm done with him, I shall turn my attention to you. Rest assured, I expect answers that you will readily provide."

CHAPTER TWO

Emily

*T*HIS CANNOT BE *happening.*

How was it that Lord Wylder St. Clair, Earl of Wyldewood, was standing in the alley alongside her, his large hand holding aloft a malnourished, erstwhile pickpocket? And all the while glaring at her as though he wanted to enact some manner of punishment upon her person.

"Please." Emily tightened her grip on Wylder's arm, her tone turning soft and pleading. "Please don't hurt him. It was a momentary lapse of judgment on his part… he meant no harm."

"He was accosting you." Wylder scowled, staring at Emily as though she'd gone mad.

"It probably appeared that way, I agree," Emily explained. "But truly, this is simply a misunderstanding. You see, I retained this young man's services as an escort of sorts. Jack mistakenly believed I would pay him in advance to see me safely returned to Blackthorne rather than when the task was complete."

The boy gaped at Emily, then bobbed his head in agreement. "That's the truth, guvnor. I wouldn't 'arm the lady, honest, I wouldn't!"

Wylder's brow rose in disbelief, but he slowly lowered Jack until the lad's feet were once again on the ground. "I suppose it was a mistake that your fingers were clutching the cord of her reticule? It appeared to me that you were attempting to rip it from her grasp and run like hell in the opposite direction."

Jack's face reddened. Wisely, he remained silent in light of that accusation, but his gaze flitted to Emily, seeking further assistance in escaping this unforeseen predicament.

Emily swallowed hard before plowing onward, her voice cheerfully optimistic. "I have also offered Jack a position in our stables, should he care to accept it. There is always a need for able-bodied lads who can handle various tasks."

Wylder scrubbed a hand over his jaw while keeping the other latched onto Jack's neck. "I shall momentarily ignore the burning question as to why you are traipsing about the streets of London at this ungodly hour and focus instead on this fantastical story. In need of an escort home from God knows where, you somehow enlisted this young ruffian's help. Expecting payment in advance, and with a job offer hanging in the balance, he decides to steal your reticule and leave you alone and helpless in this dirty, stinking alley." His silver gaze pinned Emily in place, the strength of it enough to send a frightened tingle coursing through her veins. "Is my summary correct?"

Emily crossed her arms, lifting her chin. "I see little reason why I must explain myself to you, Lord Wyldewood."

"As a courtesy to your brother and your parents, I will handle this matter in a way I deem appropriate." Wylder ignored her tiny blaze of defiance, his gaze flickering to a spot behind Emily. Only then did she notice his coachman waiting expectantly at the entrance to the alley. "Robert, please escort Lady Emily to my coach and ensure she stays in it. I shall be along once this matter is taken care of."

"Wot about my payment?" Jack protested, squirming anew. "The lady still owes me…"

"Payment?" Wylder scoffed. "You were robbing her, and you still believe you are owed something?"

"Well, he did partially complete the task, Lord Wyldewood," Emily offered. "I think it's only fair that I—"

"Robert…" The earl jerked his chin in Emily's direction, effectively cutting her off. "If you please…"

"Come along, milady. His Lordship has the matter well in hand, he does." The coachman stepped aside, allowing Emily to brush past him with a little huff of exasperation. With one last look at the blond-haired lad still caught in Wylder's grip, she reluctantly exited the alley, her mind reeling with all the varied explanations she must give to the one man who seemed capable of looking straight through her.

A groomsman stood beside the horses, his hand clutching the bridle as Robert lowered down the steps and helped Emily up into the coach. For the next few moments, she sat quietly, gloved hands nervously twisting her reticule as she waited for Wylder to appear. Of course, being alone in the earl's coach was just as scandalous as traveling the streets of London without a suitable escort.

If her parents found out what she'd done in the aid of a dear friend, they'd likely banish her to the country for an extended period. If her brother caught news of it, he would no doubt stand beside their parents and enforce their decision. And if Simon discovered she'd spent an early morning alone with the Earl of Wyldewood, he would certainly challenge his best friend to a duel.

Emily sighed heavily, removing her bonnet. The words she'd shared with Wylder in the alley were more than the past three years combined. The man avoided her as though she carried the plague, and with her heart hurt and bruised from that night in the gardens, she was also guilty of erecting an icy wall between them. Leaning back against the seat, she stared at the flickering interior lamps and wondered if she should douse them since daybreak was fast approaching.

"Allow me a moment, Robert, to determine our destination."

Wylder's rough voice startled Emily. When he jerked open the door and launched himself into the coach, she shrank back. Then, with a grim smile of determination, she collected herself, scooting farther away before positioning herself on the edge of the seat with her spine rigid and straight. One should never show fear in the presence of a man like Wylder St. Clair.

Wylder reclined against the corner of the coach, his elbow propped against the back of the seat, his thumb rubbing his bottom lip as he considered her for a long moment. Emily said nothing, but her heart was pounding in her chest as the earl's liquid silver gaze traveled over her from the top of her bare head to her now scuffed slippers.

"Where were you coming from, Emily?"

The quiet savageness in his tone caught her off guard. The way he was looking at her was almost accusatory. A flicker of fear stirred deep down in her belly, but she staunchly ignored it.

"I'd rather not say," she replied softly.

The air inside the coach changed instantly. It was hot now. Stifling. Pressing down on her until she was short of breath. That frisson of fear now unfurled and crept up her spine, leaching out all her stubbornness in tiny drips of perspiration that collected in the hollow between her breasts.

"You will tell me. The truth, goddamnit," Wylder snarled. *"Now."*

"You don't understand… I'm sworn to secrecy."

In an instant, Wylder's hands were on her shoulders, and he was yanking her up against his body. Giving her a little shake, he hissed, "Is it a man, Emily? Is that it?" Jealousy rolled off him, leaving his voice harsh and cold.

Emily stared at him, denial on the tip of her tongue in light of his bewildering fury. But when she remembered their last private conversation… and how he rejected her avowal of love… her lips tightened with renewed pain. "You once said you had no feelings for me, so why would you care if I am having an affair?"

Wylder's jaw clenched with such force, Emily wondered if it might crack apart into pieces. Digging his fingers into her shoulders, he appeared torn by indecision. "I'll have the truth out of you or so help me…"

"You are as full of empty threats now as you were three years ago," she taunted, her bravado fueled by irrational recklessness. Was it wise to remind him of that night when he'd hauled her across his lap and swatted her behind until she was dizzy with confused lust?

"And you are the same brat you were then. Perhaps more so. What were you doing out this early in the morning, little minx? I won't ask again for an explanation."

As the frustration simmering beneath his tense exterior became more apparent, Emily wondered if it would be wiser to reevaluate her stubborn refusal and give him what he wanted.

"I was not with a man, Wylder. I was helping a friend in dire need of my assistance." Biting her bottom lip, Emily carefully considered her confession. "I cannot say more as it would be a betrayal of her confidence. Suffice it to say that I was left with no method of transportation and decided it was best to hire a hack rather than try walking home."

Wylder noticeably relaxed, his fingers loosening their bite on her flesh. In the dim shadows of the coach, their breath mingled as intimately as if they shared a kiss. Emily's stomach tightened again, her skin tingling as his gaze settled on her lips.

"Does your friend require additional assistance? Is there anything I could perhaps do on her behalf?" Wylder asked softly. His hands moved from her shoulders to her upper arms, his fingers kneading with gentle persuasion.

"Nothing can be done in her situation at the moment." The words came out in a breathy exhale, and Emily silently cursed her weakness. Dear lord, she'd forgotten how easily this man's touch could turn her insides into perfect mush.

"Then that leaves me with the very simple question of what is to be done with you." His voice was a dangerous rasp of frustration, anger, and something else unrecognizable. Raising a hand, he rapped the roof with his knuckles and called out, "Robert? We're taking the lady home. Blackthorne Manor."

Emily swallowed. "I'm afraid that's impossible, my lord."

He shot her a dark look. "Why is that, precisely?"

"Well, do you think it prudent that I arrive there in your coach? I had hoped to return with no one being the wiser for my absence."

Wylder's fingers tightened again on her upper arm. "Are you saying no one knows your whereabouts?"

Emily hesitantly offered, "My mother is aware I attended the Linden ball last night. My maid accompanied me in her absence, and I was with friends."

"You are not making any sense, Emily."

Of course, she wasn't making sense. Explaining how she'd risked her own reputation while aiding her dearest friend earlier that evening was not something easily done without spilling the entire tale. Panic rose in her chest as the coach began moving in accordance with the earl's previous instruction.

"Please, Wylder. We must be reasonable about this. Surely you understand that you cannot take me home in your coach."

Releasing her, Wylder sank back against the seat, a frown creasing his brow. "Perhaps you are correct about that. But you've gone mad if you think I'll allow you to continue without a proper escort. My services are certainly preferable to those of a street urchin."

"I told you that was a simple misunderstanding. I'm sure Jack would have behaved properly if he'd only been given the chance."

A smile twitched the corners of Wylder's mouth upward. "Yes, he was the very picture of respectability with one hand clutching your reticule while you cursed him for thievery."

Emily flushed at the truth of his statement but doggedly continued as if she did not recognize the incongruity of it. "Speaking of young Jack, I did mean to obtain a position for him in our stables. He seemed quite interested in the opportunity, and I believe it was earnest on his part."

"I instructed the young man to report to my townhome later this week. Mr. George is looking for a stable boy as the last one was elevated to the position of a groom at St. Clair Manor." Wylder drummed a restless pattern on his thigh, his fingers moving rhythmically as Emily sighed with relief.

"Oh, that's very generous of you. I'm sure he will be content in your employ, but if his position does not work out, please consider sending him to our estate. It's the least I can do for the lad."

"Hmmm." His response was a noncommittal rumble of a sound. The next moment, he leaned over, lifted the coach's window shade, and stuck his head out of the opening. "Change of plans, Robert. Carry on to Davis Street, if you please. And make haste; the sun is rising as we speak."

"Aye, milord." A crack of the whip accompanied Robert's response. The coach jerked forward as the horses responded by breaking into a trot, their hooves creating a clatter on the cobblestone.

"You are taking me to your personal residence, my lord?" Emily sputtered. "You cannot possibly expect me to agree with this. If it is a scandal you wish to avoid, this is the worst possible method."

"A scandal is precisely what I intend to avoid. I will conceal you there until you can safely return home."

"This is hardly a prudent plan. Far better if you let me off just a few streets over from Blackthorne, and I walk home from there. Slipping in through the gardens will be easy enough, and I can use the servant's entrance to make my way to my bedroom. My parents are notoriously late risers, so they will never know that I arrived home this morning later rather than earlier."

Wylder shook his head. "I am astonished by the depth of your naivete." He leaned back against the seat and closed his eyes. "You sincerely believe you will succeed with this preposterous plan."

Emily bristled. "I'm not naive, nor am I innocent." Her gaze drifted over his form as he folded his arms over an impossibly broad chest. "Do you think I do not know what *you* are about this early in the morning, my lord? I have a fair idea of how you spent your evening."

"Do you now?" Wylder did not even bother to open his eyes. "Enlighten me, minx. This, I must hear."

Emily scowled at his lack of interest in her accusation. "You reek of whisky and stale cigar smoke. The aroma of a house of ill repute clings to your clothing, which is beyond rumpled." She sniffed the air and snapped, "Even worse than all that? There is the unmistakable stench of cheap perfume on your person, which can only mean one thing."

"And what is that?"

"You have been consorting with unfortunates," Emily hissed, swatting him with her bonnet and immediately regretting that decision when one of the pretty flower sprigs came loose from the brim.

"That's certainly one way to state it. Although I don't think the women considered themselves unfortunate after an evening spent in my company," Wylder drawled, his eyes still shut. "Indeed, a few nearly came to blows for the honor of warming my bed."

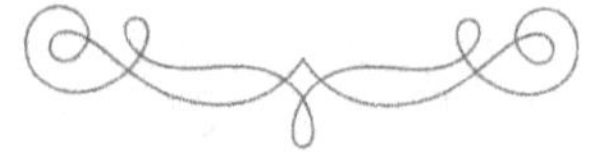

CHAPTER THREE
Wylder

WYLDER CLENCHED HIS teeth to keep the grin from spreading across his face at Emily's sharp inhale of outrage.

"You-you admit it, then," Emily stuttered.

"Without hesitation."

"Oh! You are such a cad. I don't know what I ever thought was attractive about you, Lord Wyldewood." Emily pushed herself farther into the corner of the coach with a huff of irritation. "You are uncouth. Irresponsible. Completely lacking in morals. Why my brother insists on a friendship with you is unfathomable to me."

"Fortunately, I have not sought your permission or approval on how I conduct my affairs, Lady Emily," Wylder stated calmly, daring a peek to see her cross her arms over her chest. "Or my friendships."

"Well, perhaps you should. Perhaps you would benefit from the counsel of someone other than my brother. Who, I might add, conducts himself in the same manner as you. Always flitting from one club to the next. From woman to woman. Never a thought or care for the future and the duties entailed by your title. Your family's fortunes are in a state of flux, and you... you act as though you haven't a care in the world."

Wylder's eyes snapped open, and he pinned her with a heated glare. "What would you know of the subject?"

Emily frowned at the directness of his question. "Everyone knows His Grace has squandered most of the estate's holdings. At some point, you must marry… and marry well… to salvage whatever remains of the Claymore and Wyldewood title along with all the lesser ones."

"You think my marrying an heiress will solve the problem?"

"That seems to be a logical solution." Emily shrugged, slumping against the seat cushion as though defeated by the thought of Wylder marrying another woman. "You would not be the first titled gentleman forced to such drastic measures."

Irrational anger filled Wylder. That his father's wastefulness was a topic of idle gossip among the ton was hardly surprising. But the fact that young ladies such as Emily were also aware of the matter was inexcusable. He resolved in that moment to have a very serious conversation with the duke. There must be a solution other than marriage to a woman he did not want.

"I've no intention of marrying anyone, Emily," he finally said in a harsh voice. There was only one woman he wanted, and she was far beyond his reach.

"You've made that abundantly clear, my lord," Emily slowly replied, her bright blue gaze now shuttered from his perusal. She almost seemed to shrink into herself at the remembrance of his cruel words years before.

"But if it were possible, you would be my only consideration for the role as my wife," Wylder admitted in a low voice. "Oh, you would certainly drive me mad. Vex me at every turn with your reckless, impulsive nature. And it goes without saying that your brother would quickly make you a young widow, but Emily, if I had the choice when it comes to marriage, it would be with you." Reaching out, he snagged her wrist as she stared at him in shock. "However, that is just as impossible now to make a reality as it was before."

Sorrow flickered in the indigo depths of her eyes at his unexpected confession, and all intention to maintain the distance between them melted. He could not bear seeing this girl in pain. The need to comfort her swamped him... especially since he was the cause of her distress.

"Come here, minx."

She did not resist as he pulled her to him, and without meaning for it to happen, she ended up sprawled over him. Widening his legs, she settled naturally between his thighs, her pelvis pushing against his own. Swallowing hard, Wylder raised a hand and cupped her jaw. God above, she was so damned soft. So sweet. And watching him with absolute trust shimmering in every feature of her face.

"I still do not understand why you believe that, but if you are firm in your convictions, there is nothing to be done. But if what you say is true—that you want me even if we can never be together—will you at least grant me a simple request? Will you kiss me as though I belonged to you and only you?" Emily's words were a soft whisper on his heated skin. "One day, when my future husband's touch turns my blood to ice, I'll have this memory to warm me."

The realization that Emily would one day have a husband, a man with all rights and permission to do whatever he wished with her, ignited a fire inside Wylder. How could he ignore her plea? How could he possibly exist another second without knowing what her lips felt like on his own? Simon would kill him if he ever found out, but even that was hardly a deterrent in this moment.

Ripping his leather gloves off, he curled one hand around the nape of her neck, his fingers tangled in the curls of her dark hair as he pulled her down toward him. "The things I would do to you, Emily, would shock you." His growl was feral, laced with jealousy and possession. He liked the way her eyes widened at the ferocity of his statement. Liked the glint of unease in her beautiful blue eyes that melted into awareness. "And if I acted upon them, there would be no doubt in your mind that you mean everything to a degenerate like me."

"Then shock me, Wylder. Prove to me that these are not empty words used to ease the sting of your rejection." Emily's full, tulip-pink lips parted, and Wylder's fingers tightened on her skin, his free hand skimming over her hip. She moaned low in her throat and shifted her body closer. His cock rose immediately at the contact, hard as iron and ready for her, hot blood racing through his veins as she unconsciously rocked against him in tandem with the sway of the coach.

"Emily…" he warned, but she cut him off with her mouth against his. A soft, innocent brush that made Wylder forget the danger and desire the impossible. She did it again when he didn't push her away, and with a grunt of frustration, he relented to her silent plea.

He swore silently under his breath. "I cannot resist you, and you damn well know it. Damn you, Emily. Damn us both." Then he took control before the reality of his actions had a chance to take over and bring everything to a halt.

This kiss was neither soft nor sweet. It was hard and desperate and wild with longing. The kiss they'd shared at the Blackthorne ball three years before was nothing but a fleeting caress compared to this devouring. Wylder held nothing back, his tongue lashing at hers, demanding that Emily respond.

She obeyed with a whimper, melting into him as though she'd waited for this for an eternity. Her fingers clutched the material of his waistcoat, holding on to him as he kissed her with such ferocity it felt as though their souls entwined. For a long moment, Wylder explored her mouth, tasting and teasing until her hips restlessly shifted again and again and the friction of her body left him mindless with pleasure and irrationally ready to risk his life for more.

Tearing his mouth from hers, Wylder blazed a trail of hot kisses down her throat, the hand at her hip used to shift her higher until he could taste the creamy skin swelling above the bodice of her dress. Emily's breath caught, a strangled moan of lust escaping as he nipped and licked the softness of her flesh, and her hands came up to clasp his head, holding him to her, her fingers tangled in his dark hair. Her nipples were stiff as he moved his lips back and forth over the gown's material, and another gasp of shocked delight echoed in the stillness of the coach.

"Oh, my God, Wylder. Do that again… please…"

"That's what I want to hear, little minx," Wylder growled. "Beg me not to stop. Tell me you want more. If you beg prettily enough, I'll give you what you want and fuck you with my fingers."

"More." Emily let out a tiny whimper at his filthy demand, but she obeyed as he knew she would. "More… and don't stop. Please, don't stop."

Wylder sat up, reversing their positions so that Emily lay against the cushion. Looming over her, he drank in the sight of her flushed from his kisses and desperate for his touch.

"I'm going to touch you now, Emily," he said in between scalding kisses to her mouth and along her jawline. His lips ghosted the delicate shell of her ear before catching the lobe between his teeth and giving it a sharp nip. "If you do not stop me, I will slide my hand up under your skirt and give you a memory you shall never forget."

"Yes… I want that, Wylder. Please," she said in a broken whisper. Clutching the lapels of his suit coat, she kissed him with beseeching, innocent enthusiasm. "I want—"

He cut off her words with a kiss so scorching he wondered if the two of them might not erupt into flames. And as she settled into the kiss, he swept a hand under the hem of her dress, pushing the material higher and higher until the tops of her stockings were exposed. Her thighs gleamed like satin in the dim shadows, leaving Wylder's mouth dry with lust. God help him, but if he had her laid out anywhere other than his coach, he would have immediately buried his face into the sweet juncture of her legs and feasted upon her as though she were his last meal on earth.

Instead, he settled for tracing the pink ribbons at the top of her stockings, the roughness of his fingers so different from the silk of her skin. She stilled at once, holding her breath as his hand drifted higher.

"Breathe, minx," he murmured in amusement. "I'll not have you fainting on me. Not yet anyway."

She laughed, a shaky sound that was accompanied by her body trembling almost uncontrollably. "Why would I faint?"

Wylder swallowed his own chuckle and shifted his body so that he could see her face as he petted and stroked her upper thighs. He pushed the dress higher, along with the edge of her chemise, and groaned when he caught sight of her quim through the slit of her underdrawers. "*Christ above.* If you don't faint, I just might. I've never seen anything as pretty as you are here, Emily. So pink and wet. Glistening with need for me to touch you… and that's what you want, isn't it, Emily? For me to touch you?" He ignored the warning bells ringing in his own head… that this was dangerous. Addictive. A mistake.

"Yes… God, yes."

He swept his fingers into her flesh, carefully parting the soft, dark curls until the tiny bud of her sex was exposed. Rubbing the pad of his index finger over it, he delighted in the involuntary buck of her hips. "Be still for me, Emily. And quiet, too. Otherwise, my coachmen will know that I'm pleasuring you right now."

Emily choked on a breath and brought her hand to her own mouth, biting down on her knuckles to contain a wild sob of pleasure. Wylder knew the insinuation that others might be aware of what he was doing scandalized her, but she did not stop him.

"Do you think you can be quiet for me, little minx? Or must I ensure your silence?" His fingers dipped in a shallow exploration of her tight channel, gathering up the slick dew there before returning to her clitoris. Emily trembled almost violently, her legs falling open to grant him easier access.

"Mmmm," she panted. "I don't know… it feels so good… as

though I might come apart in a million pieces..." A small cry escaped her when his finger moved too deep, her inner walls gripping his finger tight at the intrusion. "Oh! Oh, Wylder..."

"Ahh, that's what I thought." In a flash, the palm of his hand clamped over her mouth, cutting off any further sound she might have made. His index finger remained embedded inside her while his thumb stroked the nub of flesh with determined intensity. She was so wet, so ready, that Wylder knew it would not take long for her orgasm to overtake her.

His assessment was correct. Emily stiffened, her legs rigid for a long second as a low, muffled scream filled the coach. Then she shuddered, every part of her quaking with relief and satisfaction as the climax washed over her in what must have felt like endless waves.

And Wylder watched her come undone on his fingers with intense pleasure. Her release was warm and silky and so damn intoxicating that he threw all caution to the wind and bent his head so he could taste what he had done to her. Keeping his hand anchored over her mouth, he licked her quim, reveling in the creamy sweetness, swirling his tongue around and around her pulsing clit and sucking it until she was sobbing in helpless gasps and coming again.

Finally, he sat back and removed his hand from her mouth. Gently pushing her skirts back into place, he left her lying there while she caught her breath. Bloody hell, she looked like a fallen angel sprawled on the coach seat, her skin flushed pink, chest heaving for air, and her nipples hard, stiff peaks beneath the gown's thin material.

Next time, I'll feast on her nipples like the sweet little berries they are. And I'll make her come with one hand wrapped around that pretty, slender neck and my cock buried deep inside her.

No. No. No. There could never be a *next* time. What happened just now could *never* occur again in any shape or form of seduction.

His cock throbbed with angry indignation, hating that idea.

Without a word, he helped Emily sit up, appreciating how adorably rumpled and drowsy she appeared in the orgasmic aftermath. Wishing like hell they were in his bed, and he could hold her until she fell asleep while cuddled in his arms.

"Wylder?" Her voice was soft and unsure as he remained silent, her eyes searching his for any sign of cruelty or regret.

Wylder impulsively kissed her, almost roughly, but with enough tenderness that she relaxed immediately. "Shhh. Don't say anything. We've arrived at my townhome, and my men await instruction. They are very discreet, so there is nothing to concern yourself about. Just stay here, and I will decide how best to get you inside without anyone seeing you."

"We're here?" she squeaked in alarm, her cheeks flaming bright red. "At your townhome?"

"Yes, little minx." He found her shocked embarrassment to be an intoxicating element. In fact, everything about Emily Blackthorne was a delightful obsession. If she were truly his, he would strive always to turn her cheeks pink. "We arrived five minutes ago, but there was no way in hell I was going to stop pleasuring you. Now, you will do as I say. Sit here quietly, and I shall return in a moment." With another quick kiss to Emily's pouting mouth, Wylder flung open the door and leapt from the coach.

CHAPTER FOUR

Emily

EMILY PICKED UP her hat, turning the little confection over in her hands as she gathered her wits about her.

Her limbs did not seem capable of moving. Boneless satisfaction weakened her, and with her brain soft as mush, she struggled to remind herself that the longer she sat waiting for the earl to return, the more dangerous her situation became.

What had he done to her? What magic did he possess that he could so easily cause her to see stars? To give up control? The pleasure he'd given her was mind-boggling. Was it always that way between a man and a woman? Had he experienced the same soul-melting sensations? A nagging voice inside her whispered that Wylder had not found the same completion she experienced. A blush stained her cheeks as she recalled the hardness of his body and the way his own breath caught on itself when his lower half pressed against her own. She touched her lips with trembling fingers, wondering that she could taste her own musky sweetness when it transferred from his mouth to hers. Would he enjoy the same ministrations as he'd shown her? Would her mouth on his body send him into similar spasms of intense pleasure?

There was more to this perplexing connection between them. Lord help her, but Emily wanted to uncover all the mysterious emotions Wylder's touch set off inside her. Everything about the unexpected encounter intrigued her. The way he touched her… somehow rough and tender at the same time… gave her chill bumps. And when he kissed her… it was as though the heavens opened up and impaled her with dozens of lightning bolts.

She sighed heavily and retrieved her reticule from the floor where it had landed earlier. What plans did Wylder have for her now? Surely, they could not return to the stilted, formal interaction of the past three years.

Emily's jaw tightened. That was not acceptable. If anything, this interlude only proved what she'd known all along—they should be together. And despite his insistence to the contrary, his stubbornness in pushing her away and denying his feelings, Wylder must realize it as well.

But how to make her dream a reality? How could she convince the man that he was hers and she was his? What must be done to open his eyes? Ignoring her brother's objections and Wylder's own refusal to see his worth as a suitable husband seemed insurmountable obstructions, but there must be a way.

Nibbling a fingernail, Emily considered the options open to her.

She could plan her own ruination. And if it were public enough, her brother would have little recourse but to devise a marriage contract suitable for all parties involved. It would all be a terrible scandal, of course, but the end result justified the means.

Emily sagged against the coach seat. The idea of trapping Wylder in marriage left a sour taste in her mouth the longer she considered it. Could she, in good conscience, begin a marriage fueled by such an ignoble basis? In truth, she could not.

What if you make him desperate enough that he has no choice?

Jealousy? Could this be the simple answer to a complicated problem? Emily had stood steadfast in declining to accept any one of the numerous marriage proposals offered in the years following her first Season. Her parents did not understand but indulgently allowed her to do as she wished. Mother once remarked that even if she did not marry for love, it was worth holding out for at least affection. And Papa, well, he spoiled her so outrageously that Emily had no fear he would force her to accept a proposal she did not want.

Was jealousy her only recourse? Was Wylder capable of such emotion when it came to her?

Silly question. Of course, I can make him jealous. Remember how strongly he reacted when he believed I might meet another gentleman in the Blackthorne gardens that night? And just now... when I mentioned the possibility of a future husband, he reacted in a manner that indicated he did not like that idea at all. If he thinks I might become another man's wife... even if I must suffer with a faux engagement as part of my plan... he might realize how much he wants me and how difficult it will be if he lets me slip through his fingers. He could find himself so overcome that he demands to marry me, and to the devil with my brother and his objections. Perhaps this... this is the way...

A discreet knock on the coach door shook Emily from her plans. Clutching both her hat and reticule, she slid across the seat until she hovered beside the window where the shade was still pulled down tight.

"Yes?" she answered in a low voice, intensely aware of the pleasurable ache in her private areas. Wylder's large fingers had stretched thin, delicate tissues, and remembering how she melted in his hands left her voice husky and soft.

"Begging your pardon, milady, but His Lordship has instructed that the coach be brought around to the mews behind the house." Robert, the coachman, sounded apologetic and slightly tense. "I will then escort you through the servants' quarters and into the library. You are to await Lord Wyldewood there. Seems milord has had an unexpected visitor this morning, and the issue must be dealt with before he can join you."

"A visitor? At this hour of the morning?"

"Aye. It will only be a few more moments. And please, do not lift the shades, milady. This is a request directly from His Lordship."

The coachman seemed determined to say nothing more on

the subject, so Emily sat back with a murmur of confused acquiescence. But as the coach lurched forward again, the horses snorting with harnesses jingling, her damnable curiosity assailed her. Lifting the window shade, she peered beneath it despite Robert's directive. What she saw as they passed the front of Wylder's residence sent her heart beating wildly with apprehension.

A distinctive black coach with dark green trim and the Earl of Camden's title crest emblazoned upon its doors sat at the curb. The matched grays were as recognizable as the vehicle, and Emily groaned with frustration.

Why, why, why was her brother *here,* of all places? And why would Wylder continue with the plan to bring her into his home with Simon so obviously present?

While she could not know the earl's intentions, one thing was certain. There was no way she would allow herself to be escorted into Wylder's townhome. No, what she must do was make her way back out of the mews and hail a hack in accordance with her original plan. And if she happened to be caught while sneaking back into Blackthorne Manor, she would brazen it out and hope her parents understood why she'd left the Linden ball unescorted the night before. Perhaps they would understand she only wanted to help Penelope True escape inevitable ruination, and that impulsive decision did not account for a way for her to return home.

Emily sighed heavily as the coach came to a stop. No, they would not understand her actions at all, although the situation was crystal clear to Emily. They would worry that she herself would become embroiled in scandal. And while they'd proven indulgent so far in not forcing her to marry, something of this nature would certainly change their minds in that aspect.

Robert flung open the door and lowered the steps for Emily. He held out a hand, and she allowed him to help her descend from the coach.

"If you will follow me, milady, I shall take you at once to His

Lordship's library."

Emily stepped back a few steps with a shake of her head. "That won't be necessary, Mister Robert. We are only a few streets from my destination, and it's likely best that I continue on my way. Ideally, a hack will be available, but if not, perhaps one of Lord Wyldewood's grooms could escort me?"

Robert frowned, his demeanor hesitant as he glanced from the servant quarters entrance and back to Emily. "But, milady, the earl's explicit instructions were that I show you to the library."

"I understand, good sir; however, I am not a parcel of goods that requires delivery. Please relay my apologies to Lord Wyldewood, but with escort or not, I intend on making my way home. I hope you recognize my determination in this matter and choose to assist me. I believe His Lordship will understand and be grateful you aided me in my decision." She flashed the man a winsome smile. "Of course, I'm sure you have no wish to disappoint him. He is obviously concerned for my safety and well-being, the dear man."

"I'm not sure—" Robert shifted his feet and cast a glance at the groom still holding the horses by the bit.

"Oh, thank you, Mister Robert. If you can spare the young man, then he shall do perfectly for the task." Emily looked about the small courtyard and tilted her head with another broad smile for the reluctant coachman. She refused to contemplate how angry Wylder would be once he discovered she'd left without his express permission. Not that she needed it, but still, he would likely be furious that she deliberately put herself in danger by making her way home. "Now, if you will be so kind as to point me in the direction of Grosvenor Square, I shall be on my way."

CHAPTER FIVE
Wylder

WYLDER CLENCHED HIS teeth, squared his shoulders, and entered the front parlor ready to do battle.

There was only one reason why Simon Blackthorne was waiting for him. The man must have discovered that his sister was currently sitting inside Wylder's coach and was now ruined beyond all redemption.

Wylder cautiously shut the double doors behind him, ignoring the startled glance his butler cast his way at the abandonment of protocol.

Then he turned and faced his friend, bracing for the possibility that Simon would forgo the formality of a direct challenge and shoot him where he stood.

"There you are, Wyldewood. I say, you had me worried." Simon raked a hand through his thick, dark hair and plopped down into a chair with a hefty sigh of relief.

"What are you talking about? Of course, I'm all right. What possibly could have occurred since I last saw you two hours ago?" Wylder stepped to the sideboard and poured himself a glass of water. He took a healthy gulp, thanking God that Simon apparently did not know Emily waited for him just down the hall.

Simon laughed softly. "I know my intrusion at this time of the morning is unusual; however, Madam Brussard told me that you left her establishment shortly after our last game of faro. That you did not take advantage of the number of beauties clamoring for your attention is so unlike you that I worried you had fallen ill or beset by some manner of misfortune. I could not in good conscience return home without inquiring after your health. I am heartily relieved to see you are well."

"As you can see, your concern was unfounded. I won quite handily at the tables and enjoyed my time there. I trust you did as well?"

Simon cocked his head, his eyes narrowed on Wylder. "You did not find any of the women there to your liking? There was not one among that impressive selection that interested you enough to bed? Hell, man, I enjoyed three of those beauties tonight. They were most accommodating and expertly skilled in their profession."

Wylder shook his head. "I had no interest in female companionship at the time." Pouring himself another glass of water, he regarded Simon with an eyebrow raised high. "This? Or something stronger, perhaps?"

Simon shuddered. "The thought of liquor quite honestly turns my stomach at the moment."

Pouring Simon a glass, he handed it over and stepped over to the fireplace to stoke the coals in the grate. "Should we add The Grinning Cockrel to the rotation, then? It sounds as though you enjoyed yourself. And I had a fine evening winning a small fortune at the tables."

Damnation, how much longer will Simon stay? I can't be assured Emily will remain where I've placed her for much longer without my intervention.

"It is certainly an establishment worth visiting again. Madam Brussard assures me that we are always welcome. She believes that our patronage will elevate the club's reputation and increase clients." Simon slumped back in the chair, swirling the water in the tumbler and flashing Wylder a tired grin. "I highly recommend trying at least one of the three women I was with. Each one was a delectable little pigeon ripe for the plucking."

"I shall, indeed, based on your recommendation." Wylder watched his friend as he drained the glass of water. "It's been a pleasurable evening for the two of us, in different ways, of course. Now, I find myself more than eager for the comforts of my own bed."

"As do I," Simon groaned in commiseration, and with a sigh, he rose and crossed to the sideboard to set his empty glass down. "I hope you will pardon my intrusion and the foolishness of my unfounded concerns, Wylder. I should have known there was naught wrong with you, but I could not ignore the niggling thought that something was… amiss."

Oh, there is certainly something amiss. Only twenty minutes ago, my hands were beneath your sister's skirts and my tongue deep inside her despite my best efforts to resist her. Now, she waits for me in my damned library, and God help me, I will likely do the same again if she allows it.

"The hallmark of a true friend is his concern for others. You've no need to apologize, Simon. I would have done the same." Wylder stepped to the parlor door in a subtle attempt to hurry the earl along. Discreetly swiping a hand over his mouth, he savored the trace of his little minx that still existed in the corners. He prayed that Emily was still in the library, not only for his own selfish desires but also because of the trouble she'd cause if she explored a bit while waiting. What if Simon ran into his reckless sister as he was departing?

As unobtrusively as possible, Wylder made sure he was the first to enter the center hallway. His gaze darted down the wide, elegant corridor and nearly breathed aloud a sigh of relief to see it was empty. The only sound was the steady tick-tock of the long-case clock and the almost startling chimes marking the six o'clock hour.

"Bloody hell, daybreak already?" Simon groaned, raising a hand to try and straighten his wrinkled ascot.

"That it is," Wylder agreed, waving at the elderly butler to come forth. "Paulson? The door, if you please. Lord Camden is taking his leave."

"Very good, milord," Paulson replied, jumping to his post at once while also executing a stately bow.

"Shall I see you at the Jacobson ball? Should be quite the crush." Simon took his hat and gloves from Paulson and waited for Wylder to respond.

"I've no intention of being elsewhere," Wylder said calmly. *Hopefully, we will not find ourselves on opposite sides of the field in the heart of Hyde Park by the end of the evening.*

"Good. Mother is insisting I attend. Fresh influx of debutantes and all that." Simon glanced about the entry hall with an appreciative eye. "I've not pressed the matter, but I do believe I should consider securing my own place. It's become a dreadful bore returning to Blackthorne after nights like this. Enduring Father's disapproving glares over afternoon tea is beyond tiresome. Yes… I think I shall have my solicitor inquire as to which of my family's town properties are unoccupied and suitable for occupancy."

"A capital idea and one I'm surprised you've not undertaken before now."

"Yes, well, no time like the present," Simon laughed. "Good day, Wylder. I will see you at Jacobson's if not sooner. Perhaps a game of cards at White's before then?"

"I look forward to it. Safe travels." Wylder nodded, and only when the door closed behind the earl did the tension leave his body. He began down the corridor, his stride eager. "Paulson, please have Cook prepare a tray of coffee and tea, along with some toast and biscuits and deliver it to the library at once. I'm positive our guest waiting there will appreciate it."

"Begging your pardon, milord, but there is no one in the library," Paulson informed him in an apologetic voice.

Wylder paused, turning to look back at the butler. "She's not there? You put her in my study, then?"

"No, milord." Paulson swallowed. "Milady never came inside

the house. Mister Robert informed me that the lady insisted on walking home." When Wylder's expression turned thunderous, the butler hurried to say, "But not without an escort, Your Lordship! One of the groomsmen was tasked with ensuring that she safely reached her destination."

Angry disbelief mixed with bemusement bubbled up inside Wylder. *That little minx.* Her bold recklessness was not surprising, but the fact that she'd so blatantly defied him had his palm itching to exact punishment on her sweet, round bottom.

"I'm sorry for the disappointment, milord. Mister Robert is waiting to relate the whole incident and to answer any questions you may have."

"Show him to my study at once, Paulson." Regardless of why Emily had left, there remained the fact that she'd explicitly been instructed otherwise. And while waiting for Robert to join him for an early morning discussion, Wylder was already planning her punishment for when he saw her next. "And do not bother with the refreshments as there is no one to enjoy them."

CHAPTER SIX

Emily

J UST A FEW more steps and she'd be safely ensconced in her
bedroom.

She'd sent her maid home the night before so she could deal
more effectively with Penelope's problem. Now, Emily realized it
would be left to her to remove her gown and prepare herself for
bed. A somewhat daunting task, considering she was exhausted.
She and her escort had walked nearly half the way home before a
hack came along looking for a new fare. Keeping to her previous
plan, Emily requested to be let out one street over from Blackthorne Manor, paid for the groom to be returned to Wylder's
townhome, then crept through the back gardens and into the
house with only the kitchen staff witness to her arrival.

Sometime after noon, her mother would undoubtedly check
on her, as it was not customary for her to sleep in so late. A
plausible excuse was already prepared in case the matter was
pressed, but hopefully, it would not be necessary. Once she'd
gone through her first Season and the second, Lord and Lady
Blackthorne had grown more lax in their watchfulness over their
only daughter during the third. Perhaps it was because she
steadfastly refused to entertain a single one of the marriage
proposals, or mayhap it was because, as she neared the unfortunate age of twenty-one, Emily was in danger of becoming a

spinster in the eyes of the ton. Personally, Emily chose to believe it was because she'd proven herself to be both mindful of her reputation and because she'd not shown any interest in catching the eye of a man.

The exception to that was Wylder St. Clair. His attention was definitely coveted. If her parents only knew how much, they would certainly lock her in her rooms to avoid any hint of scandal with the dark, dangerous earl. Although Wylder was heir to a dukedom, she doubted her father would condone the liberties he'd taken with her.

Yawning behind her hand, Emily trudged up the back stairs used by the upper staff to access the manor wing containing her suite of rooms. As it was now nearing seven o'clock, the drapes covering the tall windows had been drawn open and secured. Warm, early morning sunshine lit the corridor in tall, rectangular sections as Emily moved along like a silent little mouse scurrying back to the safety of its den. The maids would have begun their duties of dusting and polishing, but for the moment, there was no one else about.

"What the hell do you think you are doing, Em?"

Simon's sleepy voice was so unexpected that Emily let out a little screech of surprise. Holding a hand to her rapidly thumping heart, she glared at her rumpled older brother. Fear and irritation warred for prominence inside her, with irritation eventually prevailing.

She'd been so very close to succeeding with her covert plan. Of course, it would be her overbearing, pompous brother who ruined it all.

"Oh! You wretched oaf! You frightened me!"

"Did I?" Simon muttered, moving down the hallway until he stood before her. His eyes narrowed as he looked her over, taking in her appearance. "Do not tell me you are just now coming home from your evening out, dear sister."

"Very well." Emily's chin tilted. "I shall not tell you."

"Perhaps I should wake Father, and you can explain it to him."

"That is not necessary," Emily huffed, thinking quickly of an excuse for her early morning arrival. "It's all very innocent, I assure you. The dancing went on for hours at the Linden ball, and when my feet began to ache, I found a quiet, secluded corner in which to rest, where I promptly fell asleep. Of course, I could not very well go traipsing about London in the wee hours of the morning once I awoke. And since the coach returned home without me, one of the Linden footmen kindly assisted in hiring a hack. I intended to discreetly return to my room with no one being the wiser for the embarrassing predicament I placed myself in." Her tone turned sweetly pleading. "You will keep my secret, won't you, Simon? I've no wish to upset Mother or Father."

"You truly expect anyone to believe that tall tale?" Simon's brow rose high, his expression one of bemusement. "It will be easy enough to discover the truth, you know."

"Why would I fabricate such a scenario?" Emily demanded, stomping a foot, then wincing as a bruise reminded her of the distance she'd walked. "Even Mary abandoned me. I had mentioned leaving the Lindens' to attend another ball with one of the other girls, and she must have thought I did so without telling her. This was completely my fault, however. It was very irresponsible of me." When Simon continued watching her silently, she took another approach. "Simon. Please. I rarely ask favors of you, but I'm forced to beg you now. Do not tattle to Mother or Father about this. It was a mistake that I swear will never happen again."

"Damnation. All right." Simon waved his hand after a moment of consideration. "I shall keep your secret, although I believe there is far more to the situation than you are letting on. I won't press you for it, however." His stare was inscrutable. "If I did not know you to be completely enamored of Wylder St. Clair, I might see cause for concern. I am very much aware that you've shown no interest in the gentlemen who incessantly pursue you, and I know your lack of interest is because of him. That is most unfortunate because I believe if you allowed yourself to consider someone else for a husband, you'd be quite content."

"One could say the same for you, dear brother," Emily retorted blithely. "One of your dearest friends has found happiness in marriage. You could be next to the altar and discover your aversion to matrimony is unfounded."

"No." Simon chuckled, turning toward his suite of rooms and resting a hand on the doorknob. He abruptly paused at the entrance and studied Emily for such a long moment, she wondered if he could see the truth of how she'd spent the early morning hours and with whom. "Like Wyldewood," Simon finally continued, "I have no interest in marriage."

Emily's fists clenched into tiny balls of irritation that she struggled to keep concealed. "Perhaps Lord Wyldewood does not echo your sentiments on the subject, Simon. Perhaps one day he will do as he pleases and choose a bride. Perhaps that is what he wants more than anything else in this world."

"Mayhap one day he will find a woman to match his voracious appetites," Simon muttered as if suddenly vexed by the subject. "A woman of experience, ideally. But make no mistake, Emily. I will never allow him to select you for his bride. Any hope you may still harbor of that ever happening should be erased. You do not know the man's true nature as I do. He is a fine friend, a man I admire greatly… but that is where it ends. He is not the one for you, Emily. And he never will be." He gave her an oddly sympathetic smile. "You don't believe me. God knows I would try to convince you, but such evidence is not something a young, respectable lady should ever be privy to. Go on to your bed now, dear sister. You are quite pale and certainly, you need your rest."

Then he pushed the door until it closed with a slight click, leaving Emily standing in the corridor, her heart cracking in two at the finality of his words.

IT WAS ANOTHER three days before Emily saw Penelope True. To her dismay, her friend was wan in appearance, her green eyes dark-rimmed and brimming with ill-concealed worry. While Lady True was distracted by an acquaintance's inquiry about the newest gossip, Emily pulled the girl away from her mother for a hastily whispered conversation.

"You look terrible, dear friend," Emily said in a low voice. Her gaze swept over Penelope, concerned by her subdued manner. "What happened? Did your parents find out our ploy and punish you for it?"

"N-no," Penelope replied, glancing in her mother's direction as her lips tightened into a thin line. "They do not know, thank God. But explaining how I managed to find my way home that night on my own concerned them to the point that Mother is now determined to keep me in her sight. I am unsure whether that is a welcome development or not, considering Lord Grant's insistence on courting me. It appears our scheme did not work on the man."

"But, you said he seemed repulsed by your shyness. That your refusal to talk and the constant ducking of your head greatly annoyed him," Emily murmured. "I don't understand why this did not work as it has in the past."

Penelope wrung her gloved hands. "I don't understand either. Before you helped me slip out of Lord Linden's library, Grant indicated he had a certain method to cure me of my affliction." A delicate shudder shook her body. "I do not know what he meant by that, but he had the oddest look on his face as he said it. Almost as though the possibility of physically correcting me was greatly exciting to him. It-it frightened me, Emily. And now, it appears he has set his mind on pursuing me. A development that my parents find delightful. They have all but commanded me to allow myself to be compromised by the odious man."

Emily shook her head in denial of Penelope's words. "No. *No.* We shall not allow that to happen, Pen, do you understand? And should your parents or even Lord Grant attempt placing you in a position where you will be ruined, I shall do more than extinguish the lamps and help you escape the room."

"Pray, tell, what is to be done to stop it, Emily?" Penelope asked, a helpless smile curving her full mouth. "You've done your best. You've been the truest friend I could have hoped for. And you've placed yourself in jeopardy by helping me escape marriage over the last three years. It's only a matter of time before my parents catch on to the subterfuge. Now, they've grown desperate enough to ignore all subtleties. They will force me into trapping a wealthy gentleman into marriage before the end of the Season, mark my words." She glanced around the Jacobson ballroom, noting the men her parents had already deemed worthy of the scheme but failed to catch. "The situation has grown more dire because of the past failures. I am to be sacrificed, Emily. My life and happiness for riches."

Emily ground her teeth, hating the sad reality of Penelope's statement. It was true, of course. Lord and Lady True had grown bolder over the years in their efforts to secure a wealthy husband for their only daughter. By now, their tactics were common knowledge, but rather than cease inviting Penelope to social functions, a game of sorts had somehow evolved. There were even rumors of bets placed on which unlucky man would be inadvertently captured. The wrinkle in the ton's entertainment, however, was Penelope's uncanny ability to escape situations that would have ruined any other lady. She either managed to slip away just before discovery, or the targeted gentleman refused to engage in one-sided conversations with a girl who blushed and looked down at her slippers when asked a direct question, thus saving himself.

"It isn't fair, Pen," Emily finally whispered, her despair evident as she gave her friend a quick embrace. "But at the very least, we can try and make sure you marry someone you actually like and with whom you have something in common."

"What gentleman worth his mettle would be interested in a woman who enjoys playing the 'Change and balancing accounts?"

Penelope shook her head, the gaslights of the ballroom reflecting off her glossy brown locks.

"If only your parents would listen to you. The answer to your family's financial troubles is right there inside your head. They've no idea of your brilliance when it comes to such matters. The only other person I know with similar talents is my brother." Emily huffed, then her eyes widened with a sudden thought.

"Oh, no, Emily Blackthorne. *No!*" Penelope's nervous giggle carried a hint of panic as she gripped Emily's hand. "Do *not* even consider it. I would simply die of embarrassment if my parents ever thought of trapping Lord Camden, of all people. Besides, he is far too intelligent to fall for that sort of deception, and I am too terrified of the man to say two words in passing. I fear he would react violently if he ever found himself tricked in such a manner."

"Don't be ridiculous. My brother would never harm a woman." A quadrille had begun, signaling the first dance of the evening. Emily used the gaiety of the moment to pull Penelope farther away from the watchful eye of Lady True. "I don't know why I never considered it before. Oh, Pen. My brother is perfect for you, and you for him. The pair of you are the only ones I know who find excitement in the endless tallying of numbers and stodgy, boring old stock reports."

"No, Emily." Penelope glanced about, her expression pinched when Lord Grant waved from the opposite side of the ballroom. Together, the two women watched as the man began weaving his way through the crowd toward them. "I fear I will soon have no choice but to accept my fate, horrendous though it may be." She shot Emily a sharp look, her green eyes perceptive enough that Emily nearly squirmed with dread. "You've been fortunate that your parents have not forced you to accept one of the many proposals you've received since your first Season. However, I suspect your luck will soon run out as well. There is only so much freedom they will allow us."

Emily's chin tilted higher as she saw the object of her dreams leaning against a pillar, his arms akimbo as he watched her with the mannerisms of a lounging tiger. Realizing her attention had fallen upon him, he flashed her a grim smirk of acknowledgment. Emily shivered as the earl silently conveyed his disappointment for how she'd fled from him. "I shall marry Lord Wyldewood or not at all, Penelope. Mark my word on that."

Penelope let out a delicate snort, bravely squaring her shoulders as she prepared herself for Lord Grant's imminent arrival. "If it wasn't for your imposing, arrogant brother standing in the way, I might believe it possible. But we both know he will never allow it, even if his reasons for objecting remain shrouded in mystery." Her following words were steeped in the same manner of sympathy as Simon's. "My dear, Lord Wyldewood would never consider it anyway. The man hasn't truly spoken to you in almost three years, and you think you can wrangle a proposal out of him?"

"What if I told you he is not completely adverse to the idea?" Emily confessed softly, her gaze narrowing on Wyldewood as he pushed off from the pillar. He was now sauntering his way through the crowd, staring directly at her, and her heart pounded with such force that she wondered if she might faint. *Will he truly approach me here? He must know Simon is also in attendance... and yet, something about the way he regards me says he does not care.* Her skin tingled in anticipation as he continued strolling with nonchalant determination through the crush of people.

Penelope's green eyes widened with surprise, a tiny smile playing across her delicate features. "You've had an adventure, Emily, and you will tell me everything that happened when we next find ourselves alone. Now, the saints help me, I must obey my mother's earlier directive and dance with the odious Lord Grant."

CHAPTER SEVEN
Wylder

THE PALM OF Wylder's right hand began twitching the moment he laid eyes on the dazzling Emily Blackthorne.

There was no mistake as to why his palm itched to land over and over again on Emily's pert, round arse. And while it would undoubtedly be pleasurable to mark her in such a manner, he doubted Emily would enjoy the punishment. But, punish her he would for the stunt she pulled three mornings ago.

He'd found himself consumed with worry for her safety until the groomsman returned from the Blackthorne estate with his report. For three days, Wylder debated on whether it was wise to pay a visit to Blackthorne Manor and make his displeasure known. But, how could he possibly explain that he'd come to call only on Emily and no one else?

Keeping his gaze locked on Emily, he finally reached her side. Her little intake of breath when he lifted her hand to press a kiss to the back of it was so damned gratifying that Wylder allowed himself a small smile of triumph.

"Good evening, Lady Emily. I trust you are well this evening?"

Emily's gaze darted about the ballroom, no doubt wondering where Simon might be. Normally, Wylder would have contemplated the same, but for some odd reason, he couldn't find it within him to worry overmuch when it came to his best friend's rage. In fact, he was willing to risk it for the chance to touch this girl. Now that he'd had a proper taste of her, he could not stop obsessing over when he might have her spread before him again.

"Yes, thank you, Lord Wyldewood," Emily squeaked, before clearing her throat and giving him a serene smile. "It's a fantastic crush of people. I'm sure my brother must be here somewhere, as he promised my mother he would be in attendance. Perhaps you have seen him?"

"My understanding is that he accompanied Lord Jacobson to his study to discuss some investment possibilities. Very boring stuff."

"Boring, indeed," Emily breathed, then she fell silent as Wylder's gaze slid over her. Her gown was a lovely shade of sapphire blue, matching her dark-lashed eyes almost exactly. His jaw clenched. Two mounds of plump flesh rose over the bodice of that gown, commanding his attention. Reminding him that those breasts would be the focus the next time he had her alone.

"Have all of your dances been claimed, Lady Emily?" he finally said in a husky voice.

"N-no." Her head tilted in surprise. "Why do you ask, Lord Wyldewood?"

"Because I would like to dance with you, and according to society's inane rules, I must be penciled in."

Emily fumbled for the dance card dangling from a ribbon around her wrist. After she managed to untangle it, she handed it over to Wyldewood, watching with wide eyes as he wrote his name beside one of the few spaces still available. He gave it back to her as she glanced over it before allowing him to tie the card's ribbons so that it was once again attached to her wrist.

"A waltz, Lord Wyldewood?" Her voice wavered.

"A waltz, Lady Emily," he confirmed. "I intend on having a private conversation with you before that, however."

She licked her lips, the bewitching minx, and sighed, "As you wish, Lord Wyldewood."

"Meet me on the rear terrace overlooking the conservatory in thirty minutes."

Emily shifted her feet. "But that means I must forgo my dance with Lord Bancroft."

"So you must," Wylder drawled. "Thirty minutes, Lady Emily. And please don't keep me waiting." He raised her hand once more, kissing the soft silk glove encasing her fingers, and wished her skin was bare to him. "Until then."

He left her with her lips slightly pursed as if his boldness confused her. It was understandable, of course. He'd been so very diligent in avoiding her company over the last few years; his actions now were the exact opposite of his usual behavior.

You are treading on dangerous ground, his inner voice cautioned, but Wylder ignored it. He needed more of her, even if encouraging that obsession was foolhardy. *Simon must not know...*

Wylder shut down his inner thoughts immediately when it came to that particular threat. Simon's discovery of Emily's debauchery at Wylder's hands was not ideal, but still, he put it aside for the moment. Grabbing a goblet of champagne from the tray of a passing servant, he gulped it down while contemplating the selfishness of his own nature.

With any luck, her brother would never find out.

Wylder tamped down his irritation as he continued waiting for Emily's appearance. She was already ten minutes late, and he'd spent that time devising all sorts of pleasurable ways he could punish the blatant disregard of his directive.

Not that he had any right to contemplate such things. He had no valid claim to Emily. No right to dictate her actions in any way. But the longer he stood on the shadowy terrace near the darkened conservatory, the more that rationality dissipated into mist.

Deciding that he would try cornering her before their waltz, he headed back toward the entrance to the ballroom. Before he reached them, the doors swung open and a couple emerged.

It was not Emily, that much was instantly certain. Wylder hesitated, melting into the shadows as he watched the couple. He recognized Lord Gregory Grant, but it took several moments for him to put a name to the female's face. It was one of the ladies from Emily's circle of friends. Quiet, shy Miss Penelope True.

"Miss Penelope, you and I must reach an agreement." Grant took Penelope by the elbow, and from where he stood, Wylder saw the girl wince in pain.

"It isn't proper that you and I should be alone, Lord Grant," she stated in a stern voice. She did not sound at all like the reticent girl she was rumored to be.

"Hang propriety, Miss Penelope. Your parents understand the seriousness of my intentions, and so must you."

Penelope stood her ground, pulling back even as Lord Grant tried pulling her into the deeper shadows near the railing. "I understand perfectly, sir. It is you who requires clarification."

"Dash it all," Grant hissed. "If only you'd cooperated at the Linden ball, we would not be forced to this now. Stand still now, blast you, so I may kiss you and secure this arrangement…"

Penelope let out a short, sharp cry of alarm, and Wylder's jaw clenched as he watched Grant jerk her closer. Enough of this… he would not stand idly by while the girl was ravished against her will. He stepped forward, seeing Penelope's face grow slack with confusion at the sight of him while Grant swore under his breath at the unexpected intrusion.

Just as Wylder emerged from the shadows, Emily barreled through the doors from the ballroom with two glasses in her hands. She headed straight for Penelope before catching sight of Wylder. She hesitated briefly, then continued as if nothing were the matter.

"Seems we all had the same notion of taking in a breath of fresh air," Emily exclaimed cheerfully. She flashed an apologetic smile at Wylder, then turned to Lord Grant. The man appeared frozen with shocked fury to see Wylder standing on the terrace as well. "Such kind gentlemen to provide a sense of security, don't you agree, Penelope? Why, I've never noticed how dark it is out here when the moon is not providing illumination."

Penelope took the glass, tossing back most of its contents while gaping at Wylder. A moment later, she allowed Emily to tug her away from Lord Grant. "Yes, dreadfully dark out here. And thank you, Emily, for the refreshment. I was so parched."

Emily kept hold of Penelope's arm, beaming innocently as she nodded her head at Wylder. "I believe my brother is looking for you, Lord Wyldewood. He seemed almost desperate in his search."

"I have no idea what the blazes is going on here," Lord Grant stated angrily. "But I desire a moment alone with Miss Penelope. Now, if the two of you will grant us a bit of privacy..."

Emily laughed gaily. "Oh, I declare, Lord Grant! You are such a jokester! And so scandalous! You know that being alone with a gentleman is not allowed for young ladies like ourselves. Why, the troubles that could cause... I cannot even say such things aloud."

Before Lord Grant could respond to that, a bevy of feminine voices drifted from the far end of the terrace. As they drew closer, Lord Grant's frustrated expression morphed into one of nervous concern. A group of women marched toward them, their destination obvious to the casual observer.

"Just this way," Lady True said, her strident tone of righteous indignation rising above the other ladies chattering voices. "I believe that they were headed in the direction of the conservatory. Oh, my poor, poor Penelope. I can only hope we are not too late to save the girl from ru—"

The lady, flanked by at least five of the ton's elderly, scowling matrons, rounded a corner of the terrace and immediately drew up short.

"Good evening, Lady True. Ladies." Wylder bowed at the

waist, his mouth quirking with amusement to see the shock on Penelope's mother's face. "It appears we are not the only ones seeking a breath of fresh air."

"Uh, I was just… that is to say, yes. Some fresh air, indeed," Lady True stuttered before her lips tightened into a thin line. "Good evening, Lord Wyldewood. Lord Grant." The woman studied the group before her, obviously attempting to decipher what had occurred before her arrival. Her gaze finally landed on her daughter, and her expression became even more pinched with ill-disguised fury. "Penelope? Are you all right, my dear?" The concern in her tone did not ring true as she fussed over the young lady, smoothing a wrinkle from Penelope's gown.

"Of course, Mother." Penelope smiled serenely while also sidling away. "Lady Emily and I thought we would escape the crush of the crowd for a moment and discovered Lord Grant and Lord Wyldewood doing the same." She sipped from the glass she held and tipped it toward Emily as if toasting her friend's quick thinking. "We should return the ball, Emily. I would enjoy a refill of lemonade and a brief visit to the ladies' retiring room."

Lady True's disappointment was on full display as she glared at Lord Grant. Wylder realized that the two of them had conspired to turn Penelope's ruin into a public spectacle. His presence and Emily's hasty arrival derailed that devious plan. Cocking his head, he glanced at Emily and saw her eyes narrowed at Penelope's mother. Then her features smoothed themselves into a pleasant mask.

"The lemonade is quite delicious…" she murmured, then her face split with another broad smile. "How lovely… look, Penelope! My dashing brother arrives just in time to see us safely back to the ballroom."

Wylder stifled a groan, knowing that Simon's arrival meant one thing. He had followed Emily in his search for Wylder. Finding an entire gathering of people on the dimly lit terrace would help dissipate his suspicions. At least, Wylder hoped that was the case. Honestly, he was finding new appreciation for

Emily's cleverness in the situation. She had devised a solution in which she avoided being found with Wylder in a compromising situation while also saving her friend from certain ruin with a man she obviously did not want to marry.

"Martha, it appears your daughter is quite all right, as is Lady Emily," the Countess of Marshton sniffed while patting her silver-gray hair. "I believe I shall return to the ballroom as the night air is not healthy for my constitution. Come along, Helen and Frances. Join me in a thimble of brandy so that we might combat the chill I already feel settling into my bones."

"There you are, Wyldewood," Simon said, reaching them as the group of women began strolling back toward the bright lights of the house. Lady True remained behind, a hand fluttering at the neckline of her gown.

"Camden…" Wylder nodded at Simon, noting the hard edge of his friend's jawline. Suspicion wafted off the man, setting all of Wylder's instincts on high alert. "Lady Emily says you were looking for me?"

"Yes, I—"

"Surely it can wait, Camden," Emily interrupted with a sweet grin as she stepped between the two men. "I was rather hoping that my dear brother would escort myself and Miss Penelope back to the ballroom."

Simon frowned at Emily's obvious tactics in separating everyone in this strange grouping of people, but courtesy demanded he do as his sister requested.

"Perhaps you will assist Miss Penelope while I escort Lady Emily?" Wylder broke in, moving closer to Emily. Taking the glass of lemonade from her hand, he set it on the terrace wall and offered his arm. The surprise on her face was almost comical. Wylder could not stop smiling down at her as he added, "I shall keep her company until it is time for our waltz."

"Waltz?" Simon growled, automatically holding up his arm for Penelope to take as he stared at Wylder.

"Yes. Lady Emily graciously agreed to grant me one dance

this evening. The only one left was the waltz just prior to supper." Wylder smiled benignly, then nodded his head at Lady True and Lord Grant, who stood silently watching. For her part, Lady True looked delighted by this unexpected turn of events while Lord Grant's mouth was pulled into a ferocious frown. Simon Blackthorne was far more desirable as a catch than the lesser title of Lord Grant, and now he'd been practically thrown into the mix by Emily. "I'm sure Miss Penelope would grant you the same consideration if you only asked to see her dance card."

CHAPTER EIGHT

Emily

"ARE YOU INSANE?" Emily hissed beneath her breath as Wylder tucked her hand into the crook of his arm and began walking.

"No," Wylder murmured. "But I am angry. Enough so that I have willingly thrown caution to the wind."

Emily glanced back at her brother. Penelope had accepted Simon's arm, her face a blank slate, while Lord Grant trailed behind them with Lady True in tow. Simon's brow was creased with lingering confusion, but he was silent as he followed them from a distance.

Unable to hide her panic, Emily inclined her head toward Wylder. "This is precisely what I was trying to avoid. Now, he will watch us like a hawk for the remainder of the evening. As if it were not terrible enough that my mother is also—"

"Do not worry about them, Emily. Your immediate concern should be how you will explain why you ignored my request that we meet on the terrace." Placing his free hand over hers, he squeezed it tight and said in a low, dangerous voice, "I do not like being disobeyed."

Emily dug her nails into his arm, praying he felt the sharp bite of them through the soft silk of her gloves and the broadcloth of his formal evening coat. "That was a request?" She snorted in disbelief. "That was a little more than a royal command, Wyldewood. Had I obeyed you, my brother would have found you doing God only knows what to me."

"Just what do you think I meant to do, minx?" He sounded genuinely curious.

"Something highly inappropriate, no doubt." Emily sniffed, hating how needy her voice sounded over the strains of music and the chatter of multiple guests beyond the terrace doors.

"Have no fear, Emily. Whatever you are imagining in that clever little head of yours will still occur." Leaning toward her, he whispered in her ear, "And a full explanation of your activities the night of the Linden ball will be forthcoming once I've seen to your punishment."

"There is nothing to tell," Emily replied nervously as Wylder led her to the refreshment table. Snagging a new glass of lemonade, he handed it to her and watched as she drank it down.

The mere mention of punishment had her mind flashing back to that night three years before when Wylder pulled her over his lap and struck her with the palm of his hand. Something tingled inside her at the memory, the space between her thighs clenching with a mysterious ache. She wanted more of the things he'd done to her on the bench of his coach just a few mornings ago. His beautifully stern mouth worshipping her flesh until the world exploded in a shower of sparks and lights.

She was sure her face was flushed pink as Wylder took the glass from her suddenly nerveless fingers. His iron-hued gaze was inscrutable as he studied her features.

"Hmmm," he murmured with an unmistakable note of satisfaction in his tone. "Something tells me you are remembering our interlude in the coach. I've thought of little else since then. It is something we will soon revisit, minx. I promise you that."

"But Simon will find—"

"No. Your brother will not find out." Wylder's confidence was so infectious that Emily found herself relaxing. Perhaps he was right. Maybe Simon would remain ignorant of all the liberties his little sister had allowed this man standing beside her. She sighed heavily, wondering how she could obtain what she wanted most without hurting anyone or herself.

The impossible. The unattainable. Wylder St. Clair, Earl of Wyldewood and heir to the Duke of Claymore, for a husband.

"Come with me, Emily." Wylder led her to an open spot near her mother. Lady Blackthorne smiled absently at her daughter, completely unaware of the drama that had occurred on the terrace, and turned back to the conversation she shared with two other ladies. "Stay here until I retrieve you for our waltz. My plans for later this evening must be amended due to this recent development."

"What does that mean?" Emily asked, confusion knitting her brow as Wylder bent over her hand and pressed a kiss to the back of it. Even through the thin silk of her gloves, the heat of his mouth sent shivers up her spine.

"I shall enlighten you during our waltz." Then, with an enigmatic smirk, Wylder sauntered away.

A few moments later, Penelope joined Emily on the edge of the ballroom floor. She wore a look of bemusement on her pretty face.

"I am struggling to understand what happened, Emily," she whispered. "I thought all was lost, then I saw Lord Wyldewood there on the terrace. He looked… angry. Yes, that's it. Angry. And I believe it was directed toward Lord Grant." Her voice dropped as she explained, "You see, Lord Grant had hold of me and was attempting to kiss me and… and I was resisting the odious man." Tilting her head, she regarded Emily from beneath the sweep of her lashes. "What I don't understand is why it seemed he was waiting for someone. And why you showed up."

Emily laughed softly. "Perhaps Lord Wyldewood is the moral center of the Rakehells."

Penelope smiled at that. "That's impossible. The Mayfair Rakehells have no morals. At least the two remaining ones do not." Her tone grew serious. "Will you tell me the truth?"

"I agreed to meet Lord Wyldewood." Emily sighed. "But then I saw my brother searching for him and knew that if I obeyed Wyldewood, Simon would no doubt catch us in a less than innocent situation. Then I witnessed Lord Grant practically dragging you toward the same terrace, and I realized saving you was far more important."

"Thank God that you did. But, Emily, I fear the inevitable. My parents will not stop until I am truly compromised. You saw the look on my mother's face. She has Lord Camden in her sights now, although I suspect she will still allow Grant to press his suit."

"While I would love it if my brother were to choose you for a bride, I know he is stubbornly resistant to the idea of marriage."

Penelope laughed. "I have the impression that he would rather wear a shirt made of nails than dance with a girl on the marriage mart. He was kind enough to follow through with Wyldewood's suggestion that he at least enter his name on my dance card for the last waltz of the evening."

"He may be amoral, but at least he exhibits manners when it suits him." Emily pressed her fingertips to her temple, her head aching as she tried thinking of a solution to her friend's problem. "We-we could hide you away somewhere for a while. At least until Grant loses interest in you."

"Do you think we could do that?" Penelope brightened. "It is a wonderful idea, Emily. But where would I go?"

"Let me think upon it. Your disappearance will undoubtedly have most of the ton desperate to solve the mystery, but there may be no other choice. At least right now." Emily linked her arm with Penelope, giving her a comforting smile. "And as for concealing your whereabouts, I'm sure I can find a suitable place."

EMILY RELUCTANTLY REMAINED standing where Wylder left her until the beginning strains of the last waltz began. She watched as Simon claimed Penelope for the dance, noticing how pleased their mother was to see her son dancing with the young lady. But even as the waltz progressed, Wylder still did not appear.

Worry niggled at her first, followed quickly by relief. Perhaps he had come to his senses. Realized how rash a decision it was to dance with her with Simon in the same room.

Then the relief morphed into irritation that she'd obeyed him to begin with. And the longer she stood watching from the edge of the ballroom floor as other gaily dressed women twirled by with their partners, the faster her irritation grew.

This was little more than a ploy on Wylder's part to ensure no other gentleman claimed a dance with me. He deliberately has left me standing here like an unwanted wallflower. I'm sure he finds it quite amusing that I am waiting for him. Hoping he gives me a crumb of his attention. The arrogant cad...

"Was this dance not claimed, dear?" Emily's mother, Chelsea Blackthorne, inquired with a puzzled frown. "I thought Lord Wyldewood penciled himself in."

Emily let out a silent groan. Having her mother involved in this fiasco was definitely not a good idea. Plastering a smile on her face, she decided the best way to play it off was to pretend she never wanted to dance with the earl in the first place.

"He did, but perhaps it's best he has not claimed it. His reputation is less than stellar, as well you know, Mother."

Lady Blackthorne smiled indulgently. "It's no more and no less than your brother's. However, it is certainly true that his reputation does little to keep the ladies from seeking his attention."

"He and Simon hardly require any additional boosts to their egos, do they?" Emily fingered the dance card dangling from her wrist, praying for the opportunity to rip it into tiny pieces while Wylder watched. Would it affect him, though? Or would he simply watch her, those silver eyes brimming with sardonic amusement at her fit of temper?

"Your brother and his friends have enjoyed their time as London's roguish bachelors, but eventually, those days invariably come to an end. And like Lord Ashcroft and his new bride have found each other, I wish the same for Simon and Wyldewood." Lady Blackthorne's gaze drifted from her daughter to her son. "It pleases me to see him taking an interest in Penelope. Despite the unsavory nature of her parents, the girl is sweetness and kindness itself. I've long thought that she would make a perfect wife for Simon."

Emily remained silent on that subject, hopeful that her mother remained ignorant of the truth behind Simon's waltz with Penelope, even if she herself felt the same. Simon and Pen made a lovely couple as they swirled about the dance floor, but closer inspection revealed their dance to be a tense one. Penelope wore the most miserable expression on her face while Simon's jaw was set so firmly that it might actually crack. Neither was enjoying the waltz.

"Mother, I've developed the most horrid headache. Although it is the height of bad manners, I think I shall go home." She kept watching the dance floor as she spoke, sure that if she looked at her mother, the woman would see the lie on her face.

"And not enjoy the midnight supper Lady Jacobson has planned?" Lady Blackthorne asked in surprise.

Emily nodded. "When this waltz ends, I shall take my leave as others prepare to gather in the dining room. I will have the coach sent back around for you if you would like to stay longer."

"Very well, my dear." Her mother pressed the back of her gloved hand to Emily's cheek and peered at her with questioning eyes. "You do appear rather flushed, angel. You may go, of course. I will make your excuses and see you tomorrow."

"You will stay for the entirety of the dance?" Emily asked, surprised that her mother would agree so readily to her leaving. If Lady Blackthorne did not come with her now, then she would likely not arrive home herself until the wee hours of the morning.

"Most of it, surely. I must speak with Her Grace, Lady West-ley. Lord Ashcroft and his new bride will be returning from their honeymoon by month's end, and I have requested to host a house party in their honor at Thorne Park. There are just a few details to review before we can set everything into motion. I know I will enjoy a bit of time away from the city before the winter season begins, as will your father."

Emily felt a wave of hope sweep over her. A country house party? It would mean quite a few of their particular social set would be present at the Blackthorne country estate of Thorne Park. It also provided a perfect opportunity to hide Penelope away somewhere for at least a month with no one realizing she was even missing.

"What a lovely idea, Mother. I would love to become better acquainted with Lady Ashcroft and, of course, I'm sure if Simon attends, he will welcome the opportunity to reunite with at least one of his dearest friends."

"Yes, well, I do not have much hope that the two remaining rakehells will deem a country party exciting enough to abandon London, but the invite will be extended." Lady Blackthorne smiled slyly and winked at her daughter. "And if things work out, we may even find Simon a bride while there. After all, Lord Ashcroft discovered love outside of London. The same could happen for your brother."

CHAPTER NINE

Wylder

WYLDER STALKED AWAY from Lord Jacobson's study, acutely aware that the last waltz prior to the midnight meal was nearly over.

Would Emily still be waiting for him? She'd better be. And if she were angry, well, he would handle that later in the evening in the privacy of her room.

One glance in the area where he'd left her revealed she was gone.

"Bloody hell," he muttered. If Lord Jacobson hadn't pulled him aside for an impromptu discussion regarding his father's debt, he would have kept his promise to lead her in the waltz.

His gaze swept the ballroom, and *there...* a flash of sapphire blue and dark hair exiting through one of the doors leading to the south corridor.

A predatory thrill sank into Wylder's bones. It was so potent that it swept away the lingering frustration he had when it came to his father's debts to one of their peers. The fact that he'd agreed to cover the money rankled him. It wasn't the first time he'd had to do so in the past three years, and if his father continued his reckless gambling, it would not be the last. Having already determined he would speak with the duke regarding the estate's dwindling resources, this incident tonight only strengthened Wylder's resolve.

Another look around the room, and he spied Simon waltzing with Penelope True. The pair looked individually miserable, but one could not deny the striking image they created as they swirled around the floor. Simon's height, his dark handsomeness, was well complemented by the small, curvaceous girl he held in his arms. She was an elegant, tiny bird caught in the grip of a raven… and if his friend would only allow himself to truly look at her, Simon might very well see she possessed the innately submissive nature he craved in a woman.

But that was Simon's problem, and Wylder appreciated that his friend appeared to be well occupied. He would be expected to escort the lady to dinner following the waltz. Which meant the earl could not keep track of Emily and Wylder's whereabouts.

Stepping back into the corridor, Wylder knew that if he continued straight ahead and took a left at the end of the passageway, he would intersect with the hall Emily had taken. After a few moments, he came across her standing with Lord Gregory Grant. The man gripped her elbow in his hand, and Emily looked furious.

"You may have ruined my chances with Penelope, but know this. I will not give up so easily," Lord Grant hissed. "And you will pay a dear price if you continue meddling in our affairs."

"I've ruined nothing, Lord Grant," Emily replied with exaggerated calm. "I don't know why you would think I've anything to do with—"

An ugly expression crossed the man's features. "Do you think I don't know you were behind her escape from the Lindens' library? Or that it was it simply chance when you appeared on the terrace tonight?" He angrily jerked her closer as Emily gasped in shock at his vehemence. "I suspect you've been doing this same thing with other gentlemen since last year."

"Please remove your hand from my person, or I shall be forced to call for assistance, Lord Grant." Her voice trembled a bit now, her fear evident in the higher pitch of her tone.

Wylder's hands squeezed into fists. He'd stayed hidden up to this point, hoping not to escalate the situation, but bloodlust surged through his veins. That this man dared touch Emily was unacceptable. She was his.

"I'm not a fool, Lady Emily, and I won't stand for your interference again."

"The assertion you are not a fool is debatable, but it is a certainty that if you don't take your bloody hands off her, you are a dead man," Wylder said, approaching from the end of the corridor, his stride hard and purposeful.

"This is none of your concern, Wyldewood," Grant sputtered as he released Emily and took a step back.

"That is where you are wrong. Not only is it my concern, but Lord Camden's as well. Shall we send for him and gauge his opinion on the threats you've made to his dear sister?" Wylder tsked, pushing his way between Grant and Emily. She thankfully remained silent, although her chin jutted upward in a display of stubborn independence that Wylder easily recognized.

Grant glared at Wylder, but how he retreated indicated the man had no interest in challenging either the earl or Simon. "There is no need for that. Lady Emily, I apologize if our conversation upset you. Now, if you will please excuse me. I am expected to escort Lady True to dinner this evening in the absence of her husband."

After executing a hasty bow, the man hurried down the same corridor Wylder had used, leaving him alone with a visibly relieved Emily.

"Thank you, Wylder, for coming to my rescue. I certainly did not expect to see you—"

In stony silence, Wylder snagged Emily by the arm. Without a moment's hesitation, he dragged her into the closest room.

"What the devil?" she exclaimed as he pushed her into the darkened space and locked the door behind them.

"You persist in placing yourself in dangerous situations, Emily." His hand closed over her wrist like a shackle when she would have fled.

"How could I know the man would follow me? He's angry over a perceived obstacle to his courtship of my dear friend. But as you no doubt heard while eavesdropping, his accusations are unfounded and irrational."

"I found a bit of truth in the man's statements. Indeed, I suspect you've been doing exactly what he accuses you of." He deliberately kept his voice calm, but the icy undertones had her shivering. "But that is a conversation for another time. I wish to discuss something of greater interest to me right now."

"Whatever might that be?" Emily scowled up at him, her false bravado making him smile.

"This is twice in one evening you have not obeyed me, minx," Wylder murmured as he pulled her to the room's window seat. The moon had finally appeared from behind the clouds, illuminating the room enough to recognize that they stood in an unused parlor. "And I find my patience has reached an end."

"Your patience?" Emily scoffed. "What of *my* patience while I stood like a ninny waiting for you to reappear?" She tried yanking free, but it was a useless endeavor. Wylder refused to let her go, instead spinning her around so that she now faced the window seat with her backside to his front.

"I told you I would return for you. Why did you not wait?" Still holding her wrist, he wrapped a muscled arm around her slender waist. Now she was trapped against him. "Your impetuous nature placed you in that situation just now with Lord Grant. I expect a bit more gratitude for my intervention and the restraint it took to keep from beating the man to a bloody pulp. Gratitude, minx, and I will get it from you. One way or another."

"Let me go, Wyldewood," she demanded in a frosty tone. "I have the beginnings of a dreadful headache."

"A headache? And where were you intending to go to alleviate this headache of yours?" Holding her so closely affected Wylder quicker than he would have thought possible. Her sweet scent tickled his nose, her perfectly curved arse brushing against his groin. A whimper escaped her when he dipped his head, his mouth hovering around her ear. "I'm waiting for an answer, Emily."

"You cannot order me about like this, Wylder. I'm not yours—"

Wylder nipped her earlobe, eliciting a sharp cry of alarm from his prey. "Where were you going?"

"Home," she gritted between clenched teeth. "Blackthorne Manor, to be precise. Mother will make my excuses for the remainder of the evening."

"Well, that is fortuitous. I shall be at Blackthorne Manor as well."

"What are you talking about?" Emily breathed.

"I planned on discussing this with you during our waltz. Unfortunately, I missed that opportunity." Dropping his head, Wylder nuzzled the tender curve of her neck, focusing on the area where it sloped down to her shoulder. He pressed a kiss there, following that with a grazing of his teeth. Emily shuddered in response, leaning back against him and allowing him to support most of her weight. She moaned almost silently... but loud enough that Wylder knew she was as affected as he was.

"Wylder... we shouldn't be doing this. It's too dangerous for us both."

Wylder rested his forehead against the back of her bowed head, breathing deeply of her sweet lemon and sugar scent. She was like cool lemonade to his darkly parched soul. And it was becoming apparent that he could drink until he overflowed with her essence and it would never be enough. How the hell had he managed to stay away from her for the past three years when she was a balm that soothed him?

"I know, Emily. I know. But damned if I can stay away from you now that I've tasted you." He sighed heavily, releasing her wrist and moving his hand to encircle her throat gently. His other arm remained wrapped around her waist, anchoring her in place.

"Do-do you think this hunger between us will be satisfied if we continue to feed it?" Her voice was softly questioning, seeking his guidance in matters she was terribly innocent of. "What I mean to say, if you were to satisfy my curiosity about such things, allow me to explore and experience it without expecting you to bind yourself to me, would you do it? It would be almost like you are giving me lessons. And no one would be harmed by our actions."

Wylder groaned at the explicit images exploding in his head. She had no idea what she was asking of him. And he doubted he had the necessary strength to resist taking her in all the ways he craved. But still, he found himself nodding his head. "It's said familiarity breeds contempt. Perhaps it is possible to grow tired of one another."

I will surely go to hell for that lie. If I had my way, I'd take her a dozen different ways every day for the next century and never tire of her breathy little sighs of satisfaction.

Emily relaxed even more. "Then I would like to try that, please. Because this attraction between us is just as inconvenient for me as it is for you." She shivered a little, and Wylder moved closer, wondering if she was chilled. "You will truly teach me how things are between a man and a woman? Explain why my blood races so fast when you hold me like this? Why do I feel as though I'm melting inside when you kiss me?"

"Yes," Wylder agreed hoarsely. "I will show you those things with one exception. And this is an ironclad rule, Emily. One that cannot be bent or broken. I will not take you completely. You will remain a virgin, and I will not fuck you like I want to. If you agree, then we may proceed."

"Would you have proposed the same arrangement had I not asked this of you first?" Her voice contained a hint of a smile, although he could not see her face. "Why else would you come to Blackthorne tonight? What did you expect to do in the dark of night?"

"Bend over, Emily. Place your hands on the window seat, and I will show you just a few of the things I planned for you tonight." When she hesitated, Wylder tightened his fingers around her throat just enough that she gasped with arousal. "Another rule, minx. When I command, you obey. Without question. Without thinking. Without hesitation. When I conduct these lessons, you will do as I say. And if you are afraid or unsure, you will utter a single word, at which point we shall stop and discuss your concerns before proceeding. But you are only to use this word in cases of true fear or pain beyond simply being uncomfortable."

"A word?"

"Yes, a word. Something that does not fit the situation. Something out of the ordinary but easy for you to remember." He traced her ear with the tip of his tongue, and she sighed in the most delightful way.

"Raincloud," Emily murmured in distraction. "The exact color of your eyes…"

"Hands on the window seat, minx. Now." Wylder's cock hardened into something resembling stone. This slip of a girl would surely be the death of him.

She obeyed at once, the motion resulting in her arse pushing harder into his groin.

"Spread your legs apart, my sweet. And arch your back for me. There's a good girl."

With deliberate intent, Wylder slid his arm from around her waist and used his hand to grip handfuls of her skirts. Inch by inch, he dragged the material up until swaths of it were bunched around her waist. He kept his other hand on her throat, his fingers applying enough pressure that her head was forced to tilt back toward him. He wished he could see her like this in a fully lit room, although the way the moonlight bathed her figure was sinful enough.

"Let me explain what is going to happen, Emily." He traced his fingers over the curves of her bottom, covered in the thin muslin of her underdrawers, then slipped them between her legs until he found the opening in the material. He stroked the softness of her quim, entranced by the way she moaned and pushed back against him for more. "You will come on my fingers.

You will thank me, and I will help ensure you are once again presentable. Then you will leave this room, find your coach, and go home. Upon your arrival, you will immediately retire. Undress completely and dismiss your maid. You are to remain nude with a single lamp burning beside your bed. Most importantly, you will unlock your balcony doors for me. Is any of this unclear to you?"

"N-no my lord." She was breathless now, her back arching more as Wylder's fingers circled and swirled in the honey softness of her excitement. "I understand."

"Excellent. Now, grip the seat as hard as you like and stay in this position as I pleasure you. And Emily? Try to be as silent as possible when I bring you to completion. It would not do for anyone to discover us in here."

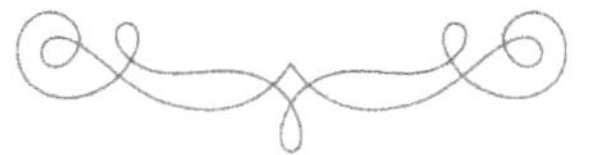

CHAPTER TEN

Emily

E MILY WRAPPED HER robe tight around her body in an attempt to quell her trembling limbs. Her gaze focused on the doors leading to her private balcony, and she wondered if she imagined the brass knob slowly turning. When the doors failed to open, her thoughts drifted to the stolen moments spent with Wylder St. Clair.

After crying out her climax twice in the silent parlor of Lord Jacobson's elegant townhouse, Wylder had pulled her upright, kissed her so fiercely she'd nearly fainted, then assisted in smoothing her skirts back into place. Then, without another word, he pushed her gently out of the room as though confident she would follow his previous orders without even a peep of protest. And the man was insufferably right about that. She'd moved as if in a daze, climbing into the Blackthorne coach then collapsing against the tufted seat as the trip home passed as though nothing more than a dream.

She'd gone straight to her room and disrobed in record time with her maid's assistance. The moment Mary exited the room, Emily quickly stripped away the nightgown she'd donned and threw a thin robe over her nakedness. Then she unlocked the doors as Wylder had instructed and plopped down in an overstuffed chair to wait for his arrival. The seconds stretched into minutes, and as the night slipped by, she nervously chewed her fingernail while contemplating the doubts running rampant in her mind.

How long would it take for him to appear? Emily shivered, wondering what the earl might do once he walked through those balcony doors. She would be completely at his mercy. What if he did not abide by his own rules? What if he took what he wanted and left her ruined?

Wylder would not do that. He is an honorable man, even if he is an unrepentant rogue. We would both suffer if he betrays the trust I have placed in him. Besides, if this is the only way I can have the man, then I must have faith in my own decision to proceed.

The way he had touched her in the darkened parlor was different from how he'd caressed her in his coach. It felt more… possessive. Darker. Ironclad. Unavoidable. As if by agreeing to his terms, she'd agreed to be his completely and without reservation. The implications of that frightened her even as it thrilled her. Wylder's touch was addictive. She would do whatever he asked if it meant that the delicious tormenting pleasure would continue.

But even as Emily acknowledged the strength of her desire to please him, she wondered what he might do if she were to defy him in some way. Would he spank her again? Or would there be some other manner of punishment concocted for her pain and his pleasure? She swallowed hard as a pang of lust speared her body. Thoughts of the weight of his hands striking her bare bottom as she struggled over his lap trickled into her consciousness. Perhaps a tiny show of defiance was warranted, if only for the opportunity to explore her own confusing reaction to being disciplined in such a scandalous way.

Frowning at the lascivious nature of her thoughts, Emily stood and shrugged out of the robe. Donning her nightgown for the second time that evening, she reasoned with herself. This was a small act, one easily explained away by saying she'd forgotten that part of his instructions. Would Wylder punish her anyway for such a small mistake?

Jumping up from the chair, Emily began pacing around her room, agitated by her own nervousness. Blast it, if the man did not appear soon, she was likely to change her mind and lock the doors against any intrusion.

The slightest whisper of cool autumn air and the soft click of the balcony doors closing alerted Emily that she was no longer alone. Before she could turn to face him, Wylder had wrapped his arms around her waist, his hard chest pressing against her back. She did not know whether to relax or resist, but she did internally melt when he whispered in her ear.

"Did you think I would not come to you, little minx?"

Emily breathed deep, unsure how to respond to his question. She both dreaded his arrival and feared he would not keep his word to come.

"I-I wasn't sure," she admitted on a sigh. Wylder carried the night wind on his clothing, the fresh scent accentuated by the woodsy sharpness of his cologne and the sweet spice of brandy.

His arms tightened when she would have turned to face him, his forearms as strong as iron bands encompassing her body. "I see we must start with a punishment after all."

"We must?" Emily hated how her voice wobbled a little bit. Would he recognize the excitement it contained? Her cheeks flushed hot when he chuckled as if she amused him. His mouth explored the nape of her neck, exposed by the braid her dark, wavy hair had been pulled into. A shudder of delight swept her as he softly kissed the skin there.

"Yes, we must. My expectations were that you would be wearing nothing, and yet, I find you clad in a garment which conceals your body from my perusal." Loosening his grip on her waist, Wylder's hands trailed up along the sides of her form, hesitating briefly to cup her breasts. A low moan trembled in Emily's chest, echoed by Wylder's groan of lust.

His fingers hooked into the bodice of the muslin gown, and Emily froze with sudden apprehension. "Wylder? You do not intend on tearing my gown from me, do you?"

He laughed again as if her hesitant question amused him. "I do."

"But you cannot. How would I explain its state to my maid in the morning?"

"Must you explain it at all, minx? I shall purchase you a new one to replace it."

Before she could protest that his buying personal items of that nature for her was highly improbable, the thin garment was ripped from collarbone to navel, and his bare hands were exploring her exposed breasts. Lifting, weighing the mounds of flesh, his fingers smoothed over her skin before encircling her peaked nipples. Emily's body shook with the force of the emotions cascading over her, the words of protest dying before she could even form them. She'd never experienced anything like this before… this wildness, this reckless urge to give herself over to him completely. Wylder's possessive touch sent her soaring, and he'd not even begun to explore her fully.

"You are so soft, minx. So smooth." He pinched her nipples until she gasped in shocked pleasure at the slight pain. "Turn around for me now. Let me see you before I decide on your punishment."

He released her then, stepping away so that she could obey the murmured command. Clutching the tattered edges of the nightgown together to conceal her nudity, Emily slowly turned. Her heart thumped harder at the look of absolute desire in Wylder's eyes. He looked as though he would eat her alive, a muscle ticking in his jaw as his gaze passed over her. A dimple in his right cheek appeared when his lips quirked upward at her display of modesty.

"Lower your hands, Emily."

Closing her eyes, she did as he instructed. The nightgown gaped open once more, and in the next second, goose bumps broke out on her flesh when his hard hands pushed the material off her shoulders. The gown hung for a few moments, then slipped away from her body, pooling in a flimsy heap of muslin at her feet. She was now entirely bare for his hot gaze and a sudden, pained embarrassment flooded her.

How terribly strange it is to be standing before him in this unclothed state when he is not similarly bare. What if he does not find me pleasing to look upon? What if I am lacking in some way compared to his other lovers? He is so much more worldly than I am... perhaps the women he has consorted with in the past were more generously endowed... their breasts fuller and their hips curved like the ones in the paintings I saw at Northumberland House last year...

"No. Don't close your eyes. Look at me, minx," Wylder commanded softly, interrupting her internal reverie. Emily's eyes flew open, meeting his when he reached out a hand to lift her braid from where it coiled around one breast. He entwined it around his fist like a silken tether. "You are by far the most beautiful thing I've ever seen. It is almost painful to look upon such beauty and know that I will be responsible for its ruination."

Releasing her, Wylder removed his coat and quickly unraveled his cravat. He tossed both into the chair she'd previously perched upon, and Emily silently watched as he shrugged out of his waistcoat. His movements were unhurried. Deliberate. Entrancing. Throwing the garment into the same chair with the rest of his clothes, he now stood before her wearing only a white muslin shirt that lay open to his waist. Emily's mouth went dry at the sight of him. What she could see of his body was smooth and lightly tanned, the expanse of exposed flesh an intriguing mix of firm muscles and ridged lines that her fingers ached to explore. That dimple in his cheek appeared once more as he tugged the shirt over his head and tossed it aside as well.

Then, as her blood raced and her knees trembled beneath the weight of her own body, Emily stared as Wylder picked up the cravat. The white strip of silk dangled from his large hand as he regarded her. His eyes glowed in the dim light of the room, chips of ice blazing with an internal flame.

"Now, what shall we do for your punishment, minx?" Wylder came closer, and Emily sucked in a breath, retreating despite herself. The enormity of the situation... the man she adored standing in the middle of her bedroom while she stood nude and quivering before him... was suddenly quite daunting. And just a tiny bit frightening, if she was truthful with herself.

Wylder's expression changed in a heartbeat, morphing from stern, hungry predator to concerned lover.

"Ah, my sweet minx. Do not be afraid." His tone was soothing and gentle. While desire still danced in the depths of his eyes, he obviously recognized Emily's reticence. "I shall not hurt you... I swear this upon my very life."

A flood of relief pinkened Emily's cheeks. "I'm not afraid. You must think me very silly and inexperienced, but I am not worried that you will hurt me. It's just that, for the briefest of moments, I found myself overwhelmed with the reality of you being here and hoping that..." Taking a deep, fortifying breath, she blurted out, "Hoping that you want me as desperately as I want you." Embarrassed by her own brazen nature, her face felt as though it were on fire as she confessed shyly, "And even if all you do is administer a punishment, I welcome it."

A slow grin curved his firm mouth. "I am heartily glad to hear this, Emily. Your concerns remind me that it's necessary to explain my actions more thoroughly due to your innocence. You see, my intention tonight is twofold if we continue this unusual relationship. I will most certainly punish you for certain infractions, the most notable being the instances you did not obey my direct instructions, beginning with the morning you fled my townhouse to make your own way home. Placing yourself in danger like that greatly offends me, and I must ensure you do not behave so recklessly again. But more importantly, my overwhelming desire is to give you such overwhelming pleasure that you seek to please me in all things. The juxtaposition of these two principles will, I believe, cause you to rethink..." Capturing her hand, he pressed a hot, open-mouthed kiss to the inner portion of her wrist, then her fingertips before biting them softly and continuing with another sinful smile, "your inherently brattish behavior."

Emily chewed at her bottom lip, her eyes wide. "I don't understand, my lord. You punished me once... the night you spanked me in the gardens of this very house. How-how can it be a punishment if I like it?"

"*Sweet Jesus,*" Wylder breathed out, his eyes fluttering shut as though her innocent confusion was too much to bear. "I suspect you will be the death of me, minx." He pulled her to him then, taking both of her hands and kissing them in reverence. When next Wylder spoke, his tone was darker but incredibly soft. "I intend on tying you up, Emily. I will first administer your punishment, then I shall bind you to your bed and worship your body until you beg for mercy. If you still want this, you shall put your hands behind your back and submit completely. This only comes to a stop if you utter the special word you selected earlier. Do you understand?"

"Yes, my lord," Emily whispered. She saw his ghost of a smile before he spun her around. When she immediately placed her hands behind her back, he quickly wound the cravat around her wrists.

She whimpered with delight, swaying back against him and loving how helpless she felt. After tying the ends into a bow, his large, warm hands slipped down over her buttocks, squeezing the globes of flesh until she was dizzy with lust. "Please, Wylder. Do that again."

"Easy, Emily. That ache you are experiencing is your body preparing itself for what is to come, but you will remain silent until I give you leave to speak. Another rule, darling, and one I must insist upon based on our present location. It would not do for your servants to hear what I'm doing to you over the next couple of hours."

Emily nearly squeaked out an alarmed protest at the length of time Wylder mentioned, but his hands tightened on the cravat as he used it to guide her toward another plush chair near the bed. He sat down on it and pulled her to stand between his open knees while still holding her wrists hostage. The position meant her upper body bowed toward his, her breasts thrusting forward with obscene eagerness.

"Bloody hell, you are a vision," he murmured almost to himself. "And one day soon, I shall enjoy having you trussed in such a manner while you are on your knees sucking my cock. You won't be able to escape as I spill down your tight throat, my hands in your gorgeous hair as I guide your movements for my pleasure."

A strangled noise slipped from Emily's throat at the arousing image Wylder's words created. It served to remind him of his purpose, for his eyes darkened even more, the silvery depths now almost black with desire.

"But that's for another time, my sweet Emily. Arrange yourself over my lap and let us begin."

CHAPTER ELEVEN

Emily

SEVEN STRIKES TO her bare bottom, and Emily was seriously reconsidering her ridiculous infatuation with Wylder St. Clair.

Tears slipped down her cheeks, landing silently on the floor beneath her head. After informing her she would be expected to count the blows upon the next occasion of punishment, Wylder enumerated each time his palm landed on bare flesh with frightening calm. The muscled hardness of his body, his arousal jutting like newly forged iron into the soft skin of her belly, were strange elements she readily accepted. The thought that the earl found this pleasurable was confusing, but no more bewildering than her own body's response. It hurt badly enough that she wept softly with barely audible gasps.

But the sharp sting was also melting into a strange ache of sorts between her legs. It was a building of pressure that must explode somehow, or else she would go mad.

"That's ten, Emily." His voice reached through the roaring inside her head. Dazed, she realized one of his hands now rested on the curve of her buttocks while the other kept her bound hands anchored in the small of her back. He was no longer counting out loud and his hand was still.

It's over? It seemed he had just begun, and yet it also felt like an eternity since she'd placed herself across his lap.

"You did so well, my sweet. And as proud as I am of you, I do hope you learned a valuable lesson from this."

Something inside Emily came alive in a rush of sensations. It was an astonishing burst that lit her from the inside out until she was sure she must be glowing. The unexpected praise, his admiration that she'd taken his punishment without calling out that single word, sent her floating and adrift on a sea of pleasure. But even as she luxuriated in the experience, her body was alive and aching for more.

More.

"Please," she whispered, instinctively knowing that she should not move until Wylder gave her permission to do so.

"Poor little minx," he murmured, a thread of sympathetic amusement in his tone. "You want more, don't you? I know that if I touch you between your legs right now, you will be wet for me. Like creamy honey dripping onto my fingers." His fingers squeezed one round globe of her arse. "Your skin is such a lovely shade of pink. Like the inside petals of a red rose."

Emily quivered, wishing he would touch her where the ache was the worst. She squirmed a little, which made Wylder heave out an agonized grunt.

"You're tempting me to forget the rest of your lesson, Emily. Be warned that I will not be swayed by the sight of your pretty arse wiggling in my lap," he laughed ruefully. "This night is for you."

"Will you take no pleasure for yourself, then?" she choked out as his fingers suddenly swept across her nether lips. She nearly bucked off his lap. *"Oh, God..."*

"Be still for me, Emily." He began tracing the damp folds of her flesh, his thumb finding the button of nerves as he'd done in the Jacobsons' front parlor only a couple of hours before. *Oh, goodness.* This was a thousand times better in Emily's opinion. She could feel his body beneath hers as she settled into the caress. She reveled in his harsh breathing and the groans he couldn't quite contain every time she moved. Closing her eyes, she let him build her orgasm to a peak, and when she cried out in helpless satisfaction, Wylder reached over and covered her mouth with his hand.

"Shhh," he chuckled. "We don't want anyone to overhear, remember?"

Emily swallowed her whimpers as the waves ebbed and undulated inside her veins. A moment later, she felt a tugging on the cravat still tied around her wrists. She'd forgotten she was still bound.

After pulling the strip of silk free of her hands, Wylder pulled Emily upright, swinging her around so that she was cradled in his lap. For a long moment, he held her, his hands softly caressing her body. Her head fell back against his shoulder, and she smiled in contentment as Wylder swiped her cheeks with the pads of his thumbs.

"Your tears, little minx, are sweet as wine." He licked his thumbs before sliding his one hand around the nape of her neck. Sliding his tongue deep into her mouth, he kissed her with languid possessiveness. "Everything about you is fucking delicious. And I'm ready to taste the rest of you."

EMILY PULLED ON the cravat, but it was no use. It held tight, her hands tethered above her head and lashed to the bed's headboard. Lower down, her feet were similarly tied with the sash of her own robe, rendering her completely immobile.

Wylder watched her test the restraints, his eyes glowing with appreciation for the scandalous sight of her trussed up on her bed. When she met his gaze, his mouth curved into a satisfied smile.

"You are not too uncomfortable?"

"N-no," she mumbled, still dazed by both the spanking and the orgasm that came after. She'd lain in a complacent stupor as

Wylder worked to secure her limbs. Even if she wished to voice a protest now, the words died on her lips, wrangled into submission by her own desire for this man.

"Good. I do not want this to be painful for you, and if you obey my instructions, it won't be. Do not tug on the restraints as it will undoubtedly leave marks behind that you will not be able to explain. My wish is that you lie completely still as I worship you, Emily. Can you do this for me?"

"Yes, my lord," Emily breathed, entranced by his possessively tender care. The combination was a fatal blow to her soul. Was he like this with all of his lovers? The thought struck a violently possessive note inside her, one she tried and failed to squelch.

"Then I shall begin. The hour is fast approaching when I must leave you."

Emily frowned, the reality of his departure intruding on the fantasy created the moment he entered through the balcony doors. "How shall you get away with no one seeing you?"

He chuckled at that, coming closer to the bed and lightly pinching her chin between his forefinger and thumb. "That is hardly your concern, my sweet. You must simply focus on me as I explore your body."

Leaning over, Wylder pressed a soft kiss to her mouth, but when Emily eagerly responded, he drew back. His gaze raked her body, his fingers trailing from her chin to her throat and then tracing the line of her collarbone. She swallowed hard as goose bumps rose as if to guide his touch.

"You are so damned beautiful, Emily. I have dreamed of this moment for so long, it does not seem real." He lightly encircled one of her pebbled nipples and Emily moaned. "I've long wondered what color your nipples would be, and the reality is so much better than my imagination. They are the loveliest shade of coral." Bending down, he traced his tongue over first one then the other. Emily's body tensed with a flood of pleasure, her hands clenching and unclenching as he drew one aching tip into the inferno of his mouth. As she shuddered beneath the onslaught of his teeth and tongue, Wylder feasted on her breasts, shaping and molding them in his hands, teasing her with little bites and a sucking motion that had her hips tilting higher to the limits of the restraints.

"So sweet," he murmured. "So responsive to my touch."

Emily blinked up at him, lost in the sensations as he carefully crawled onto the bed and settled between her open legs. She wanted her hands free. She wanted to caress the beauty of his masculine form, to commit the hard, angular lines of his chest and abdomen to memory with her fingers and her mouth. She wanted to rake her hands through the thick wealth of his dark hair and delight in the silk waves as they tumbled over her fingers. She wanted all those things and more, but blast it, she'd allowed Wylder to restrain her, and he showed little interest in releasing her.

Hovering over her body, Wylder kissed her ribs then her stomach, his mouth soft in its exploration. His hands moved down, framing her hips and grasping the curved lines as he held her steady. Emily moaned again, her lower body lifting in anticipation.

"Wylder? I want to touch you, too. Won't you let me?"

"Not this time, minx." He said nothing more as he brushed hot, lush kisses across her lower belly, his fingers slipping beneath her body. Gripping her tender buttocks, he used his tongue to part the tender folds of her vagina then licked her flesh in one scorching hot caress.

"Oh, my God…" Emily gasped, arching into his mouth in shameless, greedy abandon. "Wylder… it feels so good…"

He responded with a low growl of satisfaction, his mouth fastening over her intimate core as he proceeded to devour her. His tongue swiped and probed, applying pressure then backing off until Emily thought she was slipping over the edge into madness. Once he had worked her into a frenzy, his wicked tongue lashing at her swollen clit, he slid a finger inside her, stopping just short of full insertion.

The fullness this created, combined with the exquisite torture of his mouth working her clitoris flung Emily into the stars. When Wylder crooked that finger, rubbing an internal spot with relentless intent, she could not contain the muffled scream that escaped her. Her body clenched around his digit as she exploded, and Wylder grunted as he lapped up her release and shallowly pumped his finger in and out of her until the orgasm subsided into tremors that racked her body.

Lifting her head from the pillows that propped her up, Emily stared at the man crouched between her thighs in wonderment. What he'd just done to her was the most wonderous experience of her life. She wanted him to do it again.

After a moment, Wylder paused from licking her flesh clean and gave her a wicked grin over the flat plane of her belly.

"That—" Emily struggled to find the right words. "That was amazing."

"If it felt anything like you taste, then I must agree, little minx." He licked her again, laughing when her eyes fluttered shut. "And since I'm now hopelessly addicted to your taste, I should warn you that I intend on doing that again."

"I don't mind," she admitted shyly, her breath coming in fast pants for air.

"Not as if you have any say in the matter, bound as you are and at my mercy," he chuckled low, making sure she watched as he sucked his fingers clean of her juices. "Let's see if I can make you come again in half the time of your last climax."

CHAPTER TWELVE

Wylder

FIVE DAYS LATER, Wylder sat in the Blue Parlor at St. Clair Manor, waiting for his father to appear for their afternoon meeting.

"More tea, my dear?" his mother inquired, picking up the teapot and pouring herself a bit more of the steaming brew.

"No, thank you, Mother." Wylder smiled politely while watching the duchess from over the rim of his cup.

Annabelle St. Clair was a fragile creature. Always had been. Wylder's birth had very nearly killed her, if the stories were to be believed. He'd been a large baby and so robust during labor that the lady suffered a hemorrhage, which required a doctor to be called upon to stitch her up. The duke, while ecstatic that his newborn child was a son, had little desire to go through such a traumatic experience again. The decision to abandon his wife's bed resulted in Wylder being the sole heir to the dukedom and the slow decline of the Duchess of Claymore.

"Have you enjoyed attending the many events of the season, my dear boy?" Annabelle asked, stirring a cube of sugar into her cup. She sounded more than curious, and Wylder tilted his head as he regarded his mother.

"It passes the time," he replied with a slight shrug of his shoulders.

Annabelle smiled guilelessly at Wylder. "Of course, the gaiety of such events is certainly conducive to selecting the next Countess of Wyldewood from a variety of candidates."

If his mother only knew how he'd passed the time a few nights ago, she would likely succumb to a fit of the vapors and probably never recover.

"I've heard you've been seen with the Blackthorne girl numerous times this past week. It's said you were to dance with her at the Jacobsons' before she left with a sudden headache." Annabelle smiled brightly. "Oh, she's such a lovely little thing, Wylder. And so intelligent."

"Where did you hear that?" Wylder grunted before covering his irritation with a slight cough. After coercing Emily Blackthorne to climax so many times she finally fainted from exhaustion, he'd kept his distance from her in the days that followed the Jacobson ball. He was fearful that he'd snatch her up and claim her in front of God and everyone. It was worrisome that Simon made a point of closely watching Wylder. Even though he studiously ignored Emily's baleful glares, Wylder understood he could not be seen with her.

"Oh, Lady Blackthorne came for tea yesterday, and the subject came up. She kindly related all the gossip of the season so far. The countess was quite pleased with the prospect of you courting her daughter. And if your own mother's opinion holds any weight, I've long thought she would be perfect for you. It seems only natural you would pursue Emily, being that you are so fond of her brother. I'm sure he would love having you as a true brother, even if it be only by marriage that makes it so."

"You know that marriage does not interest me, Mother," Wylder sighed. "And a bride would only complicate matters as they stand now."

"I think a wife would help clarify things for you, my dear. Wouldn't it be lovely to have someone to share your thoughts and dreams with? Lady Emily would prove a credit to your titles and the continuation of our bloodlines."

"As much as it pains me to disappoint you, Mother, I am not in the market for a bride. I've only just set things right with my own finances, and there is so much more that needs to be done with the other estates."

Annabelle's mouth turned downward at the change of subject. "While I am not privy to His Grace's business, I have long suspected matters were unstable with the exception of Wyldewood. From all accounts, you've done a fine job with it, son."

"Thank you, Mother. I hope to convince Father to allow me to employ the same tactics with the other properties."

Annabelle set down her teacup, obviously flustered by the talk of money. It was considered unwomanly for a female to be concerned with how her family's fortunes were conceived or maintained. "He will not speak with me on such issues, but I feel confident that he will heed your advice, Wylder. Indeed, he would be foolish to ignore your expertise in matters regarding finances."

"What's this about finances?" Albert St. Clair, the Duke of Claymore and Wylder's father, entered the parlor, his voice booming in the expanse of the elegant room.

"Good afternoon, sir," Wylder said respectfully, rising from his seat to sketch a slight bow to his father. "I hoped I might have a word with you regarding some matters that have come to my attention. Your steward indicated you had time this afternoon when the appointment was made. If you are agreeable, we shall discuss it after we've finished tea with Mother."

Albert's gaze slanted toward his only son. "I can only imagine what these matters might entail, but would I be correct in assuming it involves Lord Jacobson?"

Wylder sank back down into his seat, lips thinned by irritation. "It does. I prefer that this discussion take place in the privacy of your study, Your Grace."

"Don't ruin our tea, my lord," Annabelle said to her husband with an indulgent smile for Wylder. "It is so infrequent that our son comes for a visit."

Albert looked as though he wanted to protest, but instead, he let out a sigh of resignation, dropped a kiss to his wife's forehead, and plopped down on the settee beside her. "As you wish, my dear."

⟫⟫⟫⟪⟪⟪

"WHAT IS IT that you wish to discuss?" Albert closed the door to the study behind Wylder and made his way to an imposing desk littered with slips of paper and various ledger books.

Wylder stepped over to a Rococo-style sideboard upon which rested a decanter of whisky and one of brandy. He poured himself a glass of the whisky, and after receiving a wave of acknowledgment from his father, one for him as well.

"Your letters of debt to Lord Jacobson, to start," Wylder said, handing the glass over to his father.

"Oh, a trifling thing," the duke scoffed, gulping down a healthy splash of the whisky as he sat down behind the ornately carved desk. "Jacobson would have done well not to have concerned you in my personal affairs."

"And yet, he did," Wylder mused. Rolling the crystal tumbler in his hand, he studied the amber liquid. Scolding a parent was an awkward position to be in as a son, one he heartily wished was not necessary. "I covered the amount on your behalf, but it is the last time I shall do so." He leveled a stern glare at the duke. "Your gambling must be curbed, Father. Otherwise, you will lose the estates to your debtors because I will not continue paying for your vices."

A look of real shock crossed Albert's features before he drained the amount of whisky in his glass and set it down on a ledger book. "Is it as bad as all that?" Fidgeting with a few of the papers scattered across his desk, he stacked them haphazardly while avoiding Wylder's scrutiny. The duke's embarrassment was tangible, a condition he covered with a gruffness borne of bravado.

"It is." Wylder sipped his whisky, wondering if the man would agree to his proposal. "And I have a solution to the problem, if you will entertain it."

Leaning toward Wylder, Albert's eyes lit up. "You have found an heiress to wed, have you? Your mother has despaired of that ever happening, but I've told her more than once that—"

"I have no intention of marrying an heiress, Father."

"Why not?" Albert demanded. "It is the obvious solution… and with the desirable title of 'duchess' serving as an enticement, it's only a matter of time before you snare the right girl for a bride. Perhaps one of those cheeky American heiresses… they seem almost desperate for titles. Any gentleman of nobility will suffice as a complement to their dowries."

"I have a more viable suggestion. One that will save the dukedom and the lesser estates. However, it does require a sacrifice on your part."

"Sacrifice? What the devil are you going on about?" Albert blustered while shaking a finger at Wylder. "It's high time you were wed, my boy. No more of this Rakehells of Mayfair business. Claymore needs an heir—"

"There will be no Claymore to speak of if you continue to gamble it away." Wylder heatedly interjected. "My plan… indeed, my hope… is to prevent that. To that end, you will turn over control of the finances for all of the estates to me so that I may begin rebuilding the coffers. I have enlisted the Earl of Camden's assistance with this, as he generously advised me during the recovery of Wyldewood and my personal fortune, and I trust his judgment implicitly when it comes to matters of finance. The man is an absolute genius when it comes to manipulating the 'Change. I shall grant you a reasonable allowance as I undertake this monumental task, and I will expect you to abide by the terms we set forth today." Wylder's gaze was stern and unyielding, enough so that his father swallowed nervously under the weight of his disapproving stare. "There is really no other choice, Father. If you refuse, the dukedom will be lost. If that happens, I am prepared to provide a stipend for you and Mother to live upon. However, you must be aware that it will be far below the standards you currently enjoy." Pausing, he tilted his head as he considered the duke. "Shall I choose for you? Or will you do this as a matter of honor and help me save my inheritance, pitiful though it is in its current state?"

"This is beyond the pale, Wylder," Albert feebly protested. "I've always covered my debts, son. This latest difficulty is simply a result of a string of misfortune at the tables."

"It is your choice, Your Grace. You are undoubtedly aware that you are teetering on the verge of insolvency. If I take over the accounts, you shall at least save face within your set of acquaintances and friends. And Mother would not be relegated to the country, secluded in shame. You don't wish that for her, do you?"

Dismay clouded Albert's gaze before it turned calculating. "You have me at a disadvantage, it seems, Wylder. But if I choose your solution, if I allow you to take such drastic steps, I have a request of my own."

Wylder nearly sighed with relief. Whatever his father asked, it was sure to be something easily accomplished. Most likely, it would be the payment of some debt that had not yet come to light. "What might that be?"

"I shall give you full control of the estates. I'll even abide by the terms of the allowance, but only if you agree to seek out a suitable wife. An heiress with an enormous dowry would be ideal, but even if she turns out to be as poor as a church mouse, like Lucien Westley's new bride, I will be satisfied."

"Ah, I see. You think blackmail will help your cause, Father?"

"It's hardly blackmail, my boy. I do as you request, and you do something that will make your mother very happy." Albert leaned over the desk toward Wylder. "Come on, son. Is it asking that much, considering I am giving up control of my estates? If this stipulation is not agreeable, then I shall recoup my losses at the tables. It may take a while, but I'm confident that eventually I will pull ahead."

"Fine," Wylder growled in sudden capitulation. How he would accomplish fulfilling the demands of his father, he did not know. For now, he would count this as a victory. Controlling the finances and stemming the bleeding of funds was of the utmost importance. *As for the other...* Wylder clenched his teeth to control his anger. *As for the other...*

He would focus on that later.

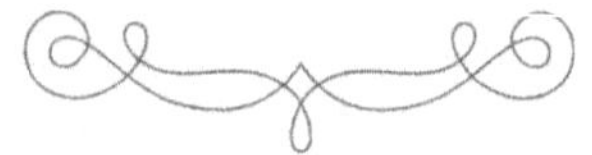

Chapter Thirteen

Emily

EMILY STALKED ACROSS her bedroom, ripping the jaunty hat from her head and sailing it without a care. The riding crop she'd forgotten to leave behind in the stables was flung upon the bed with an unladylike curse.

Beneath the obvious anger sparking her blood, bewildered hurt rippled through her fragile soul.

She'd been blissfully unaware of Wylder's visit to Blackthorne Manor today. Returning from an afternoon ride in Hyde Park, she'd discovered the earl dismounting from his horse in the circular drive. After handing her mare off to the groom, she ran to greet Wylder only to find herself reeling from the cut direct.

Wylder's dispassionate salutation deflated Emily. Any joy at seeing him collapsed when Wylder granted her a dispassionate salutation. It did not matter that his eyes spoke a different story… a spark of sadness that had she not been studying his face would have gone unnoticed. He was not happy. And, when he abruptly turned away and bounded up the steps to the manor's front doors, she stood frozen in place by his icy demeanor.

"I understand the need for discretion," she fumed aloud within the privacy of her room. "But must he be so cruel when going about it? It's as though everything that passed between us means absolutely nothing to him. How can he not comprehend how terribly it hurts when he behaves in such a manner toward me? Is it so challenging to extend even the slightest hint of affection? It wouldn't be out of the ordinary… he has known me for most of my life. He draws more attention to himself when he is so blatantly rude, but I cannot expect him to listen to reason on that particular point. He is a man… and therefore believes he knows best on every subject."

Sitting down at the dressing table, Emily stripped off the kid leather riding gloves, her hands shaking. The proper cravat around her neck was next to be ruthlessly ripped away, the pretty bow ruined in her state of anguished emotion. Shrugging off the form-fitting Spencer jacket, she threw it aside as well.

Only when it felt as though she could draw in a breath did she finally turn toward her reflection in the vanity glass. Tears streaked her cheeks, her bottom lip trembling and blood red from her teeth biting it to contain her sobs.

And as quickly as anger had overwhelmed her, sorrow now seeped through her bones. It settled deep within her, silently whispering that her hopes and dreams of making Wylder St. Clair her own were just that. Fanciful dreams that would never come true.

Dropping her head into her hands, Emily allowed the tears to flow without check as reality speared her heart. There was nothing for it… this depth of despair. Even the realization that she was reacting rather dramatically to Wylder's rejection did not make the ache any less painful. She was well aware of her spoiled nature… but wasn't it worth something that she was also kind and generous to those she loved?

Wylder had referred to her as a brat several times before, and she supposed that could be true in some instances. When she wanted something very badly, she put forth all her charm and sweetness in a bid to obtain it. When those tactics did not work, she usually resorted to pouting, tantrums, and pretty tears.

I behave as a child would.

It was a shocking self-realization. Straightening her spine,

Emily stared at herself in the mirror, stunned by this revelation while dashing the tears from her cheeks. Was it possible she had sabotaged her efforts to gain Wylder's affection? Should she accept the inevitable and move toward the future with that in mind? While it was true that contact with Wylder over the past three years had been superficial, Emily never stopped hoping that would change. Never stopped hoping that her hardheaded brother would reconsider his ridiculous objections to the relationship. It would come to that or in the alternative, Wylder would tell Simon to go to hell and to stop interfering where he wasn't wanted.

Emily sighed heavily and rose from the dressing table chair. Calmer than when she'd first stormed into her room, she retrieved the items of clothing abandoned during her fit of temper. The cravat was picked up and smoothed into order. Her riding gloves were paired once more and placed in the bureau where they belonged. And the Spencer jacket was scooped up from the floor and carefully laid across one of the plush chairs, ready for her maid to see to its cleaning.

Seeing the riding crop on the bed, Emily plucked it from the coverlet and tapped it against her outer leg. She would return it to the stable's tack room upon her next ride. For now, she set it in the same chair as the jacket.

That left one thing to be done. A new mindset that did not involve Wylder St. Clair as part of her future. She would cease this infernal hoping and waiting for the man to see reason. She would learn whatever he desired to teach her, absorb it, and save the knowledge for the future. More importantly, she would enjoy the pleasure that came with such lessons without expecting Wylder to be a part of that future.

This simple decision had a profound effect on Emily. A strange sense of peace washed over her... an acceptance of her life's path along with the knowledge that certain things about it could not be altered.

Wylder would never be hers. He would never be her husband

and she would never be his wife. But that did not mean she couldn't take some part of him for herself. She could take his kisses and his caresses and hold them as dear memories. And if the day ever came about that he realized just what he had lost, she would mourn the loss and turn her back as he'd turned his back on her.

EMILY'S FIRST OPPORTUNITY to put her new outlook into practice was at dinner that same evening.

Wylder had spent the afternoon holed up in Father's study with Simon. Emily had no idea what the two men could have possibly discussed that necessitated such serious conversations, but Wylder accepted the invitation to dinner. He appeared relaxed as the first course of white soup was served. He conversed easily with Lady Blackthorne, chuckled at her father's humorous observations, and politely inquired after Emily's well-being. Only she saw the questioning glint in his silver gaze when she coolly replied that she was fine, although a bit tired from her afternoon ride.

"I'm not surprised," Simon teased, giving Emily an affectionate grin. "I've heard tales of how you tear about Hyde Park upon Morgiana's back as though you were galloping the country meadows of Thorne." He wagged a finger at his sister and half-heartedly admonished, "Your boldness frightens half the dandies on their social rounds every time you have the reins in your hands. God help them if they actually race you."

Wylder's smile faltered at Simon's assertions. It seemed he was disturbed by some aspect of the conversation, but Emily shrugged it away. "I believe that any gentleman frightened by my style of riding would be frightened of a great many other things."

Simon and Father both laughed at her words while Mother tsked in a gentle, disapproving manner. "I at least hope you are wearing your riding gloves, my dear. Leather reins can be so harsh on a lady's hands."

Emily took a sip of water. "Of course I wore them, Mother." She deliberately remained silent on Simon's accusation of cantering through Hyde Park because it was somewhat true. She often rode through the open fields, but rarely did anyone accept the unspoken challenge of a race. She frowned playfully at Simon. "No one will race me because of my arrogant, older brother."

"You should not be engaging in such dangerous behavior," Wylder growled, taking a huge gulp of wine.

Simon's gaze shot to his friend, his dark brow raised high in question at Wylder's tone, but he said nothing.

Emily's smile was politely cool. "That sounds like something a husband might say." She flashed a charming smile at her father, knowing he would not chastise her for being so blunt. The earl rarely found fault in anything she did; his pride in both of his children was no secret among their social set. "And what else am I to do with a horse like Morgiana? She loves to run, and I do enjoy letting her have her head. So, until someone other than my father tells me I cannot, I shall do as I please."

A muscle twitched in Wylder's jaw. "A husband would not indulge nor approve of such practices like a doting father is wont to do."

Emily grinned at that. "That is probably true. And if I had a husband, I'm positive I could convince him to see things from my point of view."

"No doubt you would succeed, my dear," Lord Blackthorne laughed in delight, beaming at his daughter. "I cannot imagine any man possessing the strength to deny you once you've set your mind to something."

Emily's gaze locked with Wylder as she replied, "Oh, I'm sure one exists somewhere. However, like any other woman, I would prefer a far more reasonable spouse who will not lord his mastery over me. Perhaps I should put more effort into finding such a man this season."

Wylder's eyes were molten silver as he stared at her. Only when Simon cleared his throat in a low rumble did the earl finally break eye contact with Emily.

"Yes, well, perhaps a change of scenery will help matters, darling," Lady Blackthorne said in a cheerful voice meant to disrupt the tense atmosphere that had fallen over the dinner table. "We will indeed have a house party and ball at Thorne Park in honor of Lord and Lady Ashcroft next month. Arrangements are being made, and I've already constructed an extensive guest list."

"Oh, no," Lord Blackthorne groaned dramatically. "How extensive?"

"Do not fret, my lord," Lady Blackthorne trilled, waving her hand in the air in dismissal of her husband's concerns. "Only a hundred guests... perhaps a few more."

"I, for one, am looking forward to seeing Lucien again when he returns to London next week," Simon remarked, his attention flickering between Wylder and his sister. "I hope he is eager for a small break from domesticity and will indulge his two good friends with some time at our clubs."

Lady Blackthorne frowned at Simon. "My darling son must remember Ashcroft is now a married man and, by all accounts, besotted with his new bride. My own hope is that you find the same happiness he has."

"Here it comes," Simon groaned as the first course was removed from the table. "The not-so-subtle hints that I must settle down."

"You are not alone in that, Camden." Wylder grimaced while casting a surreptitious glance at Emily, who managed, with admirable calm, to return his stare. "My father has also increased his demands on the subject."

Lady Blackthorne clapped her hands in delight. "Would that not be the coup of the season if the two remaining Rakehells should find their brides at my house party? Even better would be that my lovely daughter finds her perfect match as well." Her mother beamed at Emily.

"You are right, Mother. In fact, I shall apply myself with greater care in finding a wonderful husband," Emily replied in a lilting voice.

Attuned as she was to the earl, Emily heard the low rumble that issued from Wylder's side of the table. Thankfully, the sound of dissent was lost in Lady Blackthorne's gay chatter regarding the guest list and what was sure to be the highlight of the season.

"Of course, your sweet friend Miss True is included. As her sponsor, I'm confident I can convince Lady True to allow her to attend, with me acting as her chaperone. She is the dearest thing."

Perhaps only Emily saw the disconcerted frown that flashed across Simon's features at the mention of Penelope. He apparently found something objectionable to the young lady attending the house party. Still, knowing how he avoided ladies of a marriageable age, Emily could not guess his thoughts on the matter.

Ideas began bombarding Emily. This would provide the perfect opportunity to help Penelope. If it could be arranged, she was sure it was possible to hide her somewhere in London while Lord and Lady True believed their daughter was still at the Thorne Park estate. Emily's heart raced as she considered the possible scenarios. While she had no qualms about deceiving Penelope's detestable parents, she realized any plan involved lying to her own mother to excuse Penelope's departure from the house party.

Complicating matters was the certainty that Wylder would be at the event. Avoiding him while scheming on her friend's behalf would be difficult. He was sure to sniff out any plot she might devise if she could not keep him at arm's length. Although Emily made it through dinner with outward calm, inside, she was a trembling mess. Feigning indifference to the man was more difficult than she had anticipated. She did not like the way her heart thumped with longing every time he looked her way, even as her brain insisted that she was doing the right thing.

The situation must be approached with dispassion if I wish to survive it.

Any attention he gave her would be filed away for the future when he was no longer in her life. And she could do it with dignity if she tried hard enough.

Every glance Wylder threw her way, every quirk of his firm mouth that made her insides flutter with desire, Emily reminded herself that she was done chasing after the man. If he wished to continue their illicit arrangement, it would be up to him to pursue her.

CHAPTER FOURTEEN

Emily

"THANK YOU, MARY," Emily said in a soft voice, pulling the robe free of her shoulders and slipping out of her slippers. She slid under the bed's coverlet, plumping the pillows into a tiny heap behind her back. "I don't need anything else tonight. Please enjoy your day with your mother tomorrow and give her my kind regards."

"I will, Lady Emily." Mary folded the robe, laying it at the foot of the bed. "Are you sure you will not need me in the morning?"

"No, it will not be necessary. I can manage to dress myself, and if I require assistance, I will call upon one of the upstairs maids." Emily slanted a glance at the girl. Mary was three years older and one of the sweetest people Emily had ever known. The maid was also amazingly gifted at accomplishing various tasks. "And you are sure you will be able to steal away for an hour or two to look over the Curzon Street townhome? I know it has a limited staff, but if Miss Penelope stays for an extended period, she will require a few things during that time. Most importantly, a maid we can trust."

"Oh, yes, milady. My cousin is available to help with this. She recently lost her post after Lord Manton passed away, and his widow was forced to address expenses." Mary smiled at Emily, her tone filled with reassurance. "And the butler at the Curzon townhome is friends with my mother. Once she became ill, he has made it a point to visit her whenever he can. I'm sure he will be happy to help, as long as you approve the venture."

"I wish Penelope could stay there with no one being the wiser," Emily mused, biting her forefinger in thought.

"It will be discreet, milady. Only the necessary staff will be aware of her stay, and they will not speak on the matter without your directive."

"I suppose you are right. I will visit it myself next week to ensure everything is in place. The house party is in a month's time, so I would like to have all plans in place before then."

Mary nodded, picking up a few more clothing items to drape over her arm, including the Spencer jacket Emily had worn that afternoon. Picking up the riding crop, she looked askance at Emily. "Shall I have this returned to the stables, milady?"

Emily shook her head. "No need. I will do it tomorrow as I plan on riding again in the afternoon. I'll take it with me then."

Mary murmured in agreement, setting the crop back down in the chair before exiting the bedroom with a soft good night for Emily.

Once alone, Emily slumped back against the pillows. Her mind raced, not only with plans for Penelope's situation but also with her own interactions with Wylder and the uneasy nature of their relationship.

He and Simon had once again disappeared into Lord Blackthorne's study following dinner. Emily overheard her mother tell their housekeeper that Lord Wyldewood would be staying the night and to ensure that his usual guestroom was prepared. Knowing he would be sleeping in the guest wing of the house made her jittery with nerves.

Her nights since the Jacobson ball and Wylder's midnight visit had been sleepless ones. She tossed and turned, dreams of Wylder's hands on her body, his eyes burning her skin while he watched her come undone. The lack of sleep was finally catching up to her. She was exhausted after seeing the earl at dinner; her efforts to remain unaffected by his presence mentally wearing her down. But even as she pondered her hopeless infatuation with the man, her eyes grew heavy. Only minutes after Mary's departure, Emily drifted off to sleep.

SHE WOKE SLOWLY, awareness dripping through her body until her eyes opened wide.

A large hand clamped over her mouth, preventing any outcry she might have made. She struggled to rise from the bed only to be pushed down onto the mattress.

"Be still now," Wylder murmured, his voice low and rough. "Do not struggle unless you would like me to lash you to the bed again. Do you want that, minx?"

Emily glared up at him in the soft lamplight and shook her head as best she could with the heel of his hand pushing her into the pillows. Her heart thumped wildly. Why was he here in her room? What could he possibly want from her? And how could he be so reckless as to try this with Simon in the same house? Indeed, on the same floor?

Wylder smelled of brandy and the sweet, smoky aroma of expensive cigars, and his eyes burned through her like molten silver. A thread of anger wove through the way he stared at her. Emily wondered if he was upset because of her coolness toward him at dinner, but then she remembered she was determined not to be concerned with his feelings on the matter.

"If I remove my hand, you will remain quiet like a good girl, won't you?"

Emily's eyes narrowed at him.

"I will remind you that you agreed to follow my orders in moments such as this," he said, his voice tight. "If that is no longer the case, then I shall leave you at once."

Emily stiffened, disturbed by the threat that he might go. This was her opportunity to prove that she could take the pleasure he gave her without expecting more. The slight shake of her head gave him permission to do as he pleased.

Wylder removed the hand from over her mouth. Emily sucked in a breath but lay silent when he snatched the coverlet back in one quick movement. His gaze traveled over her nightgown-clad form, his mouth quirking upward at the sight.

"Very pretty," he said in a low murmur. "But covered from head to toe in sprigged cotton is not how I wish to see you, Emily. Allow me to remedy that."

Wrapping his hand around her wrist, Wylder yanked her up from the bed until she was on her feet.

"Please do not tear this one, too," Emily muttered, annoyed that her body should come alive with his rough handling. "I was forced to burn the last one to prevent any questions from my maid."

"Then by all means, remove this monstrosity on your own."

"Release me, and I will do as you ask, my lord."

They glared at each other for a few moments, the tension stretching between them like a band pulled tight. Emily's gaze flickered to the set of balcony doors, her lips thinning in suspicion.

"How did you get in here?" she demanded. "I am sure I locked those doors before going to bed."

Wylder smirked. "As if a lock would keep me from you, minx." When she continued to frown, he sighed heavily. "You did not lock your bedroom door. I utilized that entrance, if the information matters."

Emily shook her head. "Are you insane? What if someone saw you come in here? What if my brother saw you? You know his rooms are just two corridors away from mine."

"I will admit to a bit of unhinged behavior when it comes to you. However, in this instance, you need not worry, as Simon retired some time ago. I was extremely cautious."

"Why are you here, Wylder?"

"Why am I here, Emily? Because it seems I cannot stay away from you. And knowing that you are just down the hall from me is more temptation than a man can reasonably endure." He sounded hopelessly resigned to that fact even as irritation tinged his words. "This obsession is a damnable sickness."

Emily sighed, her own frustration sapped by his confession. "I am similarly afflicted, Wylder. Even though I realize our lives will never entwine in the way I once hoped, I cannot deny my feelings for you. Resisting you is not possible."

The flame in Wylder's eyes burned higher. Tightening his hand around her wrist, he pulled her closer to him. "Does this mean you are willing to continue with our arrangement?"

"Y-yes." Their gazes clashed, and Emily was the first to cast her eyes downward.

Wylder's eyes softened at her display of submission before he let her go. "I can see the wheels turning in that pretty head of yours, minx. You are angry over my treatment of you this afternoon when I arrived here. I know my greeting was cold; however, there was the very real possibility that Simon would witness our interaction."

Emily nodded, rubbing her wrist to ease the marks his grip left on her tender skin. "Lord forbid that my brother sees you extending common courtesy to his only sister."

"I require his help," Wylder grumbled, scrubbing his jaw. "Far more than I ever did in the past. It is why I came to Blackthorne Manor today. Once again, I must rely upon Simon's expertise in planning out a strategy that saves my compromised inheritance."

Emily cocked her head, one slim, dark brow lifting high in question. "My brother is advising you on the search for an unsuspecting heiress?"

Wylder had the grace to flush. "It is my damnable father. I've agreed with the man in exchange for his cooperation. He is granting me full control over the estates to rebuild our coffers, but only if I pursue this repulsive task of bride hunting. He has convinced himself that a suitable heiress will overlook the lack of coin in the Claymore estates and focus instead on being a future duchess. For the moment, I am forced to oblige his delusions."

"Having intimate knowledge of your aversion to marriage, I cannot imagine how you are stomaching this travesty." Emily's voice contained a false breeziness. Her heart was shattering into pieces with the idea of Wylder searching for a bride while she watched in rejection from the sidelines. Surely God would not be so cruel as to have her watch another young woman claim the role as Wylder's wife.

"It is an illusion for Father's benefit, but one I must give every appearance of following through with. With Simon's help, I believe it is possible to turn our family's fortunes around. Once that occurs, Father's leverage will no longer be valid. Unfortunately, the appearance of my compliance with his demand is necessary right now if I am to have any success in achieving my own goals." Reaching out, Wylder tipped Emily's chin upward with the edge of a knuckle. "Do you understand what I am saying, Emily? It is all but an act worthy of the stage." Flints of gray steel hardened his eyes as he searched her face. His hand moved until that same knuckle brushed over the pulse in the base of her throat. "I fear your words at dinner tonight held a distinct ring of truth. I believe you *will* lead some unsuspecting man in a merry chase for your hand in marriage. And while I have no right to feel this way, I want nothing more than to tear that unknown gentleman to fucking shreds with my bare hands."

"Do not fret, my lord," Emily said calmly, dying inside even as she outwardly projected a resolute acceptance of the situation. "I shall not go back on our agreement before that occurs. Indeed, I still desire you to teach me about what happens between a man and a woman. And while I will remain woefully and ignorantly innocent of the ultimate act, I imagine that my future husband will enjoy the carnal results of my lessons with you. Indeed, he may even wish to thank you himself."

Wylder's fingers curled around her throat. "Damn you for that. Do you think I want it this way? Do you honestly believe for one second that I do not want you as mine? Because I do, Emily. I want every inch of you. Every breath. Every sigh. Every moan that comes from that sweet, treacherous mouth of yours. I want it all, and I am struggling with the Devil himself not to take what belongs to me."

"The Devil is not stopping you," Emily whispered against the pressure of his fingers. She was already soaring, and he'd barely touched her. "And neither am I."

Wylder groaned at her words of encouragement. "So you truly wish to continue this illicit arrangement?"

Emily's eyes fluttered shut at the enormity of her actions. She could not let go of what was between them, and neither could he. Together, they were doomed to burn. "I do."

"Fuck… I cannot help myself when I am with you, Emily. You have intoxicated me like the most dangerous of opiates." His voice was raspy with lust as he pulled her to him to kiss her hard on the mouth.

Emily felt the iron-like evidence of his arousal. His body was a mountain of rigid edges and even harder planes of muscles that she ached to explore. Pulling back from his kiss, she stared up at him.

"You will continue to show me the many ways a man can pleasure a woman? And you will teach me how to do the same for you?"

"Yes, damn you," Wylder groaned, tugging his shirt over his head to reveal the broad expanse of his chest. It gleamed like chiseled stone in the lamplight, his nipples hard, round disks of copper that made Emily's fingers twitch. A dark line of hair ran from his navel to the tops of his breeches, and she wondered if he possessed the same soft curls around his sex as she did. Her mouth watered at the erotic path her thoughts galloped down.

"Take off that nightgown, minx," he commanded hoarsely, and Emily quickly obeyed, drawing the voluminous cotton garment over her head and tossing it aside. "Unbraid your hair."

As his eyes drank in the sight of her naked body, Emily quickly unplaited her hair. She shook it until it tumbled in flowing, inky waves and curls over her shoulders and down to the middle of her back.

Wylder rubbed his palm over the front of his breeches with a low rumble of approval. "You are a goddess. Do you have any idea how many times I have pleasured myself with my own hand while thinking of you?"

Emily blinked at his confession. Men did that to themselves? She wondered if she should say that she'd done the same. The past few nights, she had explored her body with questing fingertips… wondering why the pleasure her touch invoked never came close to matching the feel of Wylder's hands roaming over her skin.

Spying the abandoned riding crop lying in the chair, Wylder picked it up and examined it before locking eyes with Emily.

"Shall I show you how to please me, Emily?" With the end of the crop extended, he traced her collarbone before moving lower. He encircled her nipples with the instrument, smirking when Emily sucked in a gasp of aroused surprise.

"Y-yes, my lord."

"And you remember your word that makes all of this stop, don't you?"

"Yes." Emily swayed toward him as if in a trance. Her stomach swooped as she uttered the word that would make all of this stop. A word she swore to herself she would *never* use in the presence of this man. "Raincloud."

"Good girl," he praised, his smile flashing at her sigh of contentment. "Now, open your mouth for me."

CHAPTER FIFTEEN
Wylder

MY LITTLE MINX will surely be the death of me.

A slight frown knitted the area between Emily's eyebrows as she absorbed what she obviously considered an odd command.

"Do not think, Emily. You simply obey."

Embers sparked in her deep-blue eyes, and her chin lifted in recognition of the mastery in his low voice. Although she clearly wished to question him, her mouth parted just enough that Wylder could see her teeth.

The pulse in her throat was beating rapidly, her chest rising and falling with excitement for the unknown. Knowing she wished to experience the pleasure he could give her... that she would use it to entice and beguile a husband one day... made Wylder want to both beat his chest in frustration and anticipation. He did not think he could stand the thought of another man seeing her beautiful form. The reality was enough to drive him mad.

He placed the crop between her teeth, recognizing her quick intake of breath at his actions. Her eyes were now wide pools of dark-blue lust and confusion.

"Do not drop this. You are not to touch it with your hands at any time," Wylder breathed. "Do you understand?"

Emily hesitated, absorbing his words before slowly nodding.

Wylder turned, locating the chair from where he'd picked up the riding crop. Sitting down, he let his gaze roam over the fetching image she made. Her slender frame was straight and proud, her breasts thrusting upward in plump perfection. From the indentation of her tiny waist, her body flowed into the curved lines of her hips and long, finely shaped legs. At the junction of her creamy thighs, a soft thatch of black curls tempted him with the delights hidden beyond. With her hair unbound and streaming in silky waves across her shoulders, she was a deity of lust he would gladly worship at the feet of.

Staring at him, unblinking, with her hands motionless by her sides, the riding crop was clenched between her teeth. But Wylder could see she was trembling, her nipples hard and pebbled with either desire or the coolness of the room. Perhaps it was both.

Settling back into the chair, Wylder spread his legs wide enough that she could stand between them and motioned that she come closer.

"Come here to me, Emily," he ordered in a deliberately soft voice. *Another time and I will have her crawl to me like this… naked… with my own riding crop between her teeth.* The thought hardened his cock to an almost painful condition. He fought the urge to ease the ache with his own hand, willing to endure this discomfort in favor of what he intended to experience next.

Emily glided forward with an innate grace. When she stood before him, Wylder could not help but run his hands down her smooth flanks, gripping her hips until the imprint of his fingers was on her skin. A small moan issued from her throat. Pulling her even closer, he leaned forward. His mouth was level with her lower belly, the nest of curls hiding her sex. With just a dip of his head, he could lap at paradise with his tongue. Inhaling deeply of her sweet scent, Wylder bent to her, latching his mouth over her sex, his tongue searching through the curls and finding the aching button of her clit.

"Fuck, you always taste so damned good, Emily," he whispered as he licked the tiny bit of flesh. "And always so fucking wet for me." She moaned again, her hands sliding onto his shoulders as she used the breadth of his body to hold herself upright. Little pants of air escaped around the crop in her mouth. "Do not let that riding crop fall," he reminded her, and she whimpered in response, her hips undulating as he nibbled and tasted her.

Wylder quickly worked her up to an orgasm, marveling how responsive she was as she shook in his arms. Before she reached the pinnacle, however, he drew back so he could stare up into her passion-dazed eyes.

"Down on your knees, little minx."

She immediately slid down into a kneeling position, placing her weight on her haunches. The riding crop remained in her mouth, and that pleased Wylder more than he could articulate.

"I am going to teach you how to please me, Emily." He lifted a chunk of her dark hair, rubbing the silky strands through his fingers. His gaze bored into her as he spoke. "It will be a bit unpleasant for you at first... at least until you become accustomed to the things I want you to do. But if you please me in this, I will reward you."

Emily's hands moved until they rested atop her thighs. Like the women in the notorious clubs he frequented, she had unconsciously assumed the position of a submissive. Her gaze never left his until, with one hand, Wylder unbuttoned the fall of his breeches. Her eyes dropped to his lap as he slowly withdrew his cock. Wrapping his fingers around his girth, he pumped his fist up and down his length twice.

A breathy sigh escaped Emily even as her teeth clamped harder on the riding crop. Wylder stifled his groan, his bollocks drawing up tight as a flare of apprehension and desire lit her eyes. She stared at his member, her hands clenching into tiny fists.

"Emily..." Wylder said in a soft voice. "Look at me."

Her gaze flickered up to meet his. Curiosity was stamped on her features, morphing with the desire and uncertainty.

"You are going to put your mouth on me and bring me to a climax." He purposefully kept his tone steady, hoping to calm any fear she had. "I will instruct you. Should you wish to stop at any time, you need only to utter the special word we previously agreed upon."

Stubbornness swept her face, her chin tilting upward in an obstinate manner, and Wylder gripped his cock even tighter as pre-ejaculate gathered on the mushroom-shaped head. She would not surrender with a safe word. She was stubborn enough to try proving herself worthy of whatever task he expected of her.

"Hand me the riding crop, minx."

With a steady hand, she reached up and removed the crop from between her teeth. With a hard swallow and a swipe of her pink tongue over her dry lip, she handed it over. While she watched, he flipped the instrument around in his hand and slid the thick end down between her legs, running it up and down her cleft.

"My lord?" Emily moaned in desperation, leaning toward him. "What will you have me do? Should I... should I kiss you *there?*"

"Bloody hell, *yes.*" Wylder closed his fist around the base of his cock, throttling off the urge to climax at the thought of her pouty, pink lips touching him. Withdrawing the riding crop from between her legs, he ignored her huff of frustration and extended his arm to sharply tap the round curve of her arse with the leather. She let out a little yelp, bowed her back, and braced herself with both hands on his thighs. Staring at him with wild eyes, she lowered her head until the head of his cock brushed against her parted lips. A moment's hesitation, then her warm, lush mouth closed over him.

"*Fuck!*" Wylder hissed, letting go of his member to shove his hand into the thick wealth of her hair. He held tight, preventing her from shuffling back in alarm. "Just like that, my sweet. Open your mouth more for me... let me slide in."

With a tiny whimper, Emily obeyed, her hands clenching into

fists as she let more of him enter her mouth. It felt so damn good. Wylder's head lolled against the chair's cushion, his eyes practically rolling backwards. His cock grew, demanding more, needing more. More of her. More of everything. Her cheeks bulged, so full of him that she gagged. Christ, he wasn't even all the way inside her mouth and already she was choking on him. His cock swelled even more, twitching in delight as his hips involuntarily thrust upward. She let out a sound of distress that melted into a moan when he snapped the crop over her buttocks once more.

"Don't you dare stop, minx. Unless it is to cry out your special word, you will not stop," Wylder muttered. The grip he had on her hair tightened as he helped guide her head up and down. Breaching her tight throat was certainly not something he could expect this first time, but he had every expectation they would work up to it. She was doing so well for him... trying so hard to please him. He gave her the opportunity to bring everything to a halt, but stubborn brat that she was, she simply hummed in acceptance and swallowed down more of him.

"You're doing so well, my naughty, sweet girl. Sucking my cock as though you love being used for my own selfish pleasure."

Emily seemed to thrive on the praise, her body rocking gently with the motions of his hand in her hair. Every so often, Wylder struck the soft flesh of her arse when he thought she needed something to ground her in the moment. Each time she responded with a soft moan and perceptible melting against him. Fuck. He wouldn't last much longer.

"I'm going to come, Emily," he groaned. "And you will not understand what that means until I explain it. My seed will erupt from my body into your mouth, and you will swallow me down unless you pull back from me right now," he warned, tossing the crop aside so he could bury both hands in her hair. Ready to yank her away at the first hint of reluctance on her part, he quivered on the cusp of an intense orgasm.

Emily did not disappoint him. She curled her nails into the

bare skin of his thighs, maintaining the inexpert sorcery of her lips and teeth on his throbbing cock. Sinking him deep into her mouth, she refused to allow the moment to end until, with a low growl of satisfaction, everything inside Wylder exploded in a glorious burst of sensations.

He'd never come so hard before in his life. It went far beyond any erotic experience he had ever enjoyed. For a long moment, he lay slumped in the chair, dazed and lightheaded as small sighs and moans issued from Emily. Her slender body was quivering, her throat closing around his erect shaft as she swallowed the fluid slowly pumping into her mouth.

When his body was wrung dry, he finally pulled her head back from him. Her lips left him with a small popping sound, and Wylder grunted at the loss of suction. With innate obedience, she remained kneeling between his widespread thighs, her eyes now a smoky, glazed blue with arousal as she stared up at him. Wylder recognized the question in her gaze. She was waiting for him to command her next move, her fingers still flexing on his thighs, her mouth beautifully swollen and pink from abuse. He could see her buttocks from this angle. The sight of those faint red stripes marring her creamy flesh was almost more than he could bear.

I've marked her as mine.

He dove headfirst into the overwhelming possessiveness that swelled inside him. She was his, even if only for a little while. The little minx had innocently taken him to the heights of desire. Now, he was eager to lick and taste the sweet frenzy he had worked her into. Tendrils of affection curled around his insides the longer he sat motionless. Tendrils that demanded he throw all caution to the wind and take Emily as his own forever. If it meant his eventual death, he would consider it an excellent reason to depart this earth.

Rising to his feet, Wylder tucked himself back into his breeches, fastening the buttons as she silently watched. What was going through her mind as she stared up at him from his feet? Was she wondering if he would leave her now? A smile that reeked of regret curved Emily's mouth, and he knew that was exactly what she was thinking.

"Come here," Wylder crooned, hooking his hands beneath her armpits and dragging her up from the floor. He pressed his mouth to hers, uncaring that his essence lingered on her lips. He kissed her with all the emotion inside him that could not be said aloud, his arms wrapping around her waist and keeping her body pressed against him. Her bare breasts felt heavenly as they branded his chest, her nipples erect and hard as diamonds scoring his skin. His cock was already beginning to harden again, aching to be deep inside her.

"I promised you pleasure if you pleased me, Emily," he whispered against her lips. "Will you allow me to do what I wish?"

"Yes," she replied softly. "If you are sure you want to stay." Her tone turned slightly accusing. "The last time you were in my rooms, you left without saying goodbye. I fell asleep, and when I woke, you were gone. Please do not do that to me this time."

"I intend to kiss and finger your sweet little quim until you faint," Wylder promised. "But I swear I will not leave you this time."

"How will you do that without being seen by anyone?"

"I will be very discreet, minx. Now, let me decide where I want to begin pleasuring you for the rest of the night," he said, his voice turning darker.

"What do you mean? We shall be in bed, of course." Shock colored Emily's voice, but she also sounded intrigued by the possibility of naughty acts occurring in different places.

Wylder laughed, truly delighted by her infectious innocence. "We are not limited to the bed, thank God. Look around your chambers, Emily. We have the chairs. Your vanity table. Even the walls can be used for my purposes."

"The walls, my lord?" she giggled softly. "I don't understand…"

Before she could say another word, Wylder spun her toward the nearest wall and pressed her against it, her breasts flattened against the cool plaster, her palms flat as well. Emily gasped in surprise at the quickness of his actions.

Using his booted feet, Wylder kicked hers apart and slipped his index finger between her thighs from his position behind her. She was so wet for him. So ready to be possessed and owned. As her creamy arousal coated his finger, he whispered in her ear, "We shall start here, I think. And you will stay in this position as I show you what I mean." Nipping her lobe and running his tongue over it to sooth the sting, he added a dark promise. "Once I've made you come in this position, I'll bend you over your vanity table next."

CHAPTER SIXTEEN

Emily

EMILY REACHED ACROSS from her side of the carriage and clasped her maid's hand. "Everything is perfect. I cannot believe you could do so much in such a short time."

Mary laughed. "It was all very simple, milady. The staff understands the need for secrecy, and the additional pay is most welcome."

Emily sighed. "I do wish it were more, but the expense has depleted my pin money considerably. If only I could liquidate a few of my financial investments to replenish my available funds. But it would require at least a month to do so, and we just do not have that kind of time."

"It's far more than enough, milady. Do not worry yourself over it," Mary assured her. "Miss True knows the plan?"

Emily smoothed a hand down the front of her dress and smiled. "Yes. Penelope will travel to Thorne Park under the pretense of attending the party and ball. Shortly after arriving, however, she will invent an illness that necessitates her return to London. And that is when you will accompany her to the Curzon Street townhome. While her parents are under the impression she is at Thorne Park, my parents will believe she has returned home. It will be at least a month before anyone even realizes she is gone."

Mary's look was skeptical. "But eventually, Miss True must return home, milady. She cannot stay hidden forever. And what then?"

Emily frowned at the reminder that there was no solution for what would occur at that point. Penelope needed help to avoid being shackled to a man she did not love. Hiding would accomplish that for a short period, but then what? Hope that Lord and Lady True relented in their unscrupulous husband hunt? Pray that Penelope would be allowed to marry a man of her own choosing? None of those seemed possible at the moment.

From her perch on the carriage seat, Emily watched other vehicles as they passed by on the busy London street. The townhome was one of her family's properties and had sat vacant for many years. The staff there saw to its upkeep so it did not fall into disrepair. Her mother once mentioned that the valuable property would likely be included as part of Emily's bridal dowry when she finally married.

This sneaking around was worrisome, but if the property was meant to be hers eventually, Emily reasoned there was nothing wrong with using it now. No one would know she would be hiding Penelope there for a short time.

"Perhaps you will find your perfect match at the house party, milady," Mary said in a gentle voice, squeezing Emily's hand. "Lord Wyldewood will be there."

Emily squirmed a bit on the carriage's cushioned seat, tilting her parasol to conceal the heated flush that stained her cheeks pink. It had been two weeks since the night Wylder snuck into her rooms. While the red marks on her arse had quickly faded, the memory of being struck with the riding crop still resonated deep within her. She closed her eyes against an unexpected swell of desire. She'd learned much of herself and Wylder during those hours. She enjoyed a bite of pain with her pleasure, and Wylder relished the implementation of that pain.

Keeping their interactions from others was weighing heavily upon her. Since the earl was still utilizing Simon's financial genius, he'd been a frequent visitor to Blackthorne Manor over the last few weeks. Wylder was distant and polite while in the presence of others, but in private, in those stolen moments hidden away in corridor alcoves and the manor library's darkened corners, he kissed and caressed her with devilish intent. His behavior was so bold, Emily wondered if he harbored a secret hope they might be caught after all.

Of course, Simon proved predictable in his scrutiny. He watched Emily and Wylder closely, searching for any hint of affection that his best friend might have shown her. His attention only wavered on those occasions that Penelope paid a call to Blackthorne Manor. Simon always found a reason to hover nearby. Penelope's presence apparently disturbed him, but he still found a way to inject himself into the conversations. Sprawled on the settee during tea. Appearing in the garden while the ladies took the afternoon air and admired the blooms. One evening in the library, he insisted on selecting a book for Penelope, interrupting the two girls as they whispered about their plans. He was so annoying that Emily eventually snapped at him to leave them in peace, to which her brother grinned and continued extolling the qualities of the book he had chosen.

Yes… he was behaving very oddly indeed, but Emily could not focus on that when she had so much occupying her thoughts. Between the illicit, stolen moments with Wylder and apprehension over being caught, the pressure to save her dearest friend from an unwanted, loveless marriage, and the relentless social swirl of the season, Emily was definitely feeling a bit overwhelmed by it all.

"I'm happy Lord and Lady Blackthorne are putting on this party," Mary remarked cheerfully. "A bit of time away in the fresh air of the country will suit you, I think. You've not been sleeping well lately."

Emily's cheeks once again grew warm, her breath more shallow than she would have liked. Of course, she was not sleeping well. Her dreams were fitful, disturbing episodes. Ones fraught with appearances of Wylder St. Clair and his dirty mouth, hard hands, and heated kisses. Taking a deep breath, she smiled at her maid.

"Yes, some time in the quiet of the country will be much appreciated."

Even as she uttered the words, something inside Emily tightened as if in warning of impending doom. She could not help feeling as though there might be some unexpected trouble. A sudden shift in her once predictable world that would forever change her. She tried telling herself she was being silly. That the stress of Penelope's situation and Wylder's attention had tainted her everyday life.

Everything will be fine. It must be. Penelope will be safe, and my relationship with Wylder will continue as it has. And if he must pursue another woman to advance the illusion that we are simply acquaintances, then I will accept it and cry when I am alone.

Yes, everything would be fine.

EMILY RAN DOWN the steps toward Thorne Park's circular drive, her skirts gripped tightly in both hands so she would not trip.

"Penelope!" she called, approaching the coach before the matched horses were pulled to a stop. "You are finally here!"

"A little more decorum, daughter," Lady Blackthorne called out in despair, but a pleased smile graced her lips as the coach finally came to a rest at the foot of the terrace steps.

Emily ignored her mother's directive, standing impatiently and shifting her feet with excitement as the groom lowered the coach's steps for the occupants to descend. A footman hopped up on the back of the vehicle and began unlashing the trunks so they could be lowered to the ground.

The first person to depart the coach was Lady Bashear, the Countess of Wentworth, and one of Lady Blackthorne's closest friends. She'd agreed to serve as Penelope's chaperone in the absence of Lady True. With a warm smile, the older lady accepted Emily's polite curtsey and then kissed her on the cheek.

"Hello, my dear girl. I see your mother has yet to curb your natural exuberance."

"She has admittedly tried her best, Lady Bashear," Emily said with a blush, looking past the woman to see Penelope climbing slowly out of the coach with the assistance of a groom. Her friend did not look well at all. Emily wondered if she was reconsidering their plan.

"It would be a shame if she succeeded," Lady Bashear said with a wink. "Now, allow me to greet your mother while you see to Miss True, my dear. The poor girl was ill for most of the journey and should be put to bed at once."

"Oh, no… Penelope, are you ill?" Emily raced to help her friend as she emerged from the coach. Her features were a shade or two paler than ivory, while tiny beads of perspiration beaded her upper lip.

"Just a little… however, there is no need to worry." Penelope's smile was faint, but she reached out to embrace Emily with a strength that belied her tired features. "You know I do not travel well. Although the journey was blessedly short, I found it difficult to stave off my usual ailment when trapped in a moving vehicle. There is no need to be overly concerned. It will pass the longer I stand on firm ground."

"Thank goodness it is nothing terribly serious," Emily said, letting out a breath of relief. "Come, I will accompany you to your room, where you can lie down and recover your bearings. I'll ring down to the kitchens and have Mrs. Crosby bring up some tea to help settle your nerves."

"That would be most welcome," Penelope said, casting Lady Bashear and Emily's mother a glance from beneath the sweep of her lashes. In a whisper, she murmured, "Lady Bashear was most adamant in questioning me on any prospects you might have at the moment. It seems she has a distant nephew by marriage who will be in attendance for the ball. She's convinced you and he have much in common, and she's looking forward to making the necessary introductions."

"Oh, bother," Emily groaned, linking an arm with Penelope as they began walking toward the terrace steps. "I'm certain she has already inquired of my mother on the subject, if she felt confident enough to bring the subject up in conversation."

"I am to be offered up as a poor second choice if you show no interest in the man." Penelope grimaced at the thought.

Emily whispered, "If we stay the course, you will be heading back to London within the week."

"My stomach has been in knots thinking of that moment," Penelope confessed quietly. "Oh, Emily! I must tell you… my situation is far more dire than it was before you departed London."

"How so, Pen?"

"Mother informed me this very morning that she and Father are crafting a marriage contract with Lord Grant." Penelope's tone was one of morose dejection. Tears welled in her lovely green eyes as she related the awful news. "Once I have returned to London, they will announce the engagement. I won't even have the opportunity to object."

Emily's heart clenched with sympathy and anger that Penelope's parents could be so cruel and exhibit such a lack of empathy for their only child. They simply saw her as a burden—one they might make a bit of money from if they were successful in trapping a wealthy husband. "You will not marry that odious man," she stated firmly. "And it is obvious to me that our plans must be put into motion. If Lord Grant cannot find you to marry you, then he is sure to lose interest and find someone else to torment."

"I fear just the opposite will occur, Emily. My mother was very sure of this arrangement. She said there would be no crying off," Penelope murmured bitterly, her eyes flashing with uncommon ire. "It hurts to realize how little value they place on my happiness. But, then, it's always been so."

Emily could only squeeze her friend's waist in commiseration, forced into momentary silence as they reached the top of the terrace, where Lady Blackthorne stood with arms open wide to embrace Penelope.

»»»«««

AFTER ENSURING PENELOPE was comfortable in her room with a nice pot of tea to settle her nerves, Emily ventured back downstairs, where more guests were arriving. Every passing hour saw another coach pulling up to the curved drive, depositing lords and ladies in excited groups. Before the end of the week, all seventy-five guests staying at Thorne Park would be settled into their rooms with the remaining fifty or so guests coming from estates within driving distance. It would make for an exciting two weeks, with the guests of honor, the Earl and Countess of Ashcroft, arriving the next night.

"Hello, dear sister," Simon called to her from the bottom of the curving staircase. "Look who has just arrived for the festivities."

Emily slowed her pace upon seeing Wylder standing alongside her brother. His head inclined in a slight nod of acknowledgment while Emily's heart skipped several beats. He looked incredibly handsome in his dark-blue suit and stark white cravat. A tingle of pleasure reminded her of the evening he had tied her hands together with a cravat similar to the one he wore now.

"Good afternoon, Lord Wyldewood," she said, venturing close enough that he could lift her hand and press a kiss to the back of it. It was swift and impersonal, executed as it was with Simon standing right there.

Simon's gaze flickered to the top of the stairs as though expecting to find someone else descending them. A tiny frown formed between his eyebrows as Emily regarded him. Her brother was acting so strangely that she could not begin to guess what was amiss with him.

"I am sure the two of you are excited by the arrival of Lord and Lady Ashcroft tomorrow," Emily ventured, calmly meeting Wylder's gaze. His silver eyes were hungrily examining her form, as it had been nearly two weeks since they'd seen one another.

Simon's attention shifted from the staircase as he slapped a hand on Wylder's back. "The three of us had drinks at White's just two nights ago. It was good to see the man was still in one piece and that marriage apparently has agreed with him. Isn't that so, Wylder?"

Wylder cleared his throat and smiled tightly. "He appeared quite content."

"I'm eager to meet the woman who could entice a rakehell to try wedded bliss," Emily said with a pointed smile for the two men standing before her. "It gives many unattached females perpetual hope."

"The new countess is a lovely girl," Wylder replied dryly. "And Lucien is devoted to her."

A guilty flush darkened Simon's face, leaving Emily to wonder if there had been an intentional testing of Lord Ashcroft's dedication to his new wife.

"That he is," Simon muttered.

"Has Miss True arrived, Lady Emily?" Wylder inquired in a sudden change of subject. His head tilted, watching her so intently that Emily wondered if he had somehow discovered the secret plot to hide Penelope away.

That would be impossible. The only ones who know are also involved with the planning and sworn to secrecy.

"She arrived a short time ago along with Lady Bashear," Emily said. "She's resting for a bit as the journey from London was not a pleasant one for her."

"With Lady Bashear as a companion, I imagine that is true," Simon quipped. "But in the interest of being polite, I do hope that Miss True recovers quickly."

"I expect her to be up and about by supper." Emily studied

her brother, noting his casual manner in mentioning Penelope. "She was feeling much better after a cup of tea."

"I'm hoping we have a moment or two to go over those reports before supper, Simon." Wylder bent at the waist, his gaze impassive as he stared at Emily. "You will both excuse me as I retire to prepare for the evening meal."

Emily watched him go before turning to Simon. "Reports?" She feigned ignorance of Wylder's statement and was rewarded by a rare bit of honesty from her brother.

"I've been helping Wylder with some financial matters." He shrugged. "We must examine the results of some recent investments and determine if those paths should continue to be pursued."

"I'm sure he is in excellent hands with you, Simon. You are a genius when it comes to such things."

Simon's brow arched high at the unexpected praise. "You've a far better head for investments than I do, Emily. If it weren't a scandalous idea, I would suggest that you provide some insight into the decisions I've made on Wylder's behalf. However, I'm positive that Father would disapprove if you began advising the gentlemen of the ton when it comes to playing the 'Change. And Mother would naturally be horrified if your instincts on financial matters became common knowledge." He recognized the look of concern that creased Emily's forehead, adding earnestly, "Don't worry, Emily. I've kept your secrets regarding your investments and the funds you've accumulated. But it must be said that whoever your future husband ends up being is in for a pleasant surprise once your dowry is settled and those accounts of yours come to light."

Emily frowned at Simon's playful teasing. "It isn't fair that those accounts will become the property of my husband when I wed."

"Fair or not, that is the way of things, my dear sister." Simon chucked her under the chin and grinned. "Perhaps the man will appreciate your remarkable talents and utilize them. I daresay he would be a fool to ignore them."

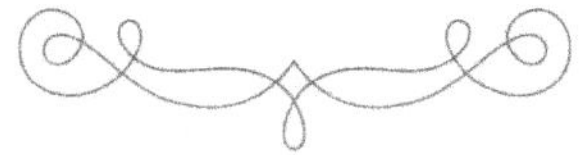

CHAPTER SEVENTEEN

Wylder

BY DIVINE INTERVENTION, or simply because of Lady Black-thorne's rather obvious scheming, Wylder found himself seated beside Emily at supper. The table was set for the thirty guests who had arrived thus far. At the other end of the dining room, Simon and Miss True had also been paired. Simon looked agitated by the seating arrangement while Miss True, in her usual fashion, shyly kept her attention focused on her plate.

Occasionally, Simon caught Wylder's eye. His expression left no doubt that he believed Wylder, or even his sister, likely had some manner of input on how guests were seated. But Wylder could honestly claim innocence in the matter. Indeed, he preferred not to be in such close proximity to Emily, afraid that his emotions would be apparent to those around them.

Taking a deep breath, Wylder wondered how he would keep his composure when Emily's sweetly perfumed body was so damned close. Each time her skirts brushed against his leg, every blood vessel in his body tightened until it was excruciatingly painful.

"How is your search for a wife progressing, Lord Wyldewood?" Emily asked in a soft voice as her wine glass was filled by one of the dining room footmen.

A muscle ticked in Wylder's jaw at the impertinent question.

"I've explained that it is simply an act for my father's benefit."

She smiled. "Yes, you've said as much. But still, you must at least pretend it for it to be real enough. How else will His Grace believe you are in earnest?"

The practical nature of her reasoning needled him. She deliberately posed the question as a way of highlighting the idiocy of his plan. Glancing down the length of the table, he focused on the young lady beside Simon, then slowly said, "You are right. Perhaps I shall consider courting Miss True. Even with her admirable skills of avoiding scandalous situations, my pursuit of her would at least appear authentic to the casual observer. It might not appease my father, but I would be upholding my end of the bargain when it comes to hunting for a wife."

If Wylder thought Emily would find his suggestion abhorrent, he was almost comically disappointed by her reaction. Her eyes lit up, a calculating gleam in the sparkly blue depths that proved so damned intoxicating he nearly forgot he meant to take her down a peg or two. She leaned toward him, her voice low and full of hopeful speculation.

"Would you truly consider it, Wylder?" Her hand came up to lightly grip his forearm, her eyes searching his. "It would be ever so helpful. Penelope and I would owe you a debt of gratitude... even if the courtship is all for show."

Wylder gaped at her, unsure if he'd heard her correctly. Did she mean that? Did she really wish to see him courting her best friend?

Then his eyes narrowed with a dawning suspicion. It was becoming obvious that the two girls were scheming something together, and now Emily was attempting to draw him into it.

"Do you mean that, minx?"

Emily frowned at him as if confused by the question. "Of course, I mean it. If Lord and Lady True have reason to believe Penelope has captured the attention of a man of your standing, they might reconsider—" She abruptly broke off whatever she was going to say next and fell silent, her hand leaving his arm.

Biting her lower lip, she quickly picked up her glass of wine and took a long sip. Wylder was left with the impression that she hoped he would let the strange statement pass without further comment.

The arrival of the first course meant an extended period where Wylder could not comment on her strange request. Other conversations continued around them as Emily politely spoke with the older man seated on her other side. Sir Gregory Brighton was a pleasant enough fellow, witty and not overbearing. He was considered handsome, although Wylder could not speak to that aspect. Sitting back in his chair, he listened as the other gentleman kept Emily engaged for the next half hour.

When he finally recaptured Emily's attention sometime after the third course of roast beef, stuffed tomatoes, and creamed peas, Wylder had decided that whatever secrets she was keeping must be uncovered. It was for her own good, he told himself. Getting to the bottom of things would keep both girls from getting into mischief.

"You will tell me the meaning behind your words, Emily," he said quietly while she pushed food around her plate and drank far more wine than she should have. "And if you think I won't obtain the truth of the matter, you are sorely mistaken."

Emily's wide-eyed look reeked of innocence. "I'm not sure what you mean, Lord Wyldewood."

"You'll have the opportunity later to explain things. And Emily?" Wylder paused, his hand moving beneath the edge of the table to grip her knee. She let out a little squeak of alarm but remained quiet as he continued, "We are both aware that I will utilize certain methods to get the information I want from you."

Her breathing grew shallow with the sensuous threat, her eyes becoming heavy-lidded as she stared back at him. "You made the offer, Wylder. I was exploring the possibilities of you courting my dearest friend and the benefits that might arise from it. It is a strategy that would draw my brother's attention away from scrutinizing our interactions too closely, wouldn't you agree?"

Wylder squeezed her knee harder, infuriated by her stubbornness in submitting to his command. "I have no interest in any woman other than you, minx."

Emily's smile was faint, but her words were strong as she stood her ground. "For the sake of others, we must play the game of indifference. I see the necessity of it, my lord, and so must you."

Once supper was done, the ladies retired to one of Thorne Park's two drawing rooms while the men remained behind to enjoy their brandies. A few gentlemen lit up cigars. Soon, the room became boisterous as various conversations centering around politics and business filled the air, accompanied by a fine haze of smoke.

"You and Emily appeared to be having a rather intense discussion," Simon dryly remarked as Wylder sipped a brandy.

"Merely polite conversation." Wylder glanced about the room, locating Simon's father. Lord Blackthorne was in deep conversation with Sir Gregory Brighton, the man who had sat on Emily's right side during supper. "In contrast, there did not seem to be any occurring between you and Miss True."

Simon snorted in disgust. "I don't know what my mother hoped to accomplish with that little stunt. The girl is so damnably shy, she barely said two words during the entire meal. The surprising thing is when I dared make mention of it, she shot me a glare that would likely ignite an ordinary man into flames." He shook his head, brow furrowed as he recalled the incident. "But perhaps I imagined that."

"It seems Lady Blackthorne is not above a bit of matchmaking," Wylder said. "I suppose we shall both be subjected to such ploys over the next two weeks."

Simon's jaw clenched at that. "I sincerely hope not. She knows you are not suitable for Emily. *You* know you are not suitable."

Wylder contained the spark of anger at his friend's statement, reminding himself that to react would only draw more attention to himself and Emily. Besides, Simon's assertion was true. His lifestyle, his multiple affairs, and pursuit of all things debauched and depraved precluded him from ever being appropriate for a woman like Emily. But still, it stung to hear it said so matter-of-factly by his best friend. "Perhaps it is her way of enticing others to court your sister? The fairer sex has a simplistic approach to matters of matrimony. They believe two people thrown together will result in the formation of a common bond."

Simon did not appear convinced by that argument, but thankfully, he turned the conversation to other matters. "Your investments appear to be doing well. Father remarked upon it when I showed him the latest report on that pottery factory in Yorkshire."

"My man of affairs tells me the accounts are already beginning to show a profit," Wylder said with a slight smile.

"Do you still intend on putting up the pretense that you are searching for a bride to please your father?"

"Bloody hell, yes, as distasteful as it is." Wylder drank the rest of his brandy. He should follow the other men trickling back into the drawing room to join the ladies.

Simon turned his glass over in his hand, his voice flat. "I hate what this directive to marry has done to the Rakehells. First Lucien… and now you."

"You know this is all a farce, Simon. One that I must play at to achieve my goal." Wylder nodded toward the drawing room in a silent invitation to join him there.

"That is true," Simon said morosely. "But once you begin searching for a bride, it's simply a matter of time before it becomes reality."

Wylder did not respond to that as he began striding toward the drawing room. Sir Brighton was also headed in that direction and would beat him there. "Are you coming to the drawing room?" he asked Simon over his shoulder. "There's sure to be a few games of whist or hazard to pass the time."

"Father has arranged for higher stakes play in the Blue

Room," Simon remarked as he trailed behind. "However, I know my mother will be disappointed if I do not at least turn a trick or two at whist with a few of the ladies."

Wylder immediately searched for Emily and found her sitting with Penelope in one of the alcove window seats. The two girls were engaged in a deep, obviously private conversation, but still, he could see Emily's eyes light up when she saw that he'd entered the room before she quickly shuttered them.

"Come join us, Lord Wyldewood," Emily's mother called out. "We just started a new game and require a fourth person since Lady Caldwell bowed out."

Wylder bowed at the waist to the older woman, a smile lifting the corners of his lips. "I fear my funds will be significantly depleted if I attempt to go up against such skilled players."

Chelsea Blackthorne grinned shamelessly at her son's best friend. "How else can we ladies replenish our pin money, my dear boy?"

Out of the corner of his eye, Wylder watched as Sir Brighton approached Emily and Penelope. Whatever the older man said to them had both girls smiling before Emily accepted his outstretched hand. He helped her rise to her feet and tucked her hand into the crook of his arm.

"Oh, I do hope Sir Brighton does not turn your daughter's head before my darling nephew can arrive," Lady Bashear said, lips pressed into a moue of disappointment. Along with Lady Blackthorne, the ladies seated around the table all turned to watch Sir Brighton lead Emily out of the double doors and onto the open terrace. Of course, the two stayed within eyesight of others in the room... a nod to respectability that Wylder found almost laughable. If there was anything he had learned of Emily Blackthorne over the last few weeks, it was the fact that she possessed a wild streak a respectable man would never be able to tame.

"No worries on that account, Caroline," Lady Blackthorne murmured, giving Wylder an audacious wink her friend did not see. "Emily is determined to let her heart lead her in matters of romance."

Lady Bashear sniffed. "A foolish endeavor, I think."

"Simon, come here, if you please." Lady Blackthorne motioned for her son to come closer. When he bent down, she whispered something in his ear and smiled when he straightened. "For my sake, dear."

"Of course, Mother," Simon replied, his jaw clenching even as he gave her a tight smile. Turning toward Penelope, sitting alone in the window seat, he threw Wylder a scowl and approached the girl.

Wylder smothered his own grin. It was apparent to him that Lady Blackthorne was determined to push Simon in Penelope's direction. But whether she was motivated by sympathy or a genuine desire to see her son with the timid girl remained to be seen.

Whatever the reason, the lady's actions were to Wylder's advantage. While Simon was busy with Miss True, Wylder was free to interact with Emily.

Now, he only needed to persuade Sir Brighton that Lady Emily was not the girl for him. And he would do that for one simple reason. Emily belonged to him, even if the relationship was one that they kept a secret for the rest of their lives.

A tragic necessity.

"My pardon, ladies." Wylder bowed to the group of older women, his eyes flicking toward the open terrace doors. Through the open portal, he could see Sir Brighton laughing with Emily. Occasionally, the man pointed up at the sky, and Wylder realized he was likely pointing out different constellations. "I believe I shall step outside for a breath of fresh air before joining the other gentlemen in the Blue Room."

CHAPTER EIGHTEEN

Emily

EMILY FEIGNED INTEREST in the night sky, only half-listening to Gregory Brighton's scientific explanations of the stars glittering in the inky darkness. All of her attention was focused on the interior of the parlor behind the terrace. More specifically, she listened for any indication that Wylder would follow her. Wasn't he even the tiniest bit curious to know what her conversation with Gregory consisted of?

"And so that cluster of stars is known as Perseus," Gregory said. "It is one of the constellations Ptolemy listed in his catalog, *Almagest*. It's all so very fascinating, wouldn't you agree?"

"Certainly," Emily murmured, shifting her feet while straining to hear if anyone else might also venture out onto the terrace.

"And there, that is Polaris, part of the Ursa Minor." Gregory pointed out an object a bit larger than the other stars. "It is the brightest star in the sky." Lowering his head, he smiled sheepishly at Emily. "But I must say, Lady Emily, that it is quite dull indeed when compared to the beauty of your eyes. Yours are by far brighter and more brilliant than any stars I've observed during my amateur attempts at charting."

"That is very kind of you to say, Sir Brighton." Emily shifted away slightly, placing a bit more distance between their bodies. Gregory placed a hand over hers where it was still tucked into the crook of his arm.

"I am very sincere in my compliments, my lady, and pray I do not offend with my brashness."

"No offense taken, sir." Emily tugged at her hand only to discover he did not seem inclined to release her.

"I would welcome the opportunity to show you the charts I've been working on, Lady Emily," he said with great enthusiasm. "Perhaps you would find it all as intriguing as I do."

"Science was never one of the areas I excelled in during my necessary studies," Emily replied apologetically. "I'm afraid that it is all truly mystifying to me. My strength was in mathematics, although I thoroughly enjoy classic literature. Especially the writings of Aristotle and even Chaucer. I read them still whenever I have free moments to myself."

"I would be happy to instruct you in matters of astronomy," Gregory offered.

Emily could not imagine a more boring endeavor, but she managed a polite smile. "I think such an endeavor would require many instances of staring up at the night sky."

He appeared delighted by that possibility, but before he could say more on the subject, there came a much-welcome interruption.

"Pardon the intrusion," Wylder murmured, stepping up to the terrace wall and leaning against it.

Even in the pale light of the moon and the glow of lamps from the drawing room, Emily could see Gregory's face darken with consternation. He released her hand, allowing her to sidle away.

"Good evening, Lord Wyldewood," Emily replied calmly, although inside she was almost faint with excitement. There was no reason for Wylder to come out to the terrace. No reason other than the fact that she was out there alone with another man.

"Lady Emily." Wylder nodded in acknowledgment. "Sir Brighton, various games are occurring in the Blue Room for the gentlemen's pleasure, if you are inclined to join us."

"Thank you, Wyldewood. Lord Blackthorne mentioned it earlier." Gregory's reply was cautiously friendly.

"Sir Brighton was just pointing out some of the constellations to me." Emily's chin tilted upward. She gazed at the sky as if entranced by the view. "It's incredible how many stars are visible on such a clear night."

Wylder commented softly, "I cannot imagine a man looking at something so insignificant as the sky when he could look at you instead, Lady Emily."

Emily swallowed hard at Wylder's unexpected compliment. *Where did that come from? And why would he say something like that so publicly?* For a long moment, she could only stare at the earl, the silence stretching until Gregory nervously cleared his throat.

"Yes, well, I did compliment Lady Emily," he offered. "I told her that her eyes are brighter than the stars."

"Well, now that we've established how sparkling my eyes are, I suppose I shall return to the parlor." Emily's voice quavered a bit. Wylder's behavior was unnerving, and she had the impression he hoped that Gregory would voluntarily leave them alone.

"Sir Brighton, I wonder if you might allow me a moment with Lady Emily?" Wylder abruptly asked, his voice firm and strong.

Gregory stood silent, apparently stunned by the request. His gaze flickered to the open doors to the parlor, which provided not even a hint of privacy. When he frowned, Wylder pressed him.

"I'm afraid I must insist, sir."

Gregory gave a tight nod, then, turning to Emily, he took her hand in his. "I'll say good evening to you now, Lady Emily. I do hope we may discuss matters of astronomy again. If it is something that interests you, that is." After pressing a brief kiss to the back of her hand, he released her.

"It would be a pleasant pastime, Sir Brighton," Emily replied, relieved that the man was obeying Wylder's directive. What was it about the earl that induced obedience?

Gregory looked as though he wished to say more, but then apparently decided against it. Bowing at the waist, he exited the terrace, leaving Emily and Wylder alone.

"Are you enjoying yourself, Emily?"

Wylder's voice was low and heated, curling around her like molten lava and just as deadly.

"Immensely, my lord," she trilled, the false bravado ringing in her tone. "Are you?"

"You should not be out here alone in the dark with a man," he replied, ignoring her question. His hands clenched into fists at his sides and in Emily's view he appeared to be holding onto his temper by a thread. Good. She hoped he was as disturbed and bothered as she was.

Emily's head tilted. "A strange thing to say, considering I am out here in the dark with you. Would you rather I leave?"

"No," he growled. "I'd rather you not try something so foolish as making me crazed with jealousy."

"Are you?" Emily asked softly, moving closer to him despite her intentions to keep her distance. Wylder St. Clair was detrimental to her sense of self-preservation. His cologne, spicy and sharp, reminded her of the moments they'd spent together in her rooms at Blackthorne Manor. His hands had explored every inch of her body, learning her secrets and using that knowledge against her until she cried out for mercy. This obsession between them was dangerous, but it could not be helped. She had to have his hands and mouth on her again... or else she would go mad with desire.

"Am I what?" Wylder demanded, his gaze falling to her mouth in a moment of distraction. The hard silver of his eyes held a warning, but Emily did not heed it.

"Jealous," she murmured. "Are you jealous?"

He was silent for a long moment, then hissed, "Bloody hell, minx. I am consumed by jealousy. I wanted to rip Brighton's eyes right out from their sockets for daring to admire your beauty in the moonlight, if you want the goddamn truth."

Emily said nothing to that, but the heated confession made her heart quiver with joy. "I would experience the same if you should stand on a dark terrace with another woman." She turned toward the parlor, noting the gaiety occurring just beyond the double doors. Simon had seated himself in the alcove with Penelope, no doubt due to their mother's urging. Pained exasperation was stamped across his features as he attempted to engage her in conversation. For her part, Penelope appeared both terrified and enraged. When she succeeded in catching Emily's eye, the girl's brows knitted together as she silently pleaded for an escape from the situation.

Penelope needed rescuing, that much was clear. Emily pursed her lips and gave her friend a slight nod in acknowledgment of the silent message. *Drat. Either Simon is making a complete ass of himself, or he is hopelessly blind to Pen's unease. My guess is the former.*

Her attention returned to Wylder for the moment. "Are you not overly concerned about my brother's reaction to the fact that we are alone on the terrace?" Since Simon had made it very clear that they must have nothing to do with one another, she was genuinely curious about Wylder's lack of care now. Not that Simon seemed even to realize she and Wylder were alone now.

"I'm beginning to believe your brother should be punched in the mouth," he drawled. "And to hell with his edicts when he is just as debauched as he claims me to be."

Emily smothered a giggle. She thought the same, but of course, it would be unseemly to voice such sentiments aloud. "I should go rescue Penelope. The poor dear is not accustomed to dealing with men like Simon."

Her rueful statement apparently reminded Wylder of why he'd ventured out onto the terrace in the first place.

"What the devil are you and Miss True planning, minx?" He snagged her by the elbow before she could flit out of his reach. "When I first entered the drawing room, the two of you were engaged in deep conversation. My instincts tell me you're up to something. A plot of some sort and one of great secrecy."

Gazing at him in surprise, Emily feigned innocence. "A plot, my lord? Your imagination is impressive, but you are also very much mistaken. You see, Miss True and I were simply discussing the various gentlemen who will be in attendance during our stay. And, of course, we are both eager to meet the new Countess of Ashcroft. Simon says she is a lovely person."

Wylder held onto her, refusing to let her loose. Emily wanted to melt into his arms, but with Simon just inside the drawing room, that would be ill-advised.

"I know a plot when I see one forming, Emily," he murmured. "You are up to something, and I will uncover the truth of it."

"I doubt it, Lord Wyldewood, but you may try if it entertains you to do so." Her lips curved in a taunting smile. "Now, please let me go before my brother has reason to believe your depraved nature has infected me. I've no wish to see either of you in a field tomorrow morning, facing one another with pistols drawn."

CHAPTER NINETEEN
Emily

S HE HOPED THAT Wylder would somehow find a way to sneak into her rooms during the early morning hours, but apparently, he was not willing to attempt such brazenness. Spending the early hours tossing and turning, she finally managed to fall asleep, only to have Mary wake her just before noon.

"The entire house is aflutter with Lord and Lady Ashcroft's arrival today, along with the Duke and Duchess of Westley. What a glorious event this will be, my lady. Lady Blackthorne has truly outdone herself with her meticulous planning."

Emily fluffed her own pillows and accepted the cup of hot chocolate Mary handed her. "Mother always throws such grand parties. She's an expert at such things. I hope one day I manage such matters with her expertise."

"I've no doubt you will, my lady." Mary bustled about the room with her usual cheerfulness. "That matter we've spoken of, do you think it will occur today or perhaps on the morrow?"

The maid was referring to the plan of sending Penelope into hiding. Emily was unsure if Penelope was ready to take that step. Last night in the parlor, she'd expressed her apprehension and fear that Emily would suffer if they were found out. All of Emily's assurances that she was willing to face the risks were not enough to persuade the girl to commit to the actual day of departure.

"Pen is naturally unsure if this is prudent. But I wholeheartedly believe she will continue with the plan we have set," Emily said thoughtfully. "She's just scared…"

Mary tsked in agreement. "Poor, dear Miss True. She's had a time of it, that's for sure."

Emily sipped her chocolate, hoping that Penelope could find the bravery within herself that was necessary to change her own destiny. But even as she worried for her friend, Emily realized how irrational that was. Expecting Penelope to challenge the path her parents set for her when Emily herself hid her own relationship with Wylder might be considered the height of hypocrisy by some.

But she was just as trapped by her circumstances as Penelope was. If she proclaimed her love for Wylder for all the world to hear, Simon would make sure the relationship was destroyed. He had warned them both to stay far away from one another. Her brother's belief that he was protecting her from Wylder was beyond foolish.

"Shall you wear the green today or the blue?" Mary pulled both dresses from the wardrobe and held them out for Emily's perusal.

"The blue," Emily said slowly. Wylder had a preference for the color, and she knew the sapphire hue was lovely on her. Perhaps he would be overcome with desire, throw caution aside, and steal a kiss when no one was looking.

Once she was up and dressed, Emily made her way to the guest room where Penelope was staying. Knocking quietly on the door, she waited for her friend to grant entrance.

"Good morning," Pen said as Emily joined her by the fireplace. "I'm sure you've had a cup of hot chocolate this morning, but would you care for more? There's enough for another cup."

"You will never see me pass up chocolate." Emily plopped into one of the two chairs and poured herself a cup as she regarded Penelope. "I wonder how you are feeling about our plan this morning, Pen. Have you changed your mind or do you wish to continue? It is your choice."

Penelope pulled a curling lock of hair over her shoulder and stared at Emily, her green eyes somber. "After Simon cornered me in the drawing room last night, I realized I must do this. Being at the mercy of a man is not something I relish. Especially a man like Lord Grant."

Emily groaned. "I'm so sorry, Pen. I knew when he sat down beside you that he would be his usual overbearing pompous self. You should have gone to sit by my mother."

"It's not that he was unpleasant. Far from it, actually. He actually tried engaging in normal conversation with me, but as usual, my blasted shyness tangled my tongue and struck me mute. And it was your mother who sent him to sit with me in the drawing room," Penelope said quietly. "And it was your mother who arranged for him to be seated next to me at supper. I cannot understand why she did so… she knows how uncomfortable your brother makes me. My hands were trembling the entire time."

"Mother means well." Emily shrugged helplessly. "I believe she has always tendered a desire to see you and Simon as a couple."

Embarrassment flushed Penelope's ivory-hued cheeks bright red. "I cannot imagine a more unlikely pairing. Lord Camden speaks to me, and I become a blithering idiot unable to stutter a proper sentence. I understand that he does your mother's bidding in seeking me out, but I do wish he would stop. He is incredibly arrogant in those moments… needling and prodding me with questions about myself… then becoming frustrated when I cannot answer."

Emily nodded in agreement. "I am sorry for Mother's persistence and Simon's arrogance. I will talk with her and explain to her your feelings on the matter. I know she does not mean to cause you undue distress."

"Oh, you mustn't do that, Emily!" Penelope cried out in alarm. "Lady Blackthorne will think me ungrateful after all that she has done on my behalf. Please… say nothing on the subject and regard my outspokenness as nothing more than a moment of venting my frustration aloud. Besides, I imagine that being told to cease speaking to me would only result in Lord Camden doubling his efforts to vex me. Please, Emily. Say nothing to your mother or even to him."

Emily's head tilted as she stared at Penelope in amazement. Was it possible that Penelope *liked* Simon's attention? The blush staining her friend's cheeks told a story… one perhaps Penelope did not even understand. Emily had always suspected an attraction existed between her friend and her brother… it was so much easier to see when the two of them were together recently. But she also knew Penelope was so shy and apprehensive around the opposite sex that she would suppress any hint of interest in Simon.

"If that is what you wish, Pen."

"It is. Thank you, Emily." Penelope visibly relaxed, her eyes studying Emily closely. "I noticed Lord Wyldewood appeared to have much to say to you out there on the terrace. Indeed, you were out there together for so long that I thought surely Simon would notice straightaway. He never did, though, thank goodness. I cannot imagine the fuss he would have created."

"Wylder was also trying his best to annoy me. He thinks you and I are plotting a misadventure, and he is quite adamant in that belief," Emily replied with a chuckle. "I did my best to assure him that it is all in his imagination."

Penelope's eyes widened with fear. "Do you think he has uncovered our plan?"

Waving a hand in dismissal, Emily set down her cup of chocolate. Something Penelope said just a few moments before had captured her attention, and she pondered it while addressing Pen's concerns. "It is unlikely. Besides, he is the type of man who would come right out and confront a person with whatever he had learned. He was more than perturbed that I would not admit a thing."

"Well, that is a relief." Penelope stood up from her chair and made her way to the bed. She gave the bell cord a sharp tug, signaling that one of the maids should come to help her dress for the day.

"Pen, I must ask you something," Emily murmured, chewing on her bottom lip. "You mentioned that Simon never noticed Wylder and me were on the terrace together. Don't you find that strange?"

A smile of faint confusion curved Penelope's full mouth. "I suppose it is. Perhaps he is finally realizing it is a futile effort to keep the two of you apart. You and Wyldewood are drawn to one another like moths to flames."

Emily laughed at her friend's striking innocence and lack of awareness. "Don't you understand what this means, Penelope, my sweet dear? Simon never noticed what Wylder was doing because he was entirely focused on *you*! You captured his interest… and held it hostage." She clapped her hands in delight. "Oh, this is the most wonderful development!"

Penelope still did not appear to understand the situation, a frown creasing her brow. "It is?"

Emily ran to Penelope, impulsively embracing her with a broad grin. "Yes. It means Simon is finally noticing your sweetness. Your beauty. Your innate goodness. And even if he does not like it, this proves he is not immune to your charms after all. This is terribly exciting, and we must take advantage of this without delay." Emily reached over and impatiently rang for the maid again as she began helping Penelope out of her robe. "If we hurry, we can probably still catch many of the guests lingering in the dining room at this time. Hopefully, Wylder and Simon will be among them. I want to see if this is a true occurrence or if last night was merely a fluke."

"Emily Blackthorne… are you using me to distract your brother?" Penelope demanded. "Just so you can flirt with Lord Wyldewood?"

"Of course, I am." Emily grinned in unabashed delight. "But don't feel as though you must only distract Simon. You may flirt with him, too, if you are so inclined."

CHAPTER TWENTY

Emily

THERE WERE A few houseguests still milling about the dining room and spilling over into the adjoining breakfast room. Wylder and Simon, however, had departed for a horseback ride into the village of Thorne Park only an hour before. The two men were not expected back until late afternoon.

Emily swallowed her disappointment, but Penelope was surprisingly vocal with her dismay.

"I wore my prettiest dress for this, Emily," she said while pouring herself a cup of tea from the sideboard. Glancing around the room to make sure no one overheard their conversation, she placed a piece of toast on a plate and sat down at the far end of the enormous dining room table. "Your brother is not even here to take notice."

Emily smiled, encouraged by Penelope's show of irritation. "He may not be here now, but no doubt by teatime he will be. Neither he nor Wyldewood will miss Ashcroft's arrival. If you like, we could change into our riding habits and look for them in the village. I know Simon enjoys an ale or two at the inn whenever we visit here."

Penelope laughed. "You know that would not be my first choice."

"I know... I continue to hope that you will grow fond of

riding. It can be so exhilarating riding a fast horse through an open field."

"This is because you crave risk in all its various forms," Penelope replied in a low voice. "That includes pursuing the earl when you know very well your brother will never allow the relationship."

Emily ducked her head, hating that Penelope's words rang so true. "Simon has been very stubborn on the subject, but then, so has Wylder. I've determined the best course of action is to neither chase the man's attention nor reject it." Sipping her cup of tea, she meant it when she said, "Whatever happens between us will occur because of destiny." But then, in teasing contradiction to her own avowal, she winked at Penelope. "But it must be said that destiny needs a little boost now and then."

⇥⇥⇥⇤⇤⇤

"LADY BLACKTHORNE INSTRUCTED that I inform you of Lord and Lady Ashcroft's arrival," Thorne Park's butler said from the door of the library two hours later. The elderly man was as cool and collected as could be, even though Emily knew the entire house would be in an uproar with the new couple's imminent arrival.

"Thank you, Seaver," Emily said, closing her book. "Miss True and I will be along in a moment."

Penelope laid her own book aside, eyes wide with sudden apprehension. "I thought they were expected later this afternoon?"

Emily gathered the stacks of books so they could be returned to the appropriate shelves. Penelope jumped up to help.

"Blast, Mother did not think they would arrive by supper, to be honest. Hurry, Pen. We can meet the new countess without a huge gathering vying for her attention."

Once all of the books were put away, the two girls quickly checked each other's dresses and made sure their hair was tidy.

Once certain of their presentability, they hurried out of the library, racing down the numerous corridors with arms linked until they finally reached the front terrace.

The Ashcroft coach had just arrived, and Emily breathlessly admired the smartness of the vehicle with its lacquered black color and blue and gold shield on the doors. A team of perfectly matched bays pulled the coach, and a groom leaped forward to secure the reins at the bit. The man struggled to hold them as the driver set the brake.

"Ah, there you are, girls," Chelsea Blackthorne said with a smile. Sliding an arm around her daughter's waist, she gave Emily a peck on the cheek before addressing the other young lady. "Penelope, dear, thank you for accompanying Emily to assist us in greeting the new couple at Thorne Park." She glanced in the direction of the stables and tsked under her breath. "I do wish Simon were here as well, but I suppose he and Wyldewood have yet to return from their trip into the village."

Lord Blackthorne patted his waistcoat before waving a hand at a second groom trotting up the gravel drive. "Jamie, my good man, take the other horse by the bit at once. They are a spirited pair, aren't they? Ashcroft has always possessed an eye for excellent horseflesh."

Emily had to agree as she sidled away to stand behind her parents alongside Penelope. Being an avid rider, she appreciated the sleek beauty of the carriage horses and wondered what treasures the earl's stables might hold when it came to thorough-breds. Perhaps an invitation to the new couple's country home could be wrangled at some point. Surely, his new countess would welcome the opportunity to form lasting friendships with other young ladies, given her relatively unknown status in society.

Lord Lucien Westley, Earl of Ashcroft, emerged from the coach, his broad-shouldered form clad in a dark-blue coat and black breeches. His thick, black hair was tousled as if someone's fingers had recently ruffled it. He quickly straightened his snowy-white cravat with a rakish grin before reaching a hand into the interior of the coach.

Lady Charlotte Westley, the new Countess of Ashcroft, stepped down from the coach with her husband's assistance. Sunlight caught on her blonde hair, turning the gleaming strands visible beneath the stylish hat she wore into molten shades of golden honey. Large blue eyes framed by dark lashes and brows looked around in curious wonder.

"Oh! Isn't she just lovely?" Penelope murmured beside Emily.

"She's stunning," Emily said when Charlotte caught sight of them and gave them a shy, but friendly smile. "And Ashcroft is a man besotted with his bride. Look at how he holds her elbow… it's the perfect blend of possessiveness and adoration."

"It's beyond romantic," Penelope sighed with envy. "They are obviously very much in love."

"Welcome, welcome, Lord and Lady Ashcroft!" Emily's father boomed, descending the terrace steps to shake Lucien's hand and bow to the countess. The young lady blushed at the exuberant greeting but did not shrink away from it. Next, Emily's mother warmly greeted the couple and then turned to motion for Emily and Penelope to come forward.

"Lady Ashcroft, this is our daughter, Emily, and her dearest friend, Miss Penelope True," Chelsea said, beaming with pride.

"I'm so pleased to meet you both," Charlotte said, nodding her head in greeting, her smile growing even wider as both Emily and Penelope crowded around her.

"I do hope you enjoy your time here at Thorne Park, Lady Ashcroft." Emily cast a teasing grin at Lucien and said, "And you as well, Lord Ashcroft. You'll be happy to know the key to the library is safely held by our housekeeper."

Lucien groaned dramatically, leaning his shoulder into his wife's with a rueful smile. "That is a subtle reminder that during my last visit, I somehow ended up locked inside the library. An unfortunate incident which kept Lady Emily from her beloved books. It was all her inebriated brother's fault, of course. He thought to teach me a lesson for some imagined slight."

"It was all in good fun," Simon injected behind them from the terrace steps.

"And well deserved," Wylder added as the two men bounded down to the gravel drive. His gaze briefly caught Emily's, the look in the deep-gray orbs unreadable, before it shifted to his friend. "It is good to see you, Ashcroft." He and Simon both vigorously shook Lucien's hand, then turned to Charlotte. Wylder took her gloved hand and kissed it. "Lady Ashcroft, you are as lovely today as you were at the wedding. I do hope this husband of yours is taking good care of you."

"Hello, Lord Wyldewood. Lord Camden," Charlotte replied, her smile affectionate and warm. "You know full well that Lucien does nothing in half-measures. Indeed, some days I wonder if he will even allow me to brush my own hair, he is so focused on caring for me. It takes a reminder that I am fully capable of taking care of myself… although I do admit to requesting his help when it comes to the procurement of pineapple ice." And then she tsked at them, "I hope we may dispense with the use of all these titles. Please call me by my given name." She glanced at Emily and Penelope. "If that is all right with you."

Emily laughed in appreciation. She immediately liked Lucien's new wife, sensing she shared a kindred spirit with the beautiful girl. "I much prefer it… keeping up with all these titles is most vexing." She gave the new countess an encouraging grin of solidarity while Penelope shyly returned Charlotte's smile. Only Emily noticed when Penelope's gaze drifted to Lucien for a brief moment before darting away, her bottom lip tugged between her teeth as if she wished to say something but could not.

While Wylder and Simon were both still clad in their riding breeches and boots, they were no less elegant and attractive beside the immaculately dressed Lucien. The men standing together were definitely an eye-catching trio of male power and good breeding. As the women discussed the guests who had already arrived for the house party and the upcoming ball, the men gathered off to the side to watch the unloading of a second coach carrying the earl and countess's trunks and their valet and lady's maid.

When a couple of footmen began carrying in the trunks, Emily cast a glance at Wylder before joining her mother, Charlotte, and Penelope as they walked up the terrace steps. Lady Blackthorne was explaining the room assignments, noting that she had placed Lucien and Charlotte in the largest and grandest of all the guest rooms, but Emily paid little heed to that. All of her attention lay centered on Wylder. How handsome he was in dark breeches and riding boots, his riding coat thrown over one arm as he watched Emily walk away. She wanted to turn and run back to him. Tell everyone just how much she loved him and that she wanted to spend the rest of her life in his arms. It would be a scandalous way of exposing their affair, but Emily had never wanted anything more in that space of a few seconds.

But that is impossible. Dangerous and impossible.

Wylder's eyes lingered upon her, an appreciative gleam within those cloud-gray depths letting Emily know that he did indeed like the color blue on her form. She gave him a small smile and was exhilarated when the firm lines of his mouth tipped upward. Then he turned back to the conversation, and the strange little moment that just passed between them was over.

WITH THE ARRIVAL of more guests, everyone had gathered to partake of the refreshments offered on the expansive lawns. With Blackthorne's statuary gardens and whimsical folly serving as the focal centerpiece, various amusements provided entertainment. On one side of the lawns, an archery range had been set up. A few gentlemen and ladies were already there practicing their skills. Emily bypassed that, headed instead toward the opposite lawn where two games of bowls were taking place.

Wylder stood off to the side of one of the alleys, watching Lucien and Simon compete against one another. Charlotte and

Penelope stood alongside him, and for a brief moment, Emily thought back to the moment Wylder indicated he might consider courting her best friend. A pang of jealousy, sharp and unrelenting, stabbed her heart with enough force that it left her breathless and her steps faltering.

If she reacted so strongly to the possibility Wylder might marry someone so dear to her, how on earth would she survive if he should wed someone she did not know? How could she stand by and impassively endure another woman claiming the honor of becoming his wife?

Biting her bottom lip, she watched her brother say something to the group that had them all laughing. The camaraderie between the three men was something special. It always had been. Even their exploits, while indeed scandalous, only added to their collective charm. But there was a definite air of change drifting through the air. Emily could see it quite clearly, and she wondered if the others would notice it, too. Lucien's attention was rarely on the game he played. Rather, his gaze strayed often to Charlotte and the charged electricity passing between them during those moments, even while standing amid a gathering of people, was breathtaking to witness.

The man was completely bewitched by his wife; that much was apparent. This left hope that the two remaining rakehells could also be captured by the right woman.

"Emily... do come join us," Charlotte called out, catching sight of Emily as she drew closer. Wylder's gaze flickered to her for a brief moment before his attention shifted back to Penelope and the conversation between them. Penelope's face pinkened with something that almost resembled guilt before her own gaze dropped from Emily's stare.

"I believe Simon has Lucien bested this time," Charlotte said with a giggle when Lucien shot her an exasperated glare over his shoulder.

"How can I win when I'm being distracted in such a manner?" Lucien grumbled. "You know very well that dress and hat are among my favorites on you. I cannot be blamed for losing two games in a row in light of such temptation."

"Might I remind you, dear husband, that it was you who selected this outfit?" Charlotte replied with a cheeky grin. "I'd say you are to blame for your own downfall, sir."

Lucien threw the curved ball down onto the ground and threw up his hands in mock surrender. "I concede the game, Camden," he laughingly said to Simon. Striding toward Charlotte, he gathered her into his arms and swung her arm. "Oh, siren. You know very well that *you* are my downfall." Not caring they'd garnered an audience, the Earl of Ashcroft gave his blushing wife a heated kiss. "And I cannot say I have any complaints at all, my lady."

Emily's heart tightened even more, envy stamping itself like firebrands across her soul. Her gaze helplessly drifted to Wylder only to find him staring at her with the same covetous gleam in his silver eyes.

Penelope cleared her throat. "I believe I'll go sit with Lady Bashear and Lady Blackthorne for a while." She looked somewhat distracted as she added, "Emily, may we speak privately?"

Emily nodded, allowing Penelope to draw her aside. Was her friend on the verge of confessing her acceptance of Wylder's courtship? She steeled herself for that possibility, hoping she was wrong.

"I know what you were thinking, Emily, and you know I would never betray you in such a manner." Penelope's soft green eyes held Emily's, her smile tremulous. "I think Lord Wyldewood was simply being kind, engaging me in conversation because God knows I would not initiate it on my own. And... perhaps I'm completely wrong, but I have the feeling he was goading Simon."

Emily deflated, ashamed that her misplaced jealousy was clouding her reason. Impulsively, she embraced Penelope, her eyes pricking with tears. "Thank you, Penelope."

Penelope laughed softly, holding Emily for a long moment. "I don't even know why you worry so. Wyldewood sees only you. If only Simon would realize it and give his blessing, things would be so much easier."

"That will never happen, but it is a lovely dream," Emily said sadly as she finally pulled away. She glanced toward Wyldewood and noted the slight frown he wore as he watched them. "What are your impressions of Charlotte?"

"She is the sweetest girl I believe I've ever met," Penelope sighed. "Almost too sweet for the ton. Thank goodness she's married Ashcroft. I cannot imagine that he would allow anyone to upset her. He dotes on her every word, and she practically worships him." Her chin trembled. "I've decided I want to follow your plan, Emily."

Emily's throat tightened with concern. "Are you sure, Pen?" She had the feeling that her friend was now looking for an escape from the uncomfortable expectations of mingling with people celebrating Lord and Lady Ashcroft's return to society instead of simply avoiding an unwanted marriage.

"Yes, I'm sure," Penelope whispered, her moss-green eyes finding Simon once more before darting back to Emily. "I'm sorry I cannot be of much help in distracting your brother. Since Ashcroft and Charlotte arrived, he seems as determined to avoid me as he was to talk to me last night. I find his behavior very confusing."

"I find it confusing as well," Emily admitted, then changing the subject, she said, "I hear that Lady Beshear's grandnephew has arrived. He is apparently not as odious as we imagined him to be. In fact, he's quite handsome."

Penelope nodded. "Yes, I met him earlier. He's very charming, too." She looked toward the clump of trees where a few of the ladies had taken shelter from the sun. "Lady Bashear is beckoning for us to come to her, but there is no need for both of us to go."

Emily groaned. "Do you think she will be offended if we don't?"

"Probably, but I will take the brunt of her displeasure," Penelope said with a small smile. "I've had enough practice dealing with my mother."

CHAPTER TWENTY-ONE

Wylder

WYLDER WATCHED EMILY and Penelope with such intensity that he did not realize Lucien was watching him with a satisfied smirk on his handsome features.

"Something is different, I think," Lucien dryly remarked.

Wylder's attention snapped to his best friend. "What do you mean?"

"Between you and Emily… there is something there." Lucien returned Wylder's heated stare with admirable calm. "Come now, do you really believe I would not see it, Wylder? Marrying Charlotte has opened my eyes to so many things in life. Things I either ignored or was blind to before her."

"And what do you believe that you see, Lucien?" Wylder's jaw tightened with annoyance. He did not like the close scrutiny. It made his skin feel hot and itchy. As if every salacious thought revolving around Emily Blackthorne was on full, unblinking display for the entire world to see.

Lucien's head tilted before his lips curved with a smile at Wylder's obvious irritation. "I think you've done something that would greatly upset Simon if he ever found out. And I think you and Emily have grown closer despite his strenuous and numerous objections."

"Simon has been assisting me in rebuilding the St. Clair accounts. At my insistence, my father has given them over to me. Emily has no part in that."

"Ah, I see. But you must give something in return, correct?"

Wylder swore beneath his breath at his friend's astute nature. "I must engage in a search for a suitable bride if I wish to retain control over the estates. My father would not agree to my plan without his own damnable stipulation."

"It should come as no surprise that I highly recommend marriage. Providing you find the right woman to spend the rest of her life with you as her husband. So, it's official? You are truly hunting for a wife?"

"Yes and no." Raking a hand through his hair, Wylder cast a glance at Simon, who was now showing Charlotte how to throw the balls for the game. "It is a bloody charade, Lucien. An act I am forced to perform for as long as it takes to rebuild the estate. I've no wish for a damned wife. You know that. How could I possibly marry a woman and not have her run screaming when she realizes the depths of my sexual proclivities?"

Lucien smiled. "It may be easier than you think to find a suitable match. After all, I did."

Wylder slanted a glance at his friend. "So you are faithful to your countess in all aspects?"

"Every single one. And I've never known such satisfaction as what I find with my wife. It is possible to fall in love and have every desire you've ever had fulfilled, Wylder." Lucien's gaze drifted to where Charlotte was laughing in delight as she managed to throw the ball straight. "It is incredible, actually. To share the most intimate moments with the woman you love. And to have her give her very soul in exchange for your own."

"Even if it were remotely possible, the woman I want is out of my reach," Wylder said slowly. He despised the envy that rose in his throat to choke him with bitterness. Regret mingled with the emotion when recalling the role he played in the attempt to subvert Lucien and Charlotte's relationship in the beginning. It had been a foolish, ill-advised endeavor, spurred mainly by

Simon. "It is because of my depravities that she remains unattainable. Simon will never—"

Lucien grunted in sudden annoyance, his jaw clenching tight. "It is because of our friendship that I nearly let the woman I love slip through my fingers. That, and my own stubborn nature." His tone turned more retrospective as he stared at Wylder, his dark-green eyes somber. "Our reputations have become an extension of ourselves, which is to be expected with the notoriety of our escapades. After all, not a single man among us fought very hard to maintain even a hint of respectability when it came to the fairer sex. We have certainly enjoyed the benefits of such a lifestyle, both privately and publicly. But I sense things are changing for you, at least. I suspect you'd rather allow that portion of our lives to fade into the past. But loyalty to the rakehells, and all the sentimentality for the camaraderie we share, is keeping you from reaching for happiness with both hands." His smile was suddenly tender and directed toward Charlotte, who was waving at him to join her in a game of bowls. "Take what you want from life, Wylder. Everything else... friends, family, responsibilities... will fall into place. And once you've chosen the woman with whom you wish to live out your days, do not hesitate to take her as well."

AFTER SPEAKING WITH Lucien, Wylder looked for Emily and found her standing with a group that included Sir Gregory Brighton and Lady Bashear's grandnephew. Lord Patrick Bashear had arrived only a short time ago and was now apparently regaling other guests with tales of his time in France. Several times, the entire bunch burst into laughter, and hearing Emily's musical giggle woven with the others made Wylder's hands tighten into twin fists. She seemed charmed by the tall, dark-blond-haired lord with the good-natured manner. But then again, she treated Gregory with the same genial pleasantness, effortlessly flirting with the two men until they were jostling one another for the honor of fetching her cups of lemonade.

Emily had no trouble juggling multiple suitors. Wylder knew that from having watched over her for the last few years. But this had a different feel to it. Before, she'd always searched him out in the crowd. She always erected an invisible wall between her and other gentlemen, but now that barrier was sagging. The knowledge struck a chord deep inside Wylder—a sense of panic he'd not experienced before. Something had indeed shifted between them. Something intangible that resulted in a coolness during their last interaction. Was it possible that Emily was drifting away from him, the hold he had on her disintegrating one fragile thread at a time? He argued with himself that this was for the best. Their association must eventually come to a natural end, but realistically, Wylder doubted he could allow that to happen. He wanted her with a desperation that overrode all sense of reason.

But was there really any other option to be made? He could not claim Emily and accomplish his goals at the same time, no matter Lucien's advice on the subject. Obviously, Lucien could not appreciate Simon's vehemence when it came to keeping Wylder far away from his sister. And it was a simple fact that Lucien was not dependent on Simon's financial expertise to save the family name and fortunes. So far, the old duke had upheld his end of the bargain. He was steering clear of the gaming tables and allowing Wylder to run things the way he desired. Now, Wylder must act the part of a reformed rakehell and search for a wealthy heiress to wed.

From his position beneath the shade trees, Wylder watched Emily break away from the group. Patrick followed close behind her while poor Sir Gregory Brighton looked positively disheartened. When Patrick reached out and took her by the arm, Wylder gritted his teeth. Having just made one another's acquaintance, what could the two of them possibly have to say privately to one another?

With a teasing smile and shake of her head, Emily pulled away from his grip and continued walking. Her purposeful strides away from the man took her to the entrance of the statuary garden. Within a few moments, she disappeared from view, leaving Wylder to realize this was an opportunity that had just presented itself. Regardless of how irrational his decision was, he would pursue her.

He waited five minutes or so before following her, wondering the entire time if she planned on meeting Patrick. God, he hoped not. He wasn't sure if he could restrain himself from destroying the man's handsome features simply because he dared to pursue Emily.

He found her standing outside the stone folly, her arms behind her as she leaned against one of the pillars. She stared out at the large lake, watching the swans and a small flock of ducks as they swam close to the shoreline. Several large weeping willows dotted the banks, the wind rustling through the long branches and making them sway. Occasionally, one or two rowboats floated aimlessly by, steered by gentlemen eager to impress the ladies brave enough to set foot in the vessels.

Wylder did not speak as he advanced upon Emily, but he knew the moment she became aware of his presence. There was a tensing of her shoulders, and her chin tilted higher. Her body seemed to brim with defiance and anticipation.

"I knew you would follow me," she said softly without even looking his way.

"Were you expecting me or that useless fop, Bashear?"

A slight smile played across her features, lifting her lips at the corners. "Do you believe Lord Bashear was inclined to follow me as you have?"

Wylder stepped closer. "I think he is entranced by you." He huffed out an exasperated sigh. "As any breathing male in your orbit would be."

"So you think I am to blame if a man finds me attractive and wishes to pursue me?" She still did not look at him, her attention centered on the tiny group of ducklings. They followed the older ducks onto the shore.

Bloody hell. I did not mean it like that.

"Are you not strong enough to resist my apparent lure, Lord Wyldewood?" Emily asked, amusement coloring her tone as she finally faced him. Her eyes were so blue in the sunlight that they sparkled like rare sapphires.

Wylder's jaw tightened, a muscle jumping there as he clenched his teeth. "You know that I am not, little minx, and that's the damnable truth of it."

Emily's expression darkened. "Should we agree that our affair is at its end? I certainly have no wish to be the cause of your distress."

He laughed, a short, sharp sound that made Emily flinch in response. "Do you honestly think I want to end things with us? Because I don't. I cannot help myself... no matter how much of you I get, I only end up wanting more."

"You make it sound as though I am an affliction you need to be cured of." Taking a piece of vine that wrapped around the column, she entwined it around her fingers. "Perhaps it is best that we keep our distance from one another."

Wylder could not stop himself in that moment. Capturing her wrists in one hand, he moved until they were no longer visible to anyone rowing past on the lake. He pressed Emily against the column, her hands trapped high above her head.

"Distance?" he murmured as she gasped in surprise. Running his nose alongside hers, he closed his eyes and let her soft perfume drift over him. "I cannot accept that, Emily, and you know it."

"Wylder... we shouldn't..." Emily's words came in a whisper, her body arching toward his despite the denial.

"You are right... we shouldn't. But we both know we will. We both know we are addicted to this. To one another. I cannot get enough of you, Emily. I want you. I want your taste in my mouth. Your hands on my body. My hands on yours…" Wylder dipped his head until his mouth brushed over hers. She tasted of lemonade and smelled like sugary citrus. His cock hardened as he coerced her lips to part, remembering when she had pleasured him with her mouth and swallowed his seed.

With a whimper, she let him in, her tongue dancing with his. His free hand wrapped around her throat, anchoring her in place as he kissed her with all the pent-up frustration racking his body. To keep her head tilted at the right angle, his thumb pressed to the underside of her chin, and she moaned in agonized delight as he controlled her.

When he pulled back, allowing her a quick breath of air, Emily was panting. Eyes glassy with desire, she begged for him just as he had dreamed she would.

"Please, Wylder. Touch me like you did before… please."

"It's too risky, Emily." His lips blazed a trail down her exposed throat, burning kisses that skated from collarbone to collarbone and down to the swell of her breasts. Fuck, if it weren't for the possibility of someone stumbling across them, he would have already dropped to his knees and sucked her sweet little quim into the heat of his mouth. But he wanted to take his time with her. Make her come again and again until she collapsed in exhausted pleasure.

"No, no, it's not," Emily moaned, her fingers flexing in his grasp. Her body trembled, tempting him to throw caution to the wind. "I need you. Don't you understand?"

"Shhh." Wylder nibbled her jaw, his fingers tightening with the slightest pressure around her throat. She quieted at once with a low hum of arousal. "I understand what you need, minx. My fingers deep in your tight, little pussy. My hand around your throat, giving you permission to breathe. My mouth sucking your sweet little nipples until they are hard and aching for me to bite them. Yes, I understand what you need."

His filthy words left her gasping with shock, but her body responded by melting into him.

"I'm sure if I touched you right now, you would be soaked for me, wouldn't you, Emily?" Wylder continued the torment, his hand leaving her throat to skim over her breasts. Beneath the thin material of the gown and half-stays, he pinched her budded nipples until she squirmed in delight. "Should I see if it's true? Should I slide my fingers inside you and make you come for me?"

"*Yes... oh yes, yes...*" Emily chanted, rocking her hips into his pelvis and making contact with his cock. The thrill that raced through him was explosive, but he had to stop before things went any further.

"I will do all of those things, Emily," he promised, releasing her hands from his tight grip. Her eyes were closed, but they drifted open to stare at him in dazed wonderment. "But not here, where anyone might discover us, naughty girl."

"Then come to my room tonight, Wylder," she replied huskily and without hesitation. She licked her lips, bringing one hand up to trace the shape of his mouth. When he turned his head and bit the inside of her wrist, she sucked in a breath of pure adoration. Then, like the brat she was, Emily challenged him without a care for the consequences. "Come to my room and you may punish me for my recklessness."

CHAPTER TWENTY-TWO

Emily

WYLDER INSISTED THAT Emily walk back through the statuary garden alone.

Of course, she knew he could not accompany her. That would mean announcing that they had spent time alone with one another. She wanted to protest, argue that she was not a secret he could keep forever, but she obeyed him. She walked out of that garden on wobbly legs, her breathing shallow as she emerged from the rows of meticulously groomed flowers and exquisitely carved marble figures.

Her gaze darted around, taking note of the guests enjoying themselves. Instinctively, she searched for her brother and found him at the archery range. He was laughing heartily at something one of the other men said when he suddenly caught sight of Emily.

A smile formed on her lips, and she waved her hand at him, praying the suspicion in his gaze would fade away. But his features darkened, his mouth turning downward into a scowl as he stared past her to the gardens. Emily knew he was waiting to see if anyone followed her out. But when no one did, his face relaxed and he smiled back at her before returning to the archery.

Letting out a sigh of relief, Emily continued making her way up the expansive lawn. She did not stop until she reached the refreshment table. Accepting a glass of lemonade from one of the footmen, she gulped it down, willing her racing heart to slow its pace.

Her body was practically vibrating with electricity. She ached in all the places Wylder intended her to ache. Swallowing hard, she remembered begging him to ease that pain deep inside her. Begged him for a release he had no intention of granting. The kisses, the caresses. All were simple methods of proving his mastery over her.

And despite her innate independence, Emily was happy to let him do it. She craved it, actually. Needed the weight of his hand around her throat, his fingers tightening until she was lightheaded and dizzy with need.

I begged him to punish me.

A pang of desire reminded her how much she loved those punishments. If he came to her tonight, she wasn't sure she could stop herself from begging him to use her body in any manner he desired.

Penelope had feigned illness and retired to her room while Emily's parents played a game of bowls with another couple. Gazing at the guests dotting the brilliant green lawn, Emily spied Lucien and Charlotte sitting on a bench beneath a sprawling oak tree. The couple laughed often together, and several times, Lucien's head bent toward his wife in the most affectionate of ways.

Emily watched them enviously and came to a sudden, sad realization. The dream she carried of her and Wylder coming together as a couple would never be realized.

All the sneaking around in the shadows. The secret kisses and caresses. The way I am forced to hide my feelings for him. Pining over him while the world twirled around in cruel ignorance.

It was suddenly far more than she could bear.

Stomach roiling, Emily pressed a hand to the back of her mouth, choking back a sob. No one must see her this upset... certainly not her parents nor her brother. And it would be an utter disaster if Wylder saw her in such a state. He would no doubt demand she tell him the reason for her distress, and her humiliation would be complete to admit she was crying over him.

With slow, deliberate movements, Emily set the glass of lemonade down on the table and turned away from the polite, yet questioning smile of the footman. For a few moments, she strolled about the lawn until it was possible to escape the gaiety with no one the wiser to her absence. And when Wylder did finally walk up the garden's terraced steps, she was not there to see the disappointment in his eyes when he discovered she had slipped away.

EMILY DID NOT appear for dinner that evening, explaining to her mother that she was not feeling well. Since Penelope suffered from the same mysterious illness, it was assumed the two girls had eaten something that resulted in the malaise.

"I will leave in the morning." Penelope's smile was pensive. "Are you certain you can manage without Mary for a few days?"

"Of course I can manage, darling Pen," Emily assured her.

"What of your mother? Do you think she will question why my illness requires me to return home immediately?" Penelope wrung her hands, overwhelmed with worry. "The worst part of all this is the numerous falsehoods I must tell."

"She will believe you, Pen. Please do not worry overmuch about that." Emily flopped back in her chair, staring at Penelope, who sat across from her. A fire crackled in the fireplace grate, the flames warm and low. "I wish you did not have to go."

"But we both know I must." Penelope's brow creased with a tiny frown. "I've no choice at this point. Mother's last letter said negotiations were moving forward with Lord Grant. They will sign the marriage contract by next week. My God, the way they have sold me into marriage really does make me ill."

Emily sighed in commiseration. "I don't know what else to do, Penelope. It is your choice to make, if you should stay or go. Whatever you decide, I will support you."

"I know, Emily." Penelope pushed her hair back from her face, revealing the tears tracking down her cheeks. "But I must go. I cannot… no… I *will not* marry that man."

"Oh, dearest," Emily whispered, pulling the girl in for a tight embrace. "They won't get away with this dastardly act. I promise you that."

When Penelope returned to her room just before midnight, Emily banked the fire and then settled herself into bed. Turning the lamp down low, she opened her book, intending to read for a little while.

The door suddenly flew open as Wylder stormed inside her room.

Emily sat up so fast that the book slipped from her lap and onto the floor. Was the earl truly in her room? Shock rendered her speechless for a long moment before she angrily stuttered, "Wh-what on earth are you doing, Wylder? Are you insane?"

Wylder's eyes narrowed as he locked the door behind him, and Emily's heart rate tripled its beat as he strode toward her. Upon reaching the bed, his hand shot out. Gripping her chin between thumb and forefinger, he stared down at her.

"What is wrong? Your mother said you were ill." His tone was harsh, although concern seeped through every word.

Emily's eyes fluttered shut. How could she possibly explain to this man that he was the cause of her condition?

"I'm waiting, Emily."

"I—" she faltered, then offered in a small voice. "I am unwell, Wylder. And I cannot do this any longer with you. Please understand and go away." Her eyes filled with tears despite every intention she had to remain strong and fierce and most of all, resistant. "Please."

"This illness you suffer from… is it because of my actions this afternoon in the gardens?" Wylder demanded. "Did I hurt you, Emily? Did I?"

Emily swallowed hard, choking back another sob. "Not physically, no. But you are killing me. Little by little, I have been dying since we began this insanity." She gripped the hand holding her chin in both of hers. "I cannot want you like this and not have you. Because while you may desire my body, you refuse to accept my love and my heart. That is why I cannot do this anymore."

Anguished rage lit Wylder's eyes, turning them a dark gray. His lips tightened into a straight, thin line of regret. "Fuck, Emily, I want all of you. Every single gorgeous inch of you. Do you think this is any easier for me?" Releasing her chin, he gripped her upper arms in his hard hands and hauled her up from the bed. "I want to kiss you in front of your parents... your damnable brother... the entire ton... and claim you as mine while the world watches."

"Then why don't you, Wylder? Why do you torment me with this half-measure of affection? Why do you torture me with talk of searching for a bride while bowing down to my brother's demands to stay away from me? You are a Mayfair Rakehell and for some reason that remains unknown, that moniker renders you unsuitable in Simon's eyes. Explain to me what you have done to warrant this sordid reputation," Emily ordered, her voice stronger now as hurt and anger flooded her veins. The emotions flared higher as Wylder remained silent. "You deny us both but refuse to tell me the truth." She tried jerking out of his grasp but failed miserably. His grip was like tempered steel, her feet barely touching the floor as he held her captive. "If you will not tell me the truth within yourself, if you do not trust me to know your secrets, then you do not deserve any part of me."

"Damn you, Emily. You want the truth?" Wylder growled, his eyes darkening even more. They were almost black now and glittering like shards of ice as he glared at her. "The truth is, if I tell you what you want to hear, you will never allow me to touch you again."

"I deserve to know what you are hiding from me," Emily replied stubbornly.

"You don't know what you are asking of me, Emily. You cannot possibly understand the darkness inside me… the overwhelming need to control and possess you in every way imaginable," Wylder hissed, nearly shaking her in his frustration. His fingers dug into her shoulders with unintentional cruelty. "The things I do to my women… the things that bring me pleasure… are not acceptable practices. The depraved acts I enjoy would disgust you. It would not happen right away but eventually you would despise me for subjecting you to such things. And, I cannot bear to have you hate me as you once did."

"Tell me, Wylder. Or else leave my room and never speak to me again." Emily's tone was so icy cold that she could hardly believe the words came from her. The tears had dried on her cheeks, leaving salty tracks behind. Wylder bent his head, his tongue tracing the paths on first one cheek then the other. Emily stood frozen, held prisoner by the unexpected tenderness, even as her heart was shattering into a thousand pieces with his continued silence.

Wylder let out a shuddering breath, then abruptly dropped to his knees before her. His muscled arms wrapped around Emily's waist, his breath warm on her stomach through the thin muslin of her nightgown.

"Emily… my little minx. You insist on uncovering my secrets… then so be it," he muttered, his dark, shaggy head tilting back so he could stare up into her eyes. "The things I've done to you thus far are mundane when compared to what I truly desire. If you were completely mine, I would bind you in ropes, securing you to various structures and rendering you immobile. I would have certain… implements… ready at my fingertips to use upon your tender skin." He rose to his feet as he confessed his darkest desires, his hands gripping hers as he loomed over her smaller form. "Riding crops, whips, birches. I would use the bite of pain to bring you to the heights of pleasure. I would use you as I see fit because every inch of you would belong to me. I would enjoy watching you crawl for me, your body bare to my gaze. I would bend you over any piece of furniture I fancied, and I would take you hard and fast with your hands bound behind your back, delighting in your tears. I would fuck your mouth. Your tight little quim. Your plump arse. My hands would wrap around your neck, and you would need my permission to breathe as I impaled you on my cock. I would command your complete submission and own every soft, silky part of you, Emily. And when morning came, you would despise me for every minute that I claimed you as mine."

A nearly inaudible whimper escaped Emily's throat as he spoke. The salacious images his words produced in her mind were shocking. But rather than being repulsed, her insides trembled with jolts of arousal and her knees wobbled beneath her weight. What on earth was wrong with her that she wanted to experience these acts that Wylder described? How was it logical that she was willing to give herself over to him for even a small taste of cruel paradise at this man's hands?

Wylder's words were a low growl, rumbling in his chest as silence fell between them. "That's the kind of man… the kind of monster… I am, Emily. Now, do you understand?"

Emily swallowed hard. "You've done these things with other women, Wylder?"

Jaw clenched tight, Wylder's eyes glittered as his gaze traced her features. "That and so much more."

"And you want to do those things to me?" Her body trembled at the thought, but still, she pressed on.

"Yes. But that would only be the beginning, minx. Which is why I cannot claim you as mine."

"But if you were to marry, you would do these acts with your wife?" Emily frowned. "I don't understand. Are you saying these… acts… are things that only loose women… can enjoy with a man?"

"I would not subject my wife to such acts of depravity. It

wouldn't be right," Wylder swore vehemently.

Emily could not comprehend the reasoning behind his words. Did ladies like herself not find pleasure in this type of sexual activity? "I am assuming Ashcroft has similar interests? Dear Lord, I suppose that includes my brother, as abhorrent as I find it to even dwell on the subject."

His eyebrows lowered, pinching together. "Without saying more, your assumptions are correct."

"Does Ashcroft seek his pleasure with others rather than his own wife?" she inquired with guileless innocence. The obvious love and affection she had witnessed between Lucien and Charlotte indicated a level of intimacy to be envied. She could not imagine the earl keeping a mistress or visiting brothels when he had a beautiful bride hanging on his every word.

"He does not." The admission was almost a snarl.

"Then…. could you not do the same with your own wife?" Emily pressed, wondering why the question seemed to upset Wylder so. She bit her bottom lip then shyly confessed, "I enjoyed it when you spanked me before. And when I pleasured you with my mouth…" She blushed, her face so hot that she wondered if she would go up in flames. "I was aroused when you took control of me… the way you commanded my movements was something I never expected to like. I want to explore and experience all things that bring you pleasure, Wylder."

Wylder let her go, rubbing his hand over his heart as he scowled. "You've granted me permission to enjoy your body, Emily. We can go no further than that. We will *not* go any further than that."

"Is that because you care more about your estates and your titles and cannot give up my brother's assistance? Is it because Simon would demand my honor be avenged with your death at his hands? Or is it because you believe you are not worthy of being with me, nor I with you?" Emily ground her teeth at his stubborn silence, her chin tilting as she regarded him. It felt as though her heart was bursting with pain and disgust. "I want you to leave now, Wylder. Please go."

Wylder raked his hands through his thick, dark hair, the strands falling over his brow. Emily wanted to brush the locks back so badly. She clenched her hands to keep from reaching for him.

"Emily…"

"Go away, Wylder." Her voice quivered, but she concealed the weakness by clearing her throat. In that moment, it felt like the earth was spinning too quickly while she floated in place. Anchored there by the savage heat of his eyes. "Before I begin screaming and bring everyone in this house running to this room."

"We both know I can make you scream for other reasons, Emily," he grunted in annoyance.

"And that would prove nothing." Taking a deep breath, she gave him a sad smile. "Unless you are brave enough to declare yourself publicly, this is where it ends. It ends *now*. Tonight. Right here. It ends with me wanting more than you can give." She wiped the tears from her cheeks and turned her back to him, her spine stiff and unyielding. "Please go. I don't want to see you anymore."

CHAPTER TWENTY-THREE

Wylder

ONE MORE WHISKY wouldn't hurt.

That's what Wylder told himself as he downed the dregs remaining in the glass and poured another.

The library was quiet, other than the sounds of the decanter clinking against the edge of the crystal tumbler. Closing his eyes, he swallowed the liquor and took a deep breath. The liquid burned his chest but that was inconsequential to the ache suffusing his entire body.

He'd been drinking since leaving Emily's room an hour before, and he would likely keep drinking for a good time to come. Maybe even until morning.

Goddamn it, I've made a mess of things.

The soft click of the door opening alerted Wylder that he was no longer alone. Squinting at the intruder, he relaxed upon seeing it was Lucien but then Simon was right behind the man. Wylder tensed again, wondering if perhaps someone had seen him storming out of Emily's rooms. How the hell would he explain his presence there?

"You left in the middle of the game and disappeared," Simon accused, stepping to the fireplace and leaning an arm against the carved marble mantel.

"My head wasn't in it," Wylder grumbled, his shoulders

drooping with unspoken relief. If Simon had any inkling that he'd spent time with Emily, he'd already be facing the round end of a pair of dueling pistols.

Lucien picked up a tumbler from the sidebar. Taking the decanter from Wylder, the earl poured himself a healthy dash of whisky and took a sip.

"Drinking will not help, my friend," he murmured, green eyes narrowing with speculation as he stared at Wylder.

"It certainly won't hurt," Wylder snapped back.

"What the devil has you all in a tangle?" Simon asked, his expression puzzled. "You've been behaving strangely since the day you arrived here."

Wylder debated even answering Simon's question. Everything was wrong, but there was no way in hell he could, or even should, explain it to his friends.

"I worry this plan you have developed to regain my fortune will collapse," he finally managed. "I worry that my father will succeed in losing our estates and I will be left penniless. He won't even need to follow through on his recurring threat to disown me if I do not marry because there will be nothing left to inherit."

Simon snorted in disbelief. "Impossible. It's a solidly developed plan, and it will not fail, Wylder. But something else is worrying you, I think."

"There is the pressure to hunt for a bride. It is stomach-turning." Wylder took a gulp of whisky. "And it is just one of many things on my mind recently."

Simon waved a hand in dismissal. "But that is nothing but a charade. No sense in turning yourself inside out over something that will never take place. I've concluded that I, too, must play the damned game." His smile was faint as his stare returned to the fire. Contemplating the flickering flames, he said nonchalantly, "Why do you think I've been dancing attendance with Penelope True? She's a mousy little thing, but whenever I engage the girl in one-sided conversations, my mother's eyes light up as though she's anticipating the arrival of her first grandchild."

"Have you actually looked at Miss True? She's quite lovely." Lucien plopped into a chair opposite Wylder, his gaze steady as he regarded Simon.

"Beauty hardly matters if the girl is as dull as a coal shuttle," Simon replied loftily, although a muscle in his jaw ticked as if he were internally protesting his own callous statement.

"Are you implying you are simply playing with Miss True?" Wylder's heart unexpectedly stirred with pity for Emily's best friend. He glared at Simon. "I've never known you to be intentionally cruel, Simon. From what I see, she is a sweet thing and undeserving of such actions."

Simon frowned. "If she is so compelling, you should pursue her, Wylder. Come to think of it, I've not witnessed you hunting a bride since you made the arrangement with your father and came to me for help. If it is all for show, shouldn't you at the very least make the effort?"

Lucien sighed and sipped his whisky. "If either one of you could possibly imagine the joys of marriage to the right woman, you would not waste time snapping at each other. And if my opinion still matters with either of you, I agree with Wylder on this, Simon. She's a close friend of your own sister. Perhaps you should not use the convenience of that acquaintance so casually."

Simon's laugh was harsh as he shook his head in disbelief. "What the devil is the matter with you both? We are the Rakehells of Mayfair, or have you forgotten that small detail? We are unapologetic. Headstrong. And spectacularly selfish in pursuing our desires and interests. We gamble too much. Practice what polite society deems depraved, and seek out women to engage with for that singular purpose. Lucien, I'll forgive your show of unabashed sentiment. After all, you are newlywed and still caught up in the rosy glow of that particular brand of bliss. And Charlotte is a beautiful wife... obviously, she accepts you as you are, since you've not sought the services of previous lovers. For God's sake, man. You've not once visited The Scarlett Petticoat since finding her in the wilds of the English countryside." Simon's hard, green gaze narrowed on Wylder, who steeled himself for the derision. Damn it to hell, if Simon did not curb his own tongue Wylder was bound to do it for him. He held his temper for the moment, realizing it was prudent to remain silent.

"But you, Wylder." Simon's head cocked as he studied his friend. "You've become a mystery to me, and I don't understand the shift. You and I are in similar positions. Our fathers have pushed us to marry, but neither one of us wants that noose around our necks. So, we must appease them without the commitment." He rubbed the back of his neck with one hand. "You and I have always desired the same things and the freedom to do them. Lately, you have not shown the same enthusiasm, and I find myself wondering if your goals have changed. I suspect you've not taken a woman to your bed in weeks, and it's a fact you declined the use of the whores at The Grinning Cockrel that night in London. Why is that?"

"My intimate relations are hardly your business, Simon." Wylder stood up from his chair, bowing slightly at the waist to his friends. "I will bid you both good night."

"Why don't you admit that something has changed, Wylder?" Simon demanded, pushing off from his stance by the fireplace. "You've changed. What the fuck is wrong with you?"

"Nothing is wrong with him," Lucien abruptly interjected, coming to stand between the two men. "Let it go, Simon."

"It's bad enough that we've lost you, Lucien," Simon slowly drawled. "But if Wylder defects, then the Rakehells are done."

"Would that be such a terrible thing?" Wylder muttered, frustrated by Simon's dogged pursuit of the subject.

"The only woman I've noticed you paying any mind to is my sister."

The room became deadly silent as Wylder's gaze met Simon's. He wasn't sure if the other man could see the truth in his eyes, but Wylder purposefully kept his expression blank. Tension stretched and vibrated until Wylder's sharp exhale shattered it into a million pieces.

"You know how I feel about Emily. But our friendship prevents me from courting her, and you know that, too."

Simon's eyes flared with immediate heat. He stared at Wylder, studying him intently, obviously searching for a flicker of guilt. Suspicion rolled off him in waves. It was so strong that even Lucien seemed taken aback. Frowning, he moved so that he firmly placed himself between the two men.

"Have you touched her?" Simon hissed. "Bloody hell, Wylder. She's my damned sister. How many times must I remind you of that?"

"I realize that." Wylder was determined not to incriminate himself or Emily. Although she had insisted their unorthodox affair was at its end, he wasn't sure if even she believed it. He calmly returned Simon's glare, willing his emotions to subside before he crumbled and shouted his love for Emily Blackthorne to the very rooftops.

And he did love her. With every breath of his soul and beat of his heart, he loved her.

But do you love her enough?

Wylder ruthlessly shut down his internal dialogue before it could go any further.

"Simon… the hour grows late, and obviously we've had our share of spirits this evening. Let us put this aside for now, and you can speak of it when you each have clearer heads," Lucien quietly urged, using the subtle force of a hand on Simon's shoulder to force more space between the two men.

Simon moved back, surprisingly conceding to Lucien's suggestion. But still, his blue eyes narrowed on Wylder, and when he spoke, his voice was low and rough with conviction.

"If you have compromised her, Wylder, I swear I will follow through on my promise I made years ago. I *will* demand satisfaction in the only acceptable manner available for gentlemen like us."

CHAPTER TWENTY-FOUR

Emily

EMILY ROSE EARLY that morning following a long, restless night. Her pillow was soaked with tears she'd shed in the dark, and while her heart ached, she was determined to forget she'd ever loved Wylder St. Clair.

After dressing with Mary's assistance, the girls made their way to Penelope's room. They helped pack her belongings. Once that was done, Emily sent Mary down to the stables to have a coach readied for the journey. It was decided that Emily would explain Penelope's departure, hoping the explanation would be sufficient to satisfy any curiosity.

"Mary will return here once you are settled in at the town-home. Remember, her cousin will serve as your maid while you are there. And I promise, I will come up with a new plan to keep this terrible engagement from *ever* taking place," Emily said, giving Penelope a quick embrace and an encouraging smile.

"I will also be thinking of a way to avoid my fate, Emily," Penelope replied softly. There was a newfound glint of strength in her pretty green eyes, along with a stubborn tilt of her chin that heartened Emily. "I've come to the conclusion that my parents cannot be allowed to abuse me in such a manner. Indeed, I shall no longer be their malleable pawn in planning the remainder of my life." Her grin was apologetic. "But I welcome this interlude to build my bravery to the heights required to enact such defiance."

"You will miss the lovely ball Mother has planned for Lucien and Charlotte tomorrow night," Emily said sadly.

Penelope pursed her lips and shook her head. "You know how such gatherings intimidate me. If only it weren't for my cursed shyness, I could perhaps engage a gentleman to show more than a passing interest in me."

"I had hoped my brother would be that man. He has behaved so strangely around you lately."

"I do not believe his attentiveness is anything more than a passing amusement. He enjoys needling me if only to see if I will snap back." Penelope's eyes flashed with a rare show of irritation. "I think he likes seeing me flustered."

Emily laughed. "He can certainly be an annoyance. Is there something more to his behavior? I cannot say with certainty."

"It doesn't matter now that I am leaving. I'm sure he will forget about me with amazing speed." Penelope's head tilted as she closely regarded Emily. "What of the situation with Lord Wyldewood? What will you do?"

Emily shrugged, ignoring the stabbing pain in her heart at the mention of Wylder. "There is nothing that I can do. He will not betray Simon's friendship, and he will not admit his affection for me. So, we stand at an impasse with no hope of resolution." She let out a heavy sigh and a rueful laugh. "It is over between us."

"I'm so sorry, Emily. I can only imagine how painful this must be."

Mentally shaking herself, Emily smiled broadly for Penelope's benefit. "I shall survive it, of course. I've pined for this man forever, hoping he would demolish the walls between us, but he will not budge from the belief that he is not good enough for me. I can no longer fight against those beliefs and must now admit defeat."

"Perhaps I should reconsider and stay. I do not wish to leave you when you need support."

"No, you must go. I'll be fine, Penelope, and so will you," Emily whispered, clasping the girl's hand tightly and fighting back tears. She'd never felt so helpless as she did in that moment, knowing she may not be able to save her friend from marrying the cold, cruel Lord Gregory Grant. "I promise."

An hour later, Penelope and Mary were on their way to London as Emily watched the coach disappear down the long drive. The coachman and groom were instructed to take her straightaway to the townhome on Curzon Street. And while the two men were not specifically sworn to secrecy, it was understood that they must be discreet regarding their destination.

It was not usual for guests to be up and about so early in the morning. When Emily stopped by the dining room for a cup of tea, she was surprised to find the new Countess of Ashcroft already seated in the adjoining breakfast room. She turned with a smile of greeting for Emily and gestured that she sit beside her.

"Good morning, Emily," Charlotte said warmly.

"Good morning," Emily replied as she perched on the empty chair. Cocking her head, she regarded the girl sitting across from her. "I did not think anyone else would be up this early in the morning."

"Oh, yes," Charlotte chuckled. "Old habits, I suppose. Before I married the earl, most of my mornings began at dawn. There was always so much to do, and it seemed very little time to do it."

"Is your life terribly different now?" Emily was truly curious. She found Charlotte vastly interesting. The young woman had been responsible for herself and her younger sister for some time following their father's death. As the daughter of a vicar, her life experiences were so different from Emily's.

"Yes." Charlotte grinned. "Lucien enjoys sleeping in late, and I find myself enjoying it as well. But my father believed that idle hands were the Devil's workshop, and so there are many mornings that I rise before my husband and have a cup of tea."

"I love riding in the morning." Emily sighed. "Galloping across an open meadow, the dew still clinging to the grass and the sun rising to turn everything a soft gold. The birds are usually just waking up, and the sound of my horse's hooves has them all twittering away. It's magical and something I rarely do unless I am here. There are always so many parties and balls to attend when we are in Town, I don't normally ride in the mornings there. Do you enjoy riding?"

Charlotte shook her head. "Occasionally, but only because Lucien likes it when I accompany him. I have the most staid mare he could possibly purchase." A giggle escaped her, her creamy complexion turning pink. "He is always so concerned that I may slip from Athena's back and hurt myself."

"It's not difficult to see the earl adores you." Emily bit her lip. "I'm quite envious, to be perfectly honest."

"He did not adore me when we first met, I can assure you of that. He considered me a dreadful inconvenience and an obstacle to his returning to London and the Rakehells." Charlotte's expression softened as she sipped her tea, a dreamy smile curving her lips. "It all still seems unbelievable, but we fell in love, despite our differences and Lucien's resistance to the idea."

"Was it—" Emily cleared her throat, hoping she was not being too inquisitive. "Was it difficult for Lucien to declare his love at first?"

"Incredibly so," Charlotte admitted. "He did not wish to disappoint your brother and Wylder. It was very hard for him to accept what our relationship had grown into. It wasn't until he thought he might lose me forever that he realized our love was the most important thing. And he rode after me, found me on a dusty lane with Ashcroft's new vicar, and begged me to become his wife. All while professing his love."

"That is such a lovely story." Emily smiled.

"Yes, and I know you wonder if the same can happen for you and Wylder."

Emily startled, her eyes wide. "What do you mean, Charlotte?"

"Oh, come now, Emily," Charlotte said gently, leaning forward to touch Emily's hand. "The yearning glances that pass between the two of you are easily noticed by someone like me. Someone hopelessly in love recognizes it in others. And you and Wylder are most definitely in love."

"No doubt that will come as a surprise to Wylder," Emily said pertly. "He kisses me, then berates himself for doing so. The man goes from fire to ice in the space of a heartbeat. And I am the one left burning in the snow."

Charlotte laughed out loud at that. "I believe Wylder is as conflicted as Lucien was before we married. They are both very loyal to their friends and do not wish to betray their solidarity."

Emily set her teacup down on the small table with a defeated thump. "It is far worse than that." She studied Charlotte and then hesitantly asked, "May I confide in you, Charlotte? The only one who knows of my dilemma is Penelope. And she has returned to London this morning after falling ill yesterday. She did not wish to burden anyone with her care." The falsehood came far too easily to her tongue. Lying was not something Emily normally practiced but if it helped save Penelope, she would.

"Oh, no! I'm so sorry to hear this. I had hoped we would have more time to become closer friends. She's such a beautiful, sweet girl," Charlotte said, dismay in her tone. "I look forward to having you both come to Ashcroft Manor for a visit once Lucien and I return home. This past month has been a whirlwind of activity. I'm very much looking forward to being home once more. And, of course, Emily, you may tell me anything your heart desires. I will not betray your confidences."

Emily settled back in her chair, glancing around to ensure they were both still alone. She experienced a surprising relief at Charlotte's earnest assurance. "Wylder's life would be in danger if anyone learned of his actions."

"Oh, goodness. Is it as serious as that?" Now it was Charlotte's turn to be shocked as Emily nodded.

"Yes. And you see, the threat comes from my own brother."

"I suspected as much," Charlotte acknowledged. "Lucien

confided in me that there was an incident last evening. He was forced to stand between Simon and Wylder as he feared they would come to blows."

Emily sucked in a breath of alarm. Had Wylder said something about their relationship? He'd been so angry when he stormed out of her room following their argument. Perhaps Simon had discovered their secret and reacted badly. "Simon believes Wylder is not suitable for me," Emily said slowly. "And Wylder believes it as well. He cares for me... I know he does... but nothing I've said or done has been enough to convince him that we should be together. Further complicating matters is the fact that he is using Simon's financial expertise to rebuild his estates. Naturally, he will abide by whatever arrangement he and Simon have made, regardless of any feelings he has for me. It's a particularly sore subject, considering I am more proficient in playing the 'Change than Simon is. Sometimes, he comes to me for advice on different investments." Biting her bottom lip, Emily shook her head before confessing softly, "Anyway, Wylder came to my room last night. We—we had a terrible argument during which I told him that our association is over. I will not seek him out, nor should he pursue me if he is unable to admit aloud what we've become to one another. He refused my demand and left."

"Oh, my poor dear." Charlotte leaned forward, her smile sympathetic and understanding. "Have you been intimate with him?"

Emily hesitated before answering truthfully. "We have engaged in intimate acts; however, I am still a virgin. He would not... he never did anything to compromise me in that way." A hot blush turned her cheeks red. "I-I did allow him to spank me after he insisted upon it. It was a shameful act that I somehow enjoyed."

Charlotte laughed softly and gripped Emily's hand. Her blue eyes sparkled with mischievous understanding. "The Mayfair Rakehells share similar interests regarding such matters. Being mindful of your innocent state, I will confess that I found myself in the same position before our marriage, Emily. Lucien and I engaged in many acts that were just shy of actual intercourse. And you should never be ashamed of finding pleasure in what you likely regard as the oddest practices." Charlotte's creamy skin flushed pink, her eyelashes fluttering down as she reminisced. "I confess that Lucien pulled me over his knee on our wedding night." Her smile was tender as she sighed. "It was a blissful experience. One I shall remember for the rest of my life. It may be difficult for others to understand, but somehow, that simple act conjures the most amazing sense of closeness and intimacy. I trust my husband in those moments with a depth that is truly astonishing. Especially when one considers that I am placing myself at his mercy."

Emily huffed in relief. "So, I am not depraved for liking it a great deal and also hoping there is a chance Wylder does it again in the future?"

A giggle escaped Charlotte at that. "He's a Mayfair Rakehell. You can be sure he will do it again. Indeed, he won't be able to help himself. And if you provoke him just a little, there is an excellent chance you will gain everything your heart desires."

"Provoke him? How?" Emily asked in confusion.

"Men such as ours enjoy many things, Emily. They love the chase. The capture. And they adore reaping the rewards. If there is an opportunity to save the woman he loves? Even better. And if they believe they may lose you once they've discovered they adore you? That is a valuable tool you must learn how to employ." Charlotte smiled encouragingly. "Wylder is in love with you. He simply does not realize it. I'm going to help you help him to realize it."

"You will do that?"

Charlotte eagerly nodded, her grin wide and hopeful. "Of course. Would you be willing to help me as well? Can you show me how you do it? Make money that way? You see, I will be opening a small school in the vicar's old cottage where I lived with my sister. And while Lucien has promised to buy me anything I need for the endeavor, I would like to fund it myself. Without his help. However, as women, we have limited options available to us in terms of financial ventures. Will you help me?"

Emily's mind raced with possibilities in light of Charlotte's offer. At the same time, her sensible nature argued it was pointless to hope. Wylder would not budge from his stance. He was as stubborn as a mule. Highhanded. Arrogant.

And she loved him more than anything in the world. That love was worth fighting for, and if it meant trying again and again to make him see that she loved him, she would.

"I most certainly will help you." She smiled at Charlotte and nodded in agreement. "Now tell me what I should do to win Wylder's heart. Because nothing I've done has worked so far."

CHAPTER TWENTY-FIVE

Wylder

WYLDER LED HIS horse out of the stables. Squinting at the sky, he considered that there might be a rain shower at some point. But he had to get away from the main house for a while. It felt as though the walls were closing in on him, and he needed the open space to stop the crushing pain in his chest.

He'd passed Simon on his way outside. The other man did not speak... merely dipped his head and continued walking. Simon was still furious, it seemed. His jaw had been clenched tight, his demeanor frigid when his gaze briefly met Wylder's. It was better that they allow more space to grow between the disagreement last night and their next conversation.

Wylder considered the inevitability of that event as Jack brought his bay around to the stable yard. The street urchin he had hired that early morning in London had proven to possess a natural affinity for horses. Wylder brought him along to Thorne Park to provide personal attention to his favorite mount. Now, as Wylder ducked his head and checked the snugness of the saddle's girth to ensure it was cinched correctly, Jack held the bay's reins. The young man stroked the horse's muzzle, murmuring in a soothing tone. After lowering the stirrups, Wylder gathered the reins and swung onto the gelding's back in one smooth movement.

The high-spirited bay danced in place as Wylder settled into the saddle. He easily controlled the animal, applying pressure with his knees, his hands light on the bit.

"Is it just you riding this afternoon, milord?" the stablemaster inquired, setting down a bucket of water and clapping Jack on the back in way of greeting.

"Yes, Thomas."

"I thought perhaps Lord Camden would ride again with you."

"No one other than myself today," Wylder replied. The wind was picking up, sending stray leaves scattering across the stable courtyard. He did not mention that his was the only company he wanted today. A solo gallop, with nothing other than his own thoughts to occupy him, was very enticing.

"Very good, milord." The elderly man peered up at one particularly dark cloud and pointed out, "That one looks like it might have a bit of rain to it."

"It doesn't seem very far away, milord," Jack offered. "Might not be long at all before it storms."

"I agree with you on that. If it does catch me unawares, I'll only have myself to blame for the soaking." Wylder turned the gelding in the direction of Thorne Park's wide, curving drive.

"I hope Lady Emily returns before the rain begins. She's riding her mare that's been cooped up for the last two months. Flighty thing, that mare is. And downright twitchy when it rains," Thomas mentioned, glancing at the sky again. "Lady Emily doesn't mind it, though. She likes her horses just on this side of wild. Between Sheba here at Thorne Park and Morgiana in London, it's a wonder milady has not been thrown more often."

"Lady Emily went riding? How long ago?" Wylder could not help the clench of apprehension that squeezed his chest. Of course, Emily was an excellent rider, and usually, he would not worry about her safety. But the approaching storm and the unpredictable nature of her mount had fear prickling the hair on the back of his neck. "Did she take a groom along with her?"

Thomas laughed. "Lady Emily never takes a groom with her

when riding here at Thorne Park. Aye, she's alone. And I'd say she's been gone maybe an hour, at the most. Said she was headed for the apple orchards and the meadows beyond that."

Bloody hell. That meant Emily would be on the far reaches of Thorne Park's vast acreage. He would go after her… just to be assured of her safety with inclement weather headed their way.

Nodding at Thomas and Jack, Wylder nudged the gelding in the direction the groom indicated. As the horse cantered away, the stable disappeared from view, and two stray raindrops hit his forehead. Thunder rumbled in the distance, and he hoped he would reach her before the rain began.

He'd been riding for no more than half an hour when the heavens opened up. It was an absolute deluge, the rain coming down in sheets so thick that Wylder could hardly see the tree line that made up the edge of the orchards. Wylder knew there was a small outbuilding where the workers kept supplies during harvest. He would stop there until the rain let up, then continue looking for her.

The building loomed ahead, glowing a ghostly white in the dark of the rainstorm. The gelding picked up speed, sensing a reprieve from the driving rain, his hooves throwing up chunks of mud and grass. Wylder leaned over the bay's neck, his face whipped by the horse's mane until it felt like a thousand needles striking him all at once.

Then out of the shadows of the apple trees, another horse burst into the clearing. The dark-gray mare might have been a shadow herself, but her eyes were wild with fright, showing white as the bridle's reins flapped around her legs. Wylder knew it was Emily's mare, but where in God's name was Emily?

His heart pounded with dread as he steered his horse to the left, avoiding the mare as she raced past them with a high-pitched, panicked squeal. She was headed back to the safety of the stables. However, there was the danger of the reins tangling about her legs, possibly causing the horse to stumble and break her neck.

Wylder could not focus on the mare. Emily was out there, somewhere. Injured, or even worse.

Nausea choked him. He must find her and get her to safety. And when this was over, he would spank her arse until she could not sit down for being so foolish as to ride a high-strung mare in the middle of a goddamn rainstorm.

Finally emerging on the other side of the orchards, Wylder urged his gelding up and over a low, stacked stone fence that marked the edge of the meadows. The open space went on for a good distance, rolling hills that on a sunny day were a delight to ride across. The grass was slightly higher than it had been in the past, and wildflowers dotted the expanse. Through the rain, Wylder picked up the path the mare had traveled, and the vegetation flattened as if it were serving as a road map. He followed it without hesitation, reasoning that Emily would be somewhere along that path.

The storm was finally letting up, the flashes of lightning and rumbles of thunder moving off into the distance. Wylder knew that beyond this section of the meadows was a stretch of deep woods that led to a secluded brook. The stream eventually became a small waterfall, emptying into a rocky gorge pool. Simon and Lucien had all swum there as young lads during the summer holidays when they were home from Eton. Shouting with wild abandon, they would try outdoing each other, leaping from the rock outcroppings into the deeper portions of the pool and holding their breaths underwater for as long as they could.

Had Emily gone to the pool? Or was she lying on the leaf-littered floor of the woods in a small heap of broken bones? Had her mare thrown her, or had Emily voluntarily dismounted when the storm began in earnest? What if she had been swept from the mare's back by a low branch? Or perhaps she tumbled off when the horse reared, causing her to strike her head.

Fear had Wylder forcing his gelding to even greater speed. He had no choice but to ignore the dangers of weaving through the trees as he searched for Emily. The bay snorted as he ran, his breath billowing out in small puffs of steam. Wylder dug his heels in, wiping the now drizzling rain from his eyes with the back of one hand.

And then he saw her. A splash of red that, in Wylder's fevered imagination, was a puddle of blood spilling across the base of a large oak. The tree's limbs were massive, stretching low and wide like a dozen arms reaching out in all directions. Wylder recognized this tree. It sat on the banks of the stream, and it was a short distance from there to reach the pool in the gorge. Emily leaned against the oak's base, her red riding habit a beacon of light calling out to him.

"Emily!"

Wylder sawed on the reins, her name choked out in a single, strangled word. The bay squealed in protest, sliding to a halt as Wylder leaped from the gelding's back. Swinging the reins around a tree to secure the animal, he then sprinted to Emily's side.

Her gaze, watery and frightened, met his as she shakily rose to her feet. She wobbled, placing a gloved hand on the tree trunk for support. The next instant, Wylder was sweeping her up into his arms. Holding her close, he felt as though he could not draw a true breath. So great was his relief that he'd found her, he momentarily forgot that she might have suffered an injury.

"Bloody hell. Thank God I found you." He embraced her tighter, barely taking notice of her tiny whimper at his unrestrained ferocity.

"Wylder..." She clutched at his shoulders, huddling closer to the heat of his body. Shivers racked her body as she trembled in the circle of his arms. She was soaked through to the bone, her red riding habit torn and muddy. The jaunty hat that matched her suit was missing, and her hair had come undone from its simple style. It hung in long, wet curls over her shoulders and down her back, twigs and leaves caught in the thick mass. Wylder leaned back, studying her heart-shaped face. A small bruise marred her cheek while a smudge of dirt lay across her forehead.

"Are you injured?" Wylder quickly asked, his hands running over her body. "Do you hurt anywhere? Let me look at you…"

"I'm fine." Emily's voice shook. "Really." But when Wylder took her gloved hands within his own, she hissed in pain. "My wrist…"

Wylder gently turned her hands, concentrating on her left wrist and watching her expression carefully as she winced. "You may have broken it. At the very least, you've sprained it. Tell me what happened." Letting her go, he quickly stripped off her riding glove, shoved it into the pocket of his coat, and then, after a moment's hesitation, quickly unwound his cravat. With efficient movements, he began wrapping the strip of silk snugly around her wrist, immobilizing it.

"It began raining, so I was headed back to the stables," Emily explained softly. "Sheba is not fond of storms, but I am well aware of that and was extra careful in handling her. When the wind picked up, I decided that it would be safer to dismount and walk her to the outbuilding by the orchard. I was gathering up the reins and preparing to slide off her back when, all at once, a big boom of thunder sounded, and there was a crack of lightning which must have struck somewhere nearby. Sheba reared up. It was so sudden that it caught me unaware. I was thrown to the ground and landed against this tree as she bolted. I suppose I hurt my wrist while bracing myself in the fall, but it all happened so quickly." A quick intake of breath revealed her pain as Wylder finished up.

"You should never have gone out in this weather in the first place. And certainly not on a horse you know to be terrified of storms," Wylder stated fiercely, his emotions getting the better of him. The thought that Emily could have been seriously injured was doing strange things to his insides. He wanted to sweep her up into his arms and shelter her from both the drizzling rain and anything that could possibly harm her.

"It's not Sheba's fault," Emily replied stubbornly, staring up at Wylder. "I've ridden her in the rain before and managed her quite well. This was a freak occurrence. An unforeseen mishap."

"A mishap?" Wylder's hands clenched to keep from shaking some sense into her. "I saw you there on the ground, and I thought you were dead, Emily." He took a deep breath to steady himself. To tamp down the overwhelming sense of panic still fluttering about his belly. "Do you understand? I thought you were *dead!*"

Emily's teeth chattered from the chill of the rain. "Why on earth would you think such a thing? I've been thrown from a horse before and survived it."

"Your riding habit, you stubborn, headstrong, foolish girl. It's bright, fucking red. So red that I believed it to be blood, and for a goddamn, heart-stopping moment, I thought my life was over as well. Because how can I possibly live in a world without Emily Blackthorne in it?"

Emily's blue eyes darkened with Wylder's impassioned confession. Raising her uninjured hand to his cheek, she peered into his eyes as if searching for something that had remained buried for far too long. "Now we seem to share the same sentiment. Because I've long wondered how I would go on with my life if you were not a part of it." Her expression softened. "There is no need to fret, Wylder. A sprained wrist will not be the end of me."

Frustration welled up inside Wylder. It was an ocean of want and need. The desire to keep her safe. A craving to keep her for himself, no matter who objected or stood in their way. He stared at her and imagined her being his... truly his. And it was enough to shatter his carefully crafted wall until it was nothing more than a pile of rubble.

"But you will be the end of *me*, Emily. Can't you understand that?" he muttered. "You have ruined me forever, and it's because of one simple, irrefutable fact. I love you. I love you so goddamn much I find it impossible to breathe sometimes from the weight of it. I love you past the point of madness, or reason, or anything that resembles sanity. I love you, knowing full well that I am not the man you should be with. And I love you despite anyone who thinks I have no right to call you my own." Wylder's hands came up, cradling Emily's face and holding her steady as she swayed into him, her expression now dazed with comprehension. Lowering his voice, he spoke with a fierceness that shocked even him. "I love you, Emily Blackthorne. I love you. I love you. I. Love. You." Then his mouth swept over hers, claiming her soft, rain-dampened lips in a heated kiss. He kissed her without mercy or tenderness, their tongues tangling in an unspoken battle until finally, a whimper of surrender came from Emily.

That tiny, breathy sound slammed Wylder back to some semblance of sanity.

What the hell am I doing? I should be carrying her to safety rather than kissing her senseless.

When he pulled away, their breaths mingling in the space between their bodies, Wylder saw Emily's eyes were wet with unshed tears. His heart clenched with worry that he may have caused her pain, but she surprised him by raising up on her tiptoes and silently pressing a soft kiss to his bottom lip.

A thread of understanding passed between them, linking their hearts together in a manner that was foreign to Wylder but felt so damned right. He kissed her brow, and a broken sob escaped her throat. "Shhh, do not cry, minx. Everything will be well, I promise. Let us get you back to the house before they form a search party to look for you. You need a hot bath, a warm bed, and your father should call for the doctor to examine your wrist and check for any other injuries." He paused, then brushed his lips tenderly across her furrowed brow. "I will take care of anything that arises from my actions today."

"What do you mean?" Emily asked, trembling even more violently. "What must be taken care of? Oh, Wylder." Her bottom lip wobbled as she apparently remembered the missing mare. "Do you think Sheba is all right? Do you think she made it back home? She was so very frightened. She did not mean to throw me today."

Her voice was softer now, and Wylder realized the heated

rush previously running through her veins was seeping away. He must get her home as quickly as possible before she slipped into a state of shock. The threat of a head injury was a consideration, as well. She needed to be carefully and closely observed for any sign of internal bleeding.

Sweeping her up into his arms, Wylder carried her to the gelding and settled her on the horse's back so that she sat perched sideways. He swung up behind her, making sure her injured wrist was cradled between their bodies. As she snuggled against his broad chest, sighing in quiet contentment, Wylder's resolve became firmly entrenched. Emily was his. He would take care of her and damn anything or anyone that stood in his way.

Squeezing Emily gently, Wylder turned the gelding homeward.

"Leave everything to me, minx."

She nodded, giving herself up to his strength as he carried her to safety. And it wasn't until much later that Wylder realized Emily never declared her love for him.

CHAPTER TWENTY-SIX
Wylder

IN AN OPEN field just a mile from the manor house, Wylder found the mare quietly grazing. Unwilling to release his grasp on Emily and attempt to catch the horse, he instead clucked at the mare. He was gratified when Sheba began following his gelding, the creature's innate need to remain part of the herd greater than the desire to graze on rain-sweetened grass. Wylder kept his gelding's pace slow and steady, worried that anything faster would harm his precious cargo. When the rooftop of the massive manor came into view above the tree line, Wylder breathed a sigh of relief.

Since Sheba had not galloped straight back to the stables, no one was aware that an accident had even taken place. Wylder approached the main house, knowing that from this point forward, his life would take a drastic turn. As would Emily's.

And despite the many years of fighting this type of scenario, Wylder could not stop the thrill that shot through him. There could only be one outcome to this. Only one thing to stave off the impending scandal. Because, despite this being a terrible, innocent accident, there was bound to be a scandal. He and Emily were returning from the seclusion of the woods. Their clothes were soaked, with Wylder missing his cravat and his jacket draped over Emily. And as for Emily... well... the fact that she was muddy, bruised, and appeared to have fainted… the rumors would paint her as being the victim of a ravishment.

Unless he could convince her parents and Simon of the truth of what had occurred, he would be required to marry Emily as a matter of honor.

Sliding off the gelding's back, Wylder carefully pulled Emily down with him and carried her up the steps to the house. The double doors were already opening, and Thorne Park's butler hurried out to meet him.

"Milord, whatever has happened?" Seaver exclaimed in distress even as he clapped his hands for two footmen to jump to attention. "You two, run fetch Lord and Lady Blackthorne at once."

"We'll need the doctor as well. Send someone right away," Wylder instructed, shouldering past the man to enter the grand foyer. "Lady Emily took a tumble off her mount and requires immediate care. Have the kitchens begin heating water and a bath prepared."

"Of course, milord. Right away. Right away." Seaver nodded, frantically tugging the bell pull by the doors. "Ah, here is Lord Camden…"

"What the devil is going on here?" Simon shouted, racing down the curved stairs. His expression was murderous as he glared at Wylder. Directly behind Simon, his mother followed. She took one look at Wylder holding Emily's body in his arms and immediately took action.

"Wylder, bring her upstairs and to her rooms."

Emily stirred at her mother's calm voice. Lifting her head from the hard planes of Wylder's chest, she smiled woozily at her and Simon.

"Hullo," she said before laying her head back down with a low sigh.

"Why is she all bruised and disheveled?" Simon demanded angrily, blocking the stairs and Wylder's path with his muscular form. "And why are you carrying her like that? Put her down this instant, Wylder. You know very well you are to keep your distance from her."

Wylder's patience with his friend snapped without warning. "Would you rather I left her back in the woods where I found her?" he snarled, sounding more like a wild animal than an aristocratic peer of the realm. "Cold and bruised? Injured? Alone? Her horse threw her off during the storm. Now, for the love of God, step aside so that I may do as your mother has asked."

"What the hell did you do to her?" Simon's accusation rang out in the large foyer, ugly and harsh and so unexpected that Lady Blackthorne gasped in shock.

"Simon Blackthorne!" she cried out in dismay. "Be silent!"

"Give my sister to me," Simon bit out, ignoring his mother. "I shall carry her, and then you can be sure I will get to the bottom of this with you."

"Try taking her from me, and I will make you wish you hadn't." Wylder's tone was icy but controlled. He stared Simon down, hating that his best friend suspected him of hurting Emily, but this was not the moment to address it. That opportunity would likely come at dawn and involve pistols. Or perhaps only fists, if he were lucky.

"Simon." Lucien emerged from the corridor to the left of the foyer, Emily's father close on his heels. "Let Wylder pass so Lady Blackthorne can care for her daughter. I'm not sure what has happened, but we certainly do not wish for the rest of the guests to become privy to it." Lucien's calm order had the desired effect as Simon reluctantly stepped aside. He still scowled at Wylder, however, and rage rolled off him until the air was thick and heavy with it.

"My thanks, Lucien." Wylder's gaze flickered from Simon to Lady Blackthorne, who came forward to lay her hand on Emily's brow, her face drawn tight with concern for her daughter. "Should we call for Miss True to attend Emily as well?" he asked her mother. "I know her friend's presence will be a great comfort to her."

"Miss True returned to London very early this morning. She fell ill yesterday and desired to recover at home," Lord Blackthorne said as Wylder continued carrying Emily up the stairs. "Emily's maid accompanied her."

"She's gone?" Simon asked suddenly. He was obviously startled by that bit of news, but he quickly recovered. Jaw clenched, his bright blue eyes shuttered themselves against Wylder's sudden scrutiny. It was a strange reaction coming from a man who claimed to care nothing about the girl. Glancing at Lucien, Wylder saw that he, too, was surprised by Simon's unexpected behavior.

Carrying Emily down the second-floor corridor, Wylder followed Lord and Lady Blackthorne into the west wing where Emily's bedroom was located. Simon and Lucien trailed behind them, hovering outside the room as Wylder placed her on the downy coverlet. Emily frowned, a whimper of protest escaping her throat as she clutched at his damp riding coat with her uninjured hand. Her fingers tightened, refusing to let go as Wylder soothed her until her grip relaxed. When Lady Blackthorne began removing her half boots, Emily stirred, her eyes fluttering open as several maids bustled into the room. The buckets of hot water they carried were poured into the slipper tub in the corner of the room.

Wylder stepped aside, allowing Emily's parents to begin caring for her, but he refused to move very far away. "Her wrist is injured, so have a care. I don't know how badly, but I wrapped it to prevent her from hurting it further."

"My poor, dear girl," Lord Blackthorne murmured, running his hand over the crown of Emily's dark hair. "I suspect she was riding Sheba. Do you know if that's the case, Wyldewood?"

"Yes," Emily mumbled, smiling up at her father. "Silly horse… she spooked at the thunder and reared up. I fell off… hit my head…" her brow furrowed, "and hurt my wrist."

"I came across the mare in a field near here," Wylder offered. "She followed us back to the house, and I imagine a groom has taken her back to a stall along with my gelding." He did not want to leave Emily, but he truly had no right to stay in the room as she was being attended to. Eventually, he moved toward the door where Simon and Lucien were informing Charlotte of the events.

"Lady Blackthorne, may I offer some assistance when the doctor arrives?" Charlotte asked softly from her position beside Lucien. "I do have some experience helping villagers with various ailments back home."

"You are all making a huge fuss over nothing," Emily said, sounding more like herself as Lord Blackthorne sat her up and helped remove her riding coat. It was silently agreed to leave the makeshift bandage crafted of Wylder's cravat in place until the doctor assessed the damage to Emily's wrist.

"Please cooperate, my dear. You've taken quite a tumble, and naturally, you're a bit woozy as a result," Lady Blackthorne said, then turned to Charlotte with a grateful smile. "Do come in, Lady Ashcroft. Any help is greatly appreciated." Glancing about the room, the woman frowned at the number of people milling about and clapped her hands. "I need everyone else to please vacate the room. We must get Emily out of these wet clothes before she catches her death of cold. When Doctor Felder arrives, send him up at once."

Emily groaned, her chin tilting up in defiance. It was enough to make Wylder's heart slow its rapid pounding of panic. If she could argue, it was clear she was already feeling better. "Oh, no. Doctor Felder is coming? Why?" She struggled to sit up, wincing when she placed too much weight on her wrist. "The man will do nothing but lecture me. I'll face enough of that from my brother and Lord Wyldewood. They are busy dreaming up things to say, I can tell just by how they are glaring at each other this very moment."

Wylder smiled at just how true her words were. Simon's expression clearly stated he wanted Wylder's blood. Although it was up to her parents, Wylder could not help but wonder if his friend would accept the offer of marriage for his sister.

"Lie back, Emily," Charlotte instructed her with a soothing smile. "Your mother and I must remove the rest of your wet clothing and get you in that warm bath before the doctor arrives to examine you." The young countess waved a hand at the men gathered at the door. "We shall update you with her condition, so please go downstairs and have a brandy to settle your nerves." She flashed Wylder a particularly encouraging smile. "Don't worry, Lord Wyldewood. Emily is in good hands now. She's young and very strong. She will be fine, I'm sure of it."

AFTER CHANGING INTO dry clothes, Wylder made his way downstairs to the earl's study, where the others awaited the doctor's arrival. A servant had brought word earlier that the mare had been checked over by the stablemaster and seemed to have suffered no injuries from the incident.

"That's a bit of good news," Lord Blackthorne sighed in relief as Wylder entered the room. "Emily loves that mare. I would have hated to have her destroyed."

"I found her after she'd already been thrown. Of course, I questioned the wisdom of riding such an unpredictable creature," Wylder said gruffly.

Lord Blackthorne laughed. "And if I know my daughter at all, I predict that she defended her actions and insinuated that you should mind your own business."

Wylder shrugged his shoulders, feeling the heat of Simon's glare upon him as he accepted a tumbler of brandy from the earl. "She did just that. I tried getting her home as quickly as possible without causing any additional damage, Lord Blackthorne."

"Why were you there to begin with, Wyldewood?" Simon demanded. "It could not be just a matter of luck that you happened to find her in that condition."

"Simon, what you are insinuating—" Lucien began angrily.

He glanced at Emily's father, who gave a subtle shake of his head, indicating he would not interfere.

"I know what I am insinuating," Simon interrupted in a cold voice. "And I want Wylder to answer my question."

"Do you believe what you are suggesting?" Wylder asked quietly, his unflinching gaze meeting his friend's. "Because if you sincerely do, then you and I have a problem that requires solving."

"Answer the question, dammit." Simon's tone held a desperation Wylder had never heard from him before. And while his hands itched to ball into fists and punch his friend in the mouth, he realized Simon struggled with the noble task of protecting his sister.

"Once I have satisfied your curiosity, you will never bring up this subject again." Wylder's stare, directed toward Simon the entire time, was hard and as cold as iron as he related the events leading up to his discovery of Emily. Explaining in great detail the actions he'd taken upon finding her, he strategically omitted the part when he declared his love and kissed her until they were both breathless. He would speak with Emily before revealing that confession to anyone else.

"Her mother and I owe you a debt of gratitude for returning her home safely, Wylder," Lord Blackthorne said, raising his glass in a silent toast to Wylder.

Simon remained silent during Wylder's explanation, but now, he let out a sharp laugh and scrubbed his face with a hand as if in complete disbelief. "Am I the only one here wondering what will happen when word of this fiasco gets out? Emily will be ruined." His accusatory glare settled on Wylder. "Not that you care if she finds herself embroiled in scandal."

Wylder stood rigid and tall, his fists balling at his sides. "I care more for Emily's happiness than you can possibly comprehend, Simon. I always have."

Simon scoffed, tossing back the rest of his brandy. "You need an heiress to help rescue your estates. Dammit, Wylder. I warned you not to pursue her. You've done just the opposite, it seems."

"That's enough!" Lord Blackthorne nearly shouted, raking a hand through thick, salt and pepper hair. He regarded his son with unconcealed, exasperated anger. "I do not know why you feel this way when it comes to an alliance between Wylder and Emily, Simon, but your mother and I have long considered the earl to be the perfect match for your sister."

"It is only with my help that he has rebuilt his fortune," Simon hissed. "You would want Emily to marry a man whose estates are on the edge of total ruin? A man whose father is himself indebted to you?"

Lord Blackthorne stared at Simon for a long moment. Then, his expression relaxed, and a small chuckle escaped him. "You and I both know if your sister were given free rein, she would likely amass a fortune greater than the gentlemen in this room combined. She's a genius when it comes to such things... although I pretend to be unaware of her dabbling on the Exchange. As for the duke's debt, I shall deduct it from Emily's dowry."

Wylder frowned. Not once had Emily mentioned her skill in monetary matters, and there had been numerous opportunities for her to do so. He could only imagine she'd kept her secret for the simple fact that she did not desire to find herself used for it. There were men in their world who would not hesitate to exploit that talent and marry her for it alone.

He might have been one of them. If his own father had his way, he would be. But knowing Emily as he did, loving her the way he did, Wylder couldn't bring himself to expect it of her.

If they indeed were married, he would wait until she trusted him enough to offer her help. And he would accept it gratefully and with much humbleness, knowing Emily Blackthorne, the headstrong, brave, loyal girl he'd loved for so long, was the one who could save him.

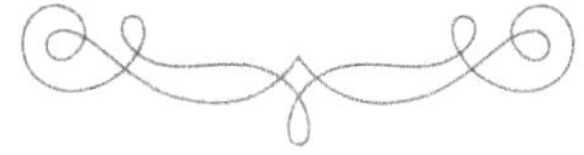

CHAPTER TWENTY-SEVEN

Wylder

IT WAS CHARLOTTE who delivered the news that the patient would make a full recovery. It was advised that Emily remain abed for the remainder of the afternoon and evening and not to overtax herself with any physical exertion. Her wrist was thankfully not broken but she had suffered a minor sprain. The doctor wrapped it properly and instructed her not to use it excessively for a few days.

"Emily is especially distraught that the doctor expressly forbade her from attending the ball tomorrow night," Charlotte related with a smile. "She argued that a sprained wrist would not affect her feet when it comes to dancing or socializing with other guests."

"That sounds like my sweet Emily," Lord Blackthorne laughed out loud. "Hearing this certainly eases my concerns."

Wylder said nothing. He was already making plans to ensure his headstrong little minx remained abed and wondered if her parents would object to his taking over the task.

"She's asked for you, Lord Wyldewood," Charlotte said, her smile widening. "To thank you personally for rescuing her."

"There are no thanks needed," Wylder gruffly replied. "However, if Lord and Lady Blackthorne have no objections, I would welcome the opportunity to visit her for a moment."

"I object," Simon rumbled from where he stood near the fireplace.

"It is not up to you any longer, Simon," Wylder said firmly. He'd reached a decision, one he would not back away from now. No longer would he allow his friendship with Simon to come between him and the woman he loved with every fiber of his dark soul.

"If you think I will allow you to debauch my sister while I stand idly by, you are mistaken," Simon stated. "Your wickedness is as great as my own, Wylder. Our reputations so sordid that we probably should not even be accepted in polite society. You *will* not drag my sister down to your level. I will not allow it—"

"Simon, Wyldewood is correct," Lord Blackthorne abruptly interrupted. "While I appreciate your concerns for your sister's future happiness and well-being, the discussion at hand concerns Wyldewood, Emily, her mother, and me." Glancing at Lucien, who stood with one arm wrapped around Charlotte, Emily's father added, "Lord Ashcroft, if you will remain behind as a witness to the initial discussion of the marriage contract, you shall have my gratitude."

"I would be honored, Lord Blackthorne," Lucien said with a sympathetic glance in Simon's direction.

Simon's face reddened. "You are seriously considering marrying Emily to Wylder?"

"I am. Of course, there are a few issues to be clarified first, but knowing Wyldewood's character, I do not anticipate there being a problem," Lord Blackthorne said in a serene voice and a broad smile. "And, son, if it eases your mind, your objections are duly noted."

⇥⟫⟪⇤

WYLDER STEPPED OUT of Lord Blackthorne's study, letting out a heavy sigh.

The negotiations took the remainder of the afternoon and once all was said and done, a tentative contract of marriage was in place.

Everything hinged on Emily agreeing to the arrangement. Wylder insisted that the final decision be left to her. As long as the circumstances behind the entire affair remained a secret, there was no urgency when it came to announcing the engagement. Paramount to all parties was the protection of Emily's reputation and the immediate squashing of any hint of scandal rising from the day's events.

With any luck, Emily will agree to this marriage. She will be mine at last.

The mere thought sent a possessive thrill streaking through Wylder's entire body. Leaning against the wall outside Blackthorne's study, he closed his eyes and savored the feeling. He hoped it would be a permanent sensation… one he would enjoy for the rest of their life.

"Hullo there, Lord Wyldewood."

Wylder's eyes snapped open, and he immediately straightened his stance as Lord Patrick Bashear strolled toward him. He appeared to have come from the billiards room, which was down that same corridor. Several of the gentlemen had gathered there for a pleasant afternoon of games and libations since the weather was still foul.

"Bashear," Wylder acknowledged with a nod of his head.

The man's smile was genial. "I do hope you can help clear up a rumor floating around the halls today." Rocking back on his heels, he regarded Wylder with a curious tilt of his head. "My great aunt tells me there was an accident today when Lady Emily went out riding and that you lent some assistance in helping her return home. I pray she is well on the way to recovery."

Wylder tamped down his suspicious nature as he regarded the other man. Patrick Bashear was blond and handsome, his manners perfectly polished and his connections impeccable. Many of the women attending the house party found him quite pleasing. He wondered if Emily fell into that group or if her reactions to the man were simply politeness on her part.

"I'm told she will suffer no ill effects."

"Ah, this is good to hear," Patrick replied. "I wish now I had gone along as planned. Perhaps, I could have done something to prevent it." He shook his head as if relieved. "However, I realized the weather would likely turn for the worse and had little desire to spend an afternoon getting soaked by rain. I tried dissuading Lady Emily from venturing out, but apparently, she is a very headstrong girl and has an unfortunate tendency to do as she pleases."

Unfortunate tendency?

"I find Lady Emily's... tendencies... entrancing." Especially since she would probably be his wife very shortly, he would have the opportunity every day to enjoy them.

Patrick waved a dismissive hand. "Of course, I see the appeal." He straightened his cravat, his expression turning thoughtful. "She's quite lovely, probably one of the most beautiful creatures I've seen since my return to England. My aunt believes we would make a perfect match; however, I'm not quite sure of it. See, I prefer my women a bit more subservient. I've a feeling Lady Emily is quite a handful and most likely impossible to tame. A challenge to some men, but such exertions are not usually to my liking. However, the considerable wealth attached to her dowry does give me a reason to reconsider my initial impression. A fortune like that could entice me to make an offer, provided the terms were agreeable."

A growl worked its way up in Wylder's chest. The words that Emily belonged to him lay on the tip of his tongue, and it was only sheer willpower that kept them from bubbling out. He'd made a promise to himself and Lord Blackthorne. He would not reveal the impending engagement until Emily agreed to it. Even if pompous arses like Lord Patrick Bashear goaded him to act irrationally.

"Perhaps I should dance a time or two with her tomorrow

night to ascertain if it is possible to overcome the obstacles between us," Patrick mused as he bowed to Wylder. "We shall see." With a bow, Patrick moved past and continued his stroll down the corridor.

And Wylder felt like punching a wall in the depths of his frustrations.

CHAPTER TWENTY-EIGHT

Emily

"THERE NOW. A bowl of hot soup should help you feel much better," Lady Blackthorne said as she settled the tray over Emily's lap.

"I already feel better," Emily replied. "I wonder if it would be more efficient to put the soup in a cup? Then I could simply drink it. Like tea."

"Oh, Emily." Her mother laughed softly. "You have the oddest ideas about things sometimes. Now, open up for a bite like a good girl."

Emily did as instructed, barely containing an eyeroll at her mother's insistence to treat her like a child. She'd only sprained a wrist. Not lost a limb. Swallowing the spoonful of soup, she examined her wrist, now wrapped in a strip of crisp, clinical white cloth. It throbbed a bit, but the doctor indicated that was to be expected. He'd also given her a small dose of laudanum for pain, but Emily did not care for the floaty feeling that came from taking the medicine. Thankfully, the effects from that first dose were finally subsiding, and she was determined not to take it more than was necessary.

"What happened to Wyldewood's cravat?" she asked in a most casual manner. Hopefully, it had not been accidentally discarded by one of the maids.

Lady Blackthorne smiled. "Do not fret, my dear. Charlotte made sure that the maids took it to be cleaned. It will be returned to Lord Wyldewood soon."

"All right." Emily bit her bottom lip, wondering how best to broach the subject of having Wylder visit her.

"Charlotte will be coming in soon to sit with you," her mother offered, her lovely features pinched with concern. "I do hate to leave you, my darling. But with so many guests in attendance and the ball happening tomorrow night, there are a thousand and one things that unfortunately require my attention."

"There is no need for anyone to sit with me, Mother. I promise I feel fine. The pain is only slightly bothersome." Taking the spoon from her mother's hand, she dipped it into the soup and swallowed it. "See? I can manage perfectly well with one hand."

"Yes, yes." Lady Blackthorne said with an indulgent grin. "You've proven your point. But, you will still adhere to the good doctor's advice and remain in bed, young lady."

"But, the ball tomorrow night," Emily protested. "It is not fair to say I cannot go. I will even promise not to dance. I shall simply sit on the sidelines… or spend the time mingling with our guests. Please, Mother. Do not confine me to my room. I will not be able to bear it." She could not bring herself to inquire about the possible scandal of Wylder bringing her home in her earlier condition. Was it all just being swept away somehow? Her lips tightened. Any other young lady of her social set would already have a hasty wedding planned, the groom standing at the ready with a special license in hand if he could obtain one. The reasons for this not happening were more than concerning. Had Wylder refused to marry her, provided the subject had been put forth? He was so intent on remaining a bachelor, certain in his convictions that he was not the man she should marry, and yet…

And yet…

Emily's heart tightened with remembrance, butterflies fluttering about in the pit of her stomach. There was that magical moment in the woods when Wylder swept her up into his arms and cradled her as though she were a precious treasure he'd just found. He'd told her that he loved her, although he might believe she was too woozy to remember his surprising confession.

She remembered it. She remembered, and she did not know what to think about it. Or even how to *feel* about it.

"We shall see, my dear," Lady Blackthorne replied in a soothing voice. "Rest tonight and then we shall see what the morning brings."

After Lady Blackthorne departed, Emily drifted off to sleep, exhaustion unexpectedly overtaking her. When she awoke some time later, she found Charlotte seated by her bedside with a book in hand.

"Hullo… how are you feeling?" Charlotte asked, setting the book aside. She poured a glass of water from the pitcher on the bedside table, then hesitated. When Emily reached for it, her jaw set at a stubborn angle, Charlotte wisely handed it over rather than attempting to hold it to Emily's lips.

"Far better than my mother will believe," Emily replied with a deep sigh, passing the glass back to Charlotte after quenching her thirst. She straightened the neckline of her nightgown and watched as Charlotte set the glass down and rearranged a stack of books.

"I thought you might wish to read while confined to your bed," Charlotte explained with a grin before shaking a finger at Emily. "Clever girl. You took my advice to heart. When I suggested that you find some way that Wylder could come to your rescue, I did not mean that you should place yourself in grave danger."

"I promise it was not intentional." The corners of Emily's mouth turned up in a slight smile at Charlotte's words. "It was a complete accident. And I had no idea he followed me. Thank goodness he did, however. I might still be propped against that tree had he not found me there."

"Well, it did the trick, I think." Charlotte straightened the covers around Emily. "Do you wish me to tell you what I have learned this afternoon?" At Emily's eager nod, Charlotte sat back down in the chair and leaned forward. "It is not much, but there is this. Wyldewood and your father have had a discussion of some sort. I was not privy to it, but Lucien was. Lord Blackthorne asked Lucien to remain in his study along with himself and Lord Wyldewood. Lucien refuses to tell me what occurred, however, the stubborn man. What I can tell you about that meeting, however, is that your brother was excluded from that meeting, and he is very upset about the whole incident. He voiced strenuous opposition to any suggestion that you and Wyldewood may need to marry before your father made him leave. He brought up the earl's reputation and how unsuitable he is for marriage."

"That happens to be Simon's favorite reason when it comes to driving a wedge between me and Wylder. And Wylder has agreed with him for as long as I can remember." Emily plucked at the coverlet's intricately embroidered design. "I was afraid to ask my mother what decisions had been made. I can only imagine what rumors are swirling, considering Wylder carried me into the house while we were both dripping wet and I was suffering an injury."

"From what I gather, nothing has been decided as of yet." Charlotte chewed the end of her finger as she considered Emily's statement. "And I've not heard any guests speaking of a potential scandal. All that's being said is you had a riding accident and require a day or two of rest."

"I wish Wylder would come to me," Emily said sadly. "But knowing my brother, he probably put up such a fuss that Wylder will not dare provoke him for fear of causing an argument."

Charlotte shook her head. "I have a feeling that Lord Wyldewood no longer cares what your brother wants when it comes to you."

HER PARENTS BRIEFLY checked in on her before they retired for the evening, but Emily was too exhausted to start any conversations regarding her future. And she wanted to speak with Wylder before broaching the delicate subject of scandal and marriage with her mother and father.

The rain, which had let up earlier that afternoon, returned during the late evening hours. It created a drumming beat against the windows, the sound rhythmic and steady. Now and then, thunder would rumble, and soft flashes of lightning lit the dimness of her room. It was unlike the violent storm she'd experienced when she was out riding. Snuggling into her pillow and being careful of her injured wrist, Emily listened to the sounds of the rain and drifted off to sleep.

She woke suddenly, not sure what had disturbed her. Struggling, she tried propping herself up against the pillows and whimpered when she bumped her wrist.

"Let me help you, little minx."

Emily startled upon hearing Wylder's low voice. It emanated from the darkness, then she heard footsteps falling softly on the hardwood floor as he approached.

"Wylder?" she breathed as he stepped into the light cast off from the fireplace.

"I'm here, Emily." He was dressed in breeches and boots and a white lawn shirt with no coat or cravat. Sinking down on the side of the bed, he reached out and tenderly brushed a stray curl away from her forehead. "How are you feeling?"

"I'm fine," she replied, feeling as though she might launch herself into his arms and never let go of him. She drank in the sight of him, noting the dark stubble on his jaw and chin and the harsh planes of his handsome face. He appeared troubled by something, but he remained silent, his eyes hooded as he regarded her.

Curving a hand around her chin, he gently turned her face until he could see the slight bruising on her cheek. Emily trembled at his touch, her body shaking in an uncontrollable reaction to his nearness.

"Are you in pain?" His gaze flickered down to her wrist, a frown marring his brow as he noted the new bandaging. "I wanted to stay as the doctor attended you, but obviously, that was impossible."

"It aches, but it is nothing I cannot bear." Emily's lashes swept down, her fingers twisting nervously as he continued to examine her. Was the coolness between them her imagination or real? She couldn't tell, especially with the lingering effects of laudanum. The drug tended to color everything in a dreamy swirl. "Do you have news of my mare? Mother said she was fine, but she does not really know horseflesh and may have told me what I wanted to hear to keep me from going down to the stables myself."

"The mare is fine, although at some point you and I will have a conversation regarding your recklessness."

There was an underlying thread of steel to Wylder's words. When Emily peeked up at him, she saw his tongue swipe at his lips as though he greatly anticipated taking her to task for her behavior. His eyes darkened to a stormy gray color, and she shivered at how ruggedly handsome he appeared in that moment. It truly felt as though he might pounce on her any second.

"I must ask you something, Emily. And I hope you think well enough of me to answer truthfully." His voice was husky, an unknown element lurking within it. It might have been uncertainty, but Emily could not credit this man with anything less than absolute strength and utter confidence in everything he did. "Why did you invite Bashear to accompany you on your ride today?"

Emily shook her head at the question before huffing out a sigh of frustration. "Don't you know why, Wylder? I think you do. During our last private conversation regarding our relationship, you made it very clear that I was not worth your effort. And Lord Bashear indicated interest in me. I would be foolish not to give the man a chance. He is very charming, even if he suffers from an intense infatuation with himself."

A muscle clenched and unclenched in Wylder's jaw. "If he had gone with you, it would have been *him* carrying you into the house. Your father would have been in deep discussions with *him* this afternoon rather than with me. There would have been no way to avoid it."

"Avoid what?" Emily asked in confusion.

"Marriage. To Bashear."

"I'm not marrying Bashear!" she sputtered.

"You would have no choice. Bashear would have insisted upon it, and your father would not be in a position to object. As it is, your reputation is still in danger of being ruined. Lord Blackthorne and I hope to avoid any hint of impropriety arising from today's incident."

"You discussed such things with my father?" Emily's voice wobbled. "Why would you do that? Charlotte says there is no indication of a scandal being bandied about. There-there will be no need for the two of us to marry without a scandal to provoke it."

"I will not marry you because of scandal, Emily," he ground out between clenched teeth.

"Then why are you here, Wylder?" she whispered in defeat. It was foolish to think he might change his mind regarding marriage. He seemed even more set against it now than ever before.

"You know why." Wylder caught her uninjured hand, pressing it against his chest and forcing her to feel the wild beat of his heart. "This... this is yours, Emily," he muttered in a raw, desperate voice. "It's always been yours. Even if I lose you now, if I lost everything in this life, my heart would remain yours. You are the only thing I've ever wanted."

CHAPTER TWENTY-NINE

Wylder

SILENCE ROARED LOUDER than the wind and rain beating against the terrace door windows. Emily stared up at him, uncomprehending his words.

"You expect me to have your heart but not give you mine in return?" she whispered, her voice trembling. "I cannot bear that, Wylder. It-it would hurt far too much. If we cannot be together, then you must let me go."

Wylder's breath in his throat caught like a man dragged back from drowning. His grip tightened on her hand, keeping her prisoner as every stone constructing the walls within him crumbled into dust.

He'd told himself for years to stay away. To honor her brother's wishes. But he could no longer ignore the fire clawing at his insides. Her plea that he should let her go, her eyes wet with unshed tears and lips parted as if to take those damned words back, broke Wylder's will.

"I cannot do it," he growled, his voice rough. "I cannot hide from the world that you are everything I want. You, my sweet, stubborn minx, own me. Do you understand that? You *own* me."

Emily's breath hitched as his words crashed over her, but still, Wylder did not stop with his confession. He careened into it full force, eyes wide open to the possibility Emily might reject him regardless of his sincerity.

"I love you. Dear God, Emily. I *ache* incessantly for you. And Simon is right… I'm not worthy of you, but none of that matters when you look at me. None of it matters when you smile at me. I'd fight him, fight the whole damned world, if that's what it takes to have you for my own." He spoke against her lips, pressing her hand harder against his heart while inhaling her sweet scent. "Every breath, every drop of blood within me, it's yours. Every filthy, depraved piece of me belongs to you. So, if you think I can stop loving you, you are wrong. You are the only thing keeping me alive. The only thing in my life worth living for. Worth dying for."

"Please, don't do this." Emily's lower lip trembled, but she did not pull away. "Do not toy with me, Wylder."

The gossamer-thin thread of mistrust in her voice shattered him, and the last vestiges of his fragile restraint snapped free. With a low, guttural sound, he cupped her face in the palm of his hand. "I tried so damn hard to stay away from you. God knows I've tried. But it's impossible." Hungry and desperate, his mouth crashed down upon hers in a fierce kiss. And the sweetness of her lips was a reminder that he'd been starving all of his life, and now a taste of true paradise lay just within reach.

Emily moaned in response, and Wylder deepened the kiss, his lips and tongue devouring and claiming her as his own. When her hand clenched around his fingers, holding onto him tighter as if she was afraid to let go for fear the moment would evaporate into the mist, he shuddered with need.

Finally tearing his mouth away, he leaned into Emily, pressing his forehead against hers. "Tell me you love me, Emily," he whispered, raw and anguished. His free hand curved around her face, careful of the tender bruise that marred her cheek. "Tell me you love me and I'll never let you go again. Not for your brother. Not for your parents nor my own. Not for the world."

"Then don't let me go, Wylder," she said in a soft voice, tilting her head back and staring up at him with heavy, molten blue eyes. "You know I love you with all of my heart." Her pale face glowed in the dimness of the room, her hair a dark, curling mass of silk cascading over her shoulders. Wylder's heart twisted with yearning for this woman. She was so beautiful… so very sweet and soft. And now, she was his.

Well, not entirely his. It would still require sliding a ring onto her finger before he could truly claim her as his own. He wanted to call Emily Blackthorne his wife as soon as possible. He'd already waited too long.

"Will you marry me?" he asked softly, still unsure of her answer, but he needn't have worried overmuch. Emily giggled and nodded, pressing a kiss against his lips.

"I will, Wylder. But only if you can promise this is not a laudanum-induced dream? That you are truly here and holding me?" Her lilting, breathless question was half-serious, half-teasing.

"If it were not for your injury, I would do more than hold you," Wylder murmured. Shifting Emily over, he slid down on the bed until he was reclining on his side and facing her. His arms wrapped around her body, carefully positioning her wrist so that it was protected from any further injury. Resting his head on the pillow beside hers, he kissed the tip of her nose. Emily sighed in contentment and snuggled closer.

"I have no objections, my lord," she whispered. "To anything you wish to do with me."

"I don't want to hurt you, my little minx. And in doing the things I wish to do, I would unintentionally cause you the wrong kind of pain. I am content to simply hold you and dream of the day I may call you my wife."

"But, Wylder, when will that be?" Emily bit her bottom lip, her eyes now brimming with sudden apprehension. "What if—"

"If you are worried that I will change my mind, I won't," Wylder interrupted with an index finger laid across her plump lips. "You *will* be my wife, Emily. And with obscene haste, once I have secured a special license. I do not doubt that, given the influence of myself, my father, and yours, one will be issued without delay. And should the archbishop refuse my request, I will carry you away to Scotland and make you my bride in Gretna Green." He nibbled at her lips with a languid seduction, enticing her to kiss him back as he swallowed any further questions she might have asked. "Now, be still and let me kiss and caress you until you fall asleep."

WYLDER LAY WITH Emily for a long while. They whispered of plans and dreams, of what their future would bring until she shifted within the circle of his arms, a whimper of discomfort escaping her. Although she stubbornly protested that she was not in great pain, he convinced her that she must take a half dose of laudanum. Soon, she was drifting off into sleep while Wylder stroked her hair and murmured endearments in her ear.

He dozed off until Emily muttered something in her sleep, waking him at once. Turning toward him, she drowsily buried her face in the crook of his neck and threw an arm around his neck. Her soft breath feathered his chin, reminding Wylder of the numerous kisses they'd shared over the last few hours.

But the interlude had come to its end. If he did not make his exit soon, there was the possibility of being discovered in her rooms when the maid came to stoke the fire.

Using great care, Wylder rose from the bed while repositioning Emily's head so that she lay cradled in the pillow's downy softness. She slept soundly, the only sign of disturbance evident in the slight furrow marring her brow. Wylder relished the odd pang of tenderness piercing his heart as he gazed down at her. Leaving her was difficult, but necessary. Moving away from the bed, he straightened his rumpled clothes and glanced toward the terrace doors.

It was nearing dawn. Now that the rain had stopped, the sky was a lovely mix of dark and light blue colors, the puffy clouds illuminated with swashes of gold, pink, and purple, and fading stars.

Bending low, he pressed a kiss to the top of Emily's dark head. "Sleep well, my sweet love."

He slipped out of her bedroom, gently closing the door behind him. For a moment, he stood there, contemplating how much his life and Emily's would change now that he had succumbed to his love for her. Things were going to be so different from this point on. Smiling to himself, he anticipated the chaos that would come from making Emily his wife. Intending to make his way back to his room he immediately drew up short at the sight before him.

Simon stood in the corridor, blocking the way with his arms crossed and eyes blazing with blue fire.

"I suspected you would be here, Wylder."

Wylder sighed heavily, leaning against Emily's door and observing Simon from beneath hooded eyes. "I merely came to check on her… to ascertain for myself her recovery. Once she agreed to become my wife, I did nothing more than hold her until she fell asleep."

"You just couldn't stay away from her, could you? After years of swearing that you would not touch her… that you would not pursue her… you betrayed our friendship." Simon's accusations stung like gunshots, and he glared at Wylder as if he wanted nothing more than to execute his friend right there on the spot.

"I tried staying away, Simon. It proved an impossible task." Wylder did not look away. He met Simon's furious gaze with a calm strength. "But, regardless of your feelings on the subject, your sister and I will be wed."

"You cannot possibly love Emily as she deserves to be loved," Simon scoffed. "You don't even know what that emotion is. Your sole interest lies in treating her as if she's just another one of your whores. Or maybe you pursue this union because it's an easy way of covering your father's debts?"

Wylder's anger ignited in a blaze. Pushing off the wall, he

rushed toward Simon and, before his friend could react, he punched him square in the jaw. "Speak of my future wife with such disrespect again," he snarled, "and I will knock your teeth out and serve them to you in a soup."

Simon wobbled on his feet but did not go down with the force of the blow. Gritting his teeth, he swung wildly in retaliation, landing a glancing blow to Wylder's midsection. The impact knocked Wylder back a few steps, which opened some space between them. The two men stood silently, facing one another. Two best friends finding themselves at odds over a woman they both cared deeply for.

"Do you truly love her?" Simon heaved, brushing a hand over his busted lip. Worried anguish for his sister made his voice harsh. "Do you *love* her, goddammit?"

Wylder raked a hand through his disheveled hair, glancing back at Emily's bedroom. Hopefully, she'd slept through the brief ruckus right outside her door. "Yes, you hardheaded jackass. I love her. I love her with every drop of blood in my body. I love her more than you can possibly comprehend." He regarded Simon with more than a bit of sympathy. "You cannot understand it until you experience it, Simon. I don't care what happens to me. I don't care if the world ends as long as Emily is with me when it happens." His laugh was self-deprecating. "Lucien was right, after all. This is like nothing I've ever experienced or will ever experience. I suppose it's true. When a rakehell falls in love, it's all-consuming."

"Have you compromised her?" Simon choked out, his face red with embarrassment at the intimate question. It competed with the darkening bruise beginning to bloom across his jawline. "Your life depends on your answer, Wylder."

Wylder stared at Simon, unsure if he should take the threat seriously. But he answered slowly and truthfully. "She is untouched, Simon. I never allowed the situation to go too far."

Simon slumped, relief evident as he leaned against the wall for support. "Then there is still time to talk some sense into her.

To stop her from making the greatest mistake of her life."

"If you think you can talk Emily out of it, you do not know your sister very well," Wylder drawled, striding past Simon in dismissal of his words. "And if you think you'll stop me from taking her as my wife, then you must know the only way of accomplishing that is if you manage to kill me."

"As you wish, Wyldewood."

Wylder turned, mildly surprised by the conviction in Simon's tone. "Think upon your words carefully, Simon. I entered into a marriage contract for your sister's hand with your father's enthusiastic blessing. It is binding in the eyes of English law. You cannot stop this. You shouldn't *want* to stop this. I love Emily. I will be a good husband to her, and she will never want for anything as my wife."

Simon's features were carved from stone. "And your... proclivities? Will you continue visiting places like The Scarlett Petticoat? Because if you do, you most certainly will be unfaithful to her. And that is unacceptable."

"I'm not discussing intimate matters regarding my future wife with you, Simon. Suffice to say, I've no intention of becoming a philandering husband, nor will my particular brand of desire go unsatisfied." Wylder walked back to Simon and gripped his friend's shoulder in subtle warning. "Either we continue from this point as enemies or as brothers, old friend. I hope like hell it is as brothers, but this decision is yours to make. Not mine. But, and mark my words well, Simon, Emily will be my wife. Your father is hopeful to announce our engagement tomorrow evening. I'm leaving immediately for London where I shall apply for a special license from the archbishop."

Simon jerked free of Wylder's grip. "I told you once, long ago, that if you ever laid a hand on my sister, I would demand that you answer for it. And now that day has come. I don't give a damn if you obtain a special license. I don't care if you obtain a marriage contract. I don't even care that my sister loves you or that you say you love her. This is a matter of honor to be settled between the two of us, and settle it we shall. When you return, be prepared to meet me in Cedar Alley, where we shall put this to rest. I suggest you locate a second willing to stand with you as I intend to ask Lucien to serve as mine."

CHAPTER THIRTY

Emily

EMILY STRETCHED HER arms above her head, carefully minding her wrist. She lay still for a long moment, wondering if what had happened during the night was nothing more than a dream.

Was it? Was it all just a wonderful, fantastical dream?

Had Wylder truly asked her to marry him? Had he really confessed his love? Rolling over, she burrowed down into the pillows and took a deep breath. He had been there… his spicy cologne lingered on the pillowcase.

She sighed, submerged in absolute wonderment. It was coming true. Her dreams of becoming Lady Emily St. Clair, Countess of Wyldewood, were within reach. All that was required was the announcement of their engagement and the wedding to follow.

I wish Penelope were here to share in the news.

Emily frowned, dismayed by the reality of why that was not possible. Penelope's absence created a unique, heartbreaking problem. How could she marry Wylder without her dearest friend in attendance? Penelope would surely be missed from the celebrations, and there would be no reasonable way of explaining why she was missing. People would begin asking questions and Penelope's parents would most certainly inquire as to her whereabouts.

After all the planning to secure Penelope's disappearance,

Emily could not stomach giving up the scheme meant to prevent Lord and Lady True from selling their daughter to a wealthy predator like Lord Gregory Grant.

The only solution was a hasty, quiet wedding to Wylder. That would ensure Penelope remained concealed for the immediate future. And once Emily became Countess of Wyldewood and the future Duchess of Claymore, she would have more power to help Penelope. With Wylder as her husband, few would dare protest if she enfolded her vulnerable friend under a wing of protection.

Wylder would most certainly not object to a small, intimate wedding that took place sooner rather than later. Emily knew that if she indicated she preferred that above the pomp and circumstance of the usual wedding ceremony, her parents would concede if it made her happy. That left only the Duke and Duchess of Claymore to protest, but by all accounts, they would be ecstatic if their only heir wed as soon as possible.

Simon will be furious. He will no doubt blame Wylder, and there is no telling what he might do in his anger.

Emily sighed, propping herself against the headboard and hugging a pillow to her chest. Her brother presented a very real problem, considering his strenuous objections to any relationship between her and Wylder. Simon would stubbornly refuse to engage in a rational discussion, laboring under the mistaken belief that he knew what was best for his sister. Emily could only imagine the arguments that would erupt between the two men. Arguments that had the potential to turn deadly.

But perhaps there was a solution... Lord Ashcroft could be utilized in convincing Simon to grant his blessing on the union. He was, after all, one of Simon's closest friends. A great deal of mutual respect and affection existed between all three men. If anyone could talk Simon into accepting Wylder as Emily's husband, it would be Lucien. She would broach the subject today with the man and gauge his reaction. She would also employ Charlotte's assistance in the matter as well since Lucien seemed inclined toward his new wife's tiniest wish.

Carefully turning her wrist, Emily tested the level of pain the motion caused. It did not hurt as badly as the day before. There was no reason why she could not attend the ball that evening. Mother would probably put up a fuss, but Emily thought she could convince her to allow it.

There was a slight click of the doorknob turning, and Emily sat up straighter, her heart pounding with anticipation. Could it be Wylder? Was he daring enough to return with the morning sun shining brightly on their newly forged status as future husband and wife? She hoped so…

She sank back against the pillows, disappointment swamping her. Her mother bustled into the room, closely followed by one of the upstairs maids carrying an ornate silver tray.

"Good morning, my darling," Lady Blackthorne trilled. "How are you feeling today?"

"Much better, Mother." Emily smiled as her mother came closer to lay a hand across her forehead. "In fact, I am well enough to resume my normal activities. With my wrist securely wrapped, of course."

Lady Blackthorne laughed at Emily's confident statement. "Impertinent miss." She affectionately patted Emily's cheek while nodding to the maid to place the tray on the bedside table. "You shall have your breakfast in your bed and spend the day recovering from your ordeal. You are still warmer than I would like."

Emily stifled a sudden grin. If she were indeed warmer to the touch, then Wylder was undoubtedly to blame for that particular ailment. Thinking of the future pleasures to be unveiled once she became his wife turned the blood in her veins into molten liquid. Giving her mother an innocent smile, she determinedly pushed the lascivious thoughts aside.

"If I promise not to dance tonight and lift nothing heavier than a teacup in my uninjured hand, may I at very least attend the ball tonight, Mother?"

Lady Blackthorne scrutinized Emily as if determining the

wisdom of allowing her to have her way, then gave a slow nod of assent. "Yes. Yes, I suppose you shall. For you see, there have been some exciting developments following your accident, and it certainly would not be fair to exclude you at this point." Plopping carefully on the side of Emily's bed, she beamed at her daughter. "Now, while you eat, I shall tell you the extraordinary news. If you are in agreement, my dear, and I am certain that you are, you and Lord Wyldewood shall have your engagement announced this evening."

Emily did not dare indicate that this was news she was already aware of. After all, she could not very well inform her mother that Wylder had spent most of the night in her bed while she lay curled against him. Taking her mother's hand, she squeezed it hard. "You have no idea how happy this makes me, Mother. I have loved Wylder for as long as I can remember. And he loves me, too. I know he does."

"Then, all will be well," Lady Blackthorne said, pulling Emily into a tight embrace and kissing her forehead. "Wyldewood left for London this morning to secure a special license. Upon his return, you may wed as soon as you wish."

LATE IN THE afternoon, Emily convinced her mother that she was well enough to go downstairs. Although her wrist throbbed a bit, she barely noticed it. The happiness in her heart overwhelmed everything else until she was floating on air.

The entire household was abuzz with excitement for the ball that evening. Servants rushed here and there, bringing in fresh flowers, polishing furniture even where it was unnecessary, and dusting chandeliers and candelabras. Guests chattered and laughed in groups as a general atmosphere of gaiety permeated every corner of the enormous manor.

Emily successfully avoided going into much depth regarding

her injury and the faint bruising that shadowed her cheek. Mother had fluffed a bit of rice powder over the mark, which toned its coloring down, but one could not mistake the fact that it was there. Settling onto a chaise in the Sapphire parlor, she gazed out the open windows and pondered Wylder's return. It was a three-hour carriage ride from Thorne Park to London. Depending on how long it took to obtain the license, Emily believed it was possible he could be back at the manor before midnight.

She shivered, thinking how wonderful it would be if Wylder enfolded her in his arms upon his return without a care that others might witness the embrace.

Soon. Very soon, there will be no reason to hide our love.

There was a commotion at the doorway of the parlor, and glancing in that direction, Emily watched Patrick Bashear enter the room. He escorted his great aunt on his arm, and the elderly lady immediately noticed Emily. She smiled at Emily while whispering something in private to Patrick. His gaze landed on her as he nodded in apparent agreement to whatever Lady Bashear said. Within an internal groan, Emily watched him seat the lady in a small grouping of other ladies before he determined-ly headed in her direction.

"There you are, Lady Emily." Patrick smiled as he bowed to her. "Would it be acceptable to sit with you for a few moments?"

"Of course," Emily replied graciously, nodding at the chair opposite the chaise. Once he was settled, Emily waited for him to begin the conversation since she was unsure what he might say. After all, had he not declined her invitation, he would have been with her during the thunderstorm.

Patrick's gaze ran over her face and form, a critical glint in his brown eyes. "I am relieved to see you are relatively well following your unfortunate accident yesterday." His eyes flickered down to her ungloved hands and the bandaging that wrapped her wrist. "Does it pain you very much?"

"Oh, no," Emily said with a breezy smile. "A minor ache is the extent of it, Lord Bashear."

"That is certainly good news." He relaxed into the chair. "The rumors swirling about last evening were dreadful to hear. Especially when your father spent the whole of the evening ensconced in his study with Lords Wyldewood and Ashcroft. Word is that your brother was absent from whatever discussions were taking place. And now, Lord Wyldewood has gone to London on mysterious business." The grin that flitted across the man's handsome features gave Emily pause. Obviously, he was searching for any nugget of information she would supply, but she refused to indulge Patrick's curiosity.

"I'm not sure what they might have discussed, other than maybe an expression of gratitude to Lord Wyldewood for ensuring my safe return. I was unseated from my mare during the thunderstorm and injured my wrist," she explained blandly. She'd not seen her brother since that hazy moment Wylder had carried her into the foyer. That he had not sought her out made her more than nervous. Emily did not blink as she regarded the man. "I'm very fortunate that Lord Wyldewood came by when he did. Otherwise, I faced a very long, unpleasant walk home in the rain."

"I see," Patrick murmured, cocking his head as he studied her intently. Then he brightened, his tone turning almost jovial. "Are you well enough to attend the ball this evening?"

"Most certainly. Of course, I will refrain from taking part in any of the dancing, but there is little reason why I cannot visit with guests and stroll about the ballroom and the terrace. 'Tis only my wrist that pains me... not my feet. And if the binding remains tight so that I cannot move it, it should be fine."

Patrick's gaze dropped to her wrist once more, the corners of his lips quirking upward as though she'd uttered something amusing. A twinge of unease settled in Emily's stomach as she realized the man found something intimate in her words. Wylder exhibited a fascination with tying her up. Perhaps Lord Bashear was interested in the same pursuits. She felt her cheeks turning pink, the flush warming her entire face.

"I look forward to escorting you on your strolls this evening, Lady Emily." His charming smile was meant to put her at ease, but it failed miserably. "And if you are feeling up to it, perhaps a waltz may be attempted?"

"That would be lovely." Hopefully, Wylder would return in time to prevent that from happening, but until their engagement was announced, Emily was left no choice but to politely accept the offer. From the corner of her eye, she saw Charlotte enter the parlor. The countess's gaze skimmed the room's inhabitants, her face lighting up with a smile once she caught sight of Emily. Just as quickly, Charlotte's brows knitted together when she realized Patrick was seated with her.

"Very good." Patrick rose from the chair, taking Emily's uninjured hand and pressing a quick kiss to the back of it. "I've more reason now than ever to look forward to this evening. Now, if you will please excuse me, I must inquire of my aunt if she needs my assistance. Some of the gentlemen are engaging in a game of billiards this afternoon, so she may find my absence unsettling." He bowed a second time and took his leave as Emily sighed in silent relief.

Once Patrick sauntered off, Charlotte hurried over to Emily and sank into the chair he had just vacated. Grateful to see her new friend, Emily scooted closer along the chaise so that the two of them might carry on a more private conversation.

"It's a good thing Wyldewood was not here to see that," Charlotte said with a grin. "If he is anywhere near as possessive as Lucien, we might have had a true brawl right in the middle of your mother's pretty parlor."

Emily stifled a laugh. "Do you think Wylder would actually do that?"

"I believe he would." Charlotte smoothed a hand down the front of her dress. "In my own personal experience, once a rakehell falls in love, he finds himself overcome with the need to protect. And that includes fending off any threats, both real and perceived, to his claim on you." She gave Emily a half-serious smile. "I only mean to warn you, in case you are shocked by *your* rakehell's inevitable behavior."

"I am aware," Emily replied in a more somber tone. "Wylder is definitely the possessive type."

"The two of you have come to an understanding, then?"

Emily nodded. "He came to my room late last night." Her features softened with remembrance of the magical time Wylder spent in her bed that morning. "He says he loves me and has asked me to marry him. Of course, I said yes."

"Lucien told me Wyldewood left for London early this morning. It seems he will seek to obtain a special license. And being the son of a duke, as well as having high-ranking friends and being a powerful earl himself, he'll have little problem receiving one."

"I can hardly believe it's true." Emily smiled and explained, "You see, I've been in love with him forever, and while it was obvious he had an affection for me, my brother worked very hard at keeping us apart." She ran a finger over the edge of the bandage around her wrist before asking, "I've not spoken with Simon about any of this. He's been so determined... I worry Simon's over-protective anger will escalate into something horrible. I hope I may speak with Lord Ashcroft and see if his intervention will prevent that from happening."

Charlotte smiled sympathetically. "Lucien is aware of the issue. Before I came here to speak with you, he told me he was going to speak with Simon and try to make him see reason. Hopefully, he succeeds." She paused and gently changed the subject. "How is your wrist?"

Emily grimaced. "Sore, but if I admit that out loud to anyone but you, my mother or Wylder will place me on bedrest for a month."

"You are most likely correct about that." Charlotte's bright blue eyes twinkled with sudden mischief. "However, there are certain benefits to such a scenario that you cannot fully appreciate yet. A month in bed with your husband? You will soon find that to be something to look forward to."

CHAPTER THIRTY-ONE
Emily

THE BALL WAS in full swing when Emily finally came down the stairs.

Her heart was a thousand times heavier than she could have ever thought possible. Smoothing a gloved hand down the front of her violet shade, silk ballgown, Emily blew out a steadying breath in hopes of calming her jangled nerves.

Her lady's maid, Mary, had returned from London only two hours before bearing news which was far from ideal. Although Penelope was now safely hidden away in the Curzon Street town home, it was now a solution fraught with danger. It seemed Simon was purchasing the town home from her parents. As Mary understood it from the Curzon Street butler's explanation, the funds from the sale would be relayed into Emily's dowry accounts. It was not yet final, as Lord Blackthorne still had not signed off on the transaction, but the sale was progressing rapidly. In fact, Simon was already planning some minor renovations to the residence with a renowned architect on standby to oversee the project.

Which meant Penelope could only stay there until Simon took possession. Emily pinched the bridge of her nose, fighting off the headache threatening to take over. She wondered if Wylder knew of the sale, then realized her father must have surely informed him of it during the marriage negotiations.

And Simon was likely paying a pretty bit of coin for the property. Those funds would become part of Emily's dowry, which Wylder could certainly use to restore his own estates. No, none of that truly concerned her. The real problem lay in the fact that Penelope would soon require a new hiding spot.

"I'll worry about it later," Emily muttered to herself. "Once Wylder and I are wed, I shall convince him that he must help Penelope. She'll be out of that house before Simon ever takes up residency there."

Entering the ballroom, Emily found her mother standing with Lady Bashear. Gritting her teeth, she approached the two women with a sweet smile plastered on her face.

"There you are, my darling." Lady Blackthorne smiled at her daughter. "With your gloves on, no one can even notice the bandaging."

"Yes, Mother," Emily replied. "It doesn't even really hurt anymore. Just a slight ache now and then. Mary helped with applying some cold compresses before wrapping it tonight."

"Very good, dear," her mother said, examining Emily's features for any sign of discomfort. "I'm glad she made it back from London in time to assist you tonight." She tsked suddenly, her mouth forming a moue of disappointment. "I do wish Penelope had not taken ill and was forced to miss the ball. Poor dear."

Emily simply nodded before addressing Lady Bashear. "My lady, are you enjoying the ball to honor Lord and Lady Ashcroft? Mother has certainly done an excellent job arranging it all. I'm sure it will be the social event of the season."

"Oh, certainly," the lady said, waving an ornate fan to stir the air around her face. "Lord and Lady Ashcroft are to dance the first waltz of the evening. Is that right, Lady Blackthorne?"

"Yes, the first waltz." Lady Blackthorne sighed, holding a hand to her heart. "They are such a lovely couple. It's a shame Lord Ashcroft's parents could not attend, but apparently Her Grace was feeling poorly and could not make the trip."

"I'm sure Lady Ashcroft is disappointed by their absence. It's said the duke and duchess are quite fond of their new daughter-in-law and she of them," Lady Bashear commented.

Lady Blackthorne clapped her hands as the musicians in the balcony began strumming the beginning strains of the evening's first waltz. "Oh, it's time for the evening's highlight!"

The entire ballroom fell into a reverent hush as Lucien led Charlotte into the middle of the gleaming ballroom floor. Great, crystal-laden chandeliers illuminated the space in an ethereal glow as the evening's honorees faced each other.

Lucien bent at the waist in an elegant bow as Charlotte sank into a perfect, gracefully executed curtsey. Then, taking his wife's hand, Lucien swung her into the intricate steps of the dance. Their movements were perfectly in tune with one another as guests murmured amongst themselves how lovely the new couple was and how attentive the earl was to his new bride.

Emily watched wistfully, her heart aching at the beauty of the scene. It truly resembled something out of a fairytale, and she eagerly anticipated her own waltz with Wylder once they were wed.

Glancing about the ballroom, Emily let out a sigh of exasperation when her eyes landed on her brother. He stood off to the side of the ballroom near the open terrace doors, and his handsome features were screwed into a scowl. When he noticed her, his scowl deepened as Emily's hands curled into twin balls of frustration. On the opposite side of the ballroom near the refreshment table was Patrick Bashear. The gentleman's brown eyes lit up with anticipation when he spied Emily, his grin widening. He immediately had a second cup of ratafia poured and began strolling in Emily's direction. With a groan of dread, Emily turned to her mother with a bright smile.

"I have spied Simon, Mother, by the terrace doors. I must speak with him. If you will both excuse me?"

"Be kind to him, dear," Lady Blackthorne murmured. Leaning forward to embrace her daughter, her words were for Emily's ears only. "He had made it very clear that he does not sanction a marriage between you and Wyldewood. His reasons, however, are his own and have no bearing on the decision your father and I have made."

"Thank you, Mother." Emily gratefully nodded. Dipping a slight curtsey to Lady Bashear, she hurried away, eager to confront her brother and avoid the attentions of Patrick.

In addition to the guests staying at Thorne Park, local gentry were also in attendance, as well as many of the ton with their own country houses nearby. There were easily close to two hundred guests enjoying the evening's festivities. The sheer number of people helped her evade Patrick and she sighed with relief when she finally reached Simon.

"Simon Blackthorne," Emily scolded as he took a sip of champagne. He steadfastly refused to look at her. "You've avoided me since I was deposited safely in my bed. Why on earth have you done that? What's gotten into you?"

Simon's dark-blue eyes swept the ballroom as if looking for someone before settling on her. His jaw tightened, a muscle clenching there as his gaze flicked to her injured wrist.

"Why have you not checked on me yourself?" Emily demanded in exasperation. "Are you so angry that Wyldewood came to my rescue that you ignored my well-being?"

"I'm glad to see you are feeling well, Emily. But yes, I am furious that Father granted Wyldewood permission to marry you, despite my numerous objections. And you have capitulated to the earl's demands," he muttered, his expression stony and unforgiving. Dark hair tumbled over his brow as though he'd raked his hands through it numerous times. It pained Emily's heart to see her brother in such a state of distress when there was no cause for it.

Looking about to ensure no one overheard their conversation, Emily admitted, "It's true. I have accepted Wylder's offer of marriage. I love him very much, Simon. I always have." She rested a gloved hand on his arm, her smile beseeching. "This is what I've always wanted. Why can you not accept the fact that Wylder and I belong together?"

"You have no idea what kind of man he is, Emily."

Taking hold of Simon's coat sleeve, she quickly dragged him out onto the open terrace. He followed without protest, but Emily suspected that no matter her arguments on the subject, he would not be swayed from his position. He truly believed Wylder was wrong for her.

"You are wrong, Simon." Emily glared at him. Simon had always possessed a stubborn nature. She felt a twinge of pity for whoever his future wife might be. The woman was sure to face her brother's obstinate nature on a regular basis. The sounds of the ballroom drifted on the cool evening breeze. It was only a matter of time before other guests began using the terrace, and this momentary privacy was lost. She sighed heavily, determined to convince him she knew what she was doing. "I do know, and I love Wylder for who he is. He is intelligent and strong. Surprisingly kind, and even gentle at times. Honorable. Loyal. So loyal, in fact, that rather than betray you, he did as you asked and ignored his own heart. That's the type of man he is. A man that you should be glad your sister will marry."

"There are things about him that you do not know. Things I hope you never do," Simon snapped, his face turning red as he broached this sensitive subject. "His… sexual appetites…"

"They do not frighten me," Emily stated firmly. "And those intimate moments between me and Wylder are none of your concern." Her head cocked as she regarded Simon with such solemness that he finally looked away from her intense stare. "Oh, Simon. Do you honestly believe I'm unaware of what Wylder desires of a woman? Of course, I know because I asked him and he explained in great detail just what he expects of me. So, while you may be embarrassed by this rather frank discussion, you must understand that Wylder and I are compatible in such matters. Simon, my dearest brother, please be happy for me and your best friend. Because we will marry regardless of your feelings on the subject."

Simon blew out a frustrated breath and said from between clenched teeth, "He's bewitched you."

"You are wrong, Simon," Wylder said from the doors to the ballroom, his voice startling both Emily and Simon. He was dressed in black evening attire, his features drawn and tired but his jaw was set with grim resolve.

Emily choked back a little cry of joy at seeing him. She wanted to run to his arms and press kisses to every inch of his face, but struck by uncertainty, she did not dare move. Must she still keep their relationship a secret? Or would he finally claim her publicly?

"She's bewitched me. Entranced me. Captivated me." Stalking toward the pair, Wylder's gaze held Emily's as he spoke softly but with steel-tempered conviction. His sudden appearance and the determined glint in his eyes made her realize secrecy was no longer necessary. The Earl of Wyldewood had come to claim her.

"She is my heart and soul. Without her, I am doomed to a life of misery." Going straight to Emily, Wylder reached out a hand and cupped her jaw. A faint smile lifted the corners of his mouth when she let out a breathy sigh of adoration. His words remained directed to Simon, although he continued staring down into Emily's eyes. "I have assured you that I love her, but what I feel truly goes beyond that. I will worship her for the rest of my days."

Emily's knees wobbled at Wylder's declaration. Hearing him state such lovely things out loud was doing strange things to her insides. When Wylder finally spared Simon a glance, it was blatantly sympathetic. Emily peeked at her brother to gauge his reaction and saw his jaw clench. A flicker of uncertainty crossed his features but his hands balled into tight fists, as though he wanted nothing more than to punch Wylder.

"Betrayal does not sit well with me, Wylder," Simon said bitterly. "You were my friend before you became her suitor. You kept this courtship hidden from me, knowing I have never approved of your infatuation with her. And must I remind you of the vow we made to resist the plans of our fathers and the shackles of marriage?"

Wylder's head cocked. "If you must despise me, then so be it. But I will not allow you to punish Emily for my weakness."

"You will be the one answering for your actions. Not Emily," Simon shot back. "Will you keep the appointment we previously made so that satisfaction may be gained?"

Wylder straightened at once, his hand moving down to grip Emily's. He meshed their fingers together, reassuringly squeezing hers. He stared back at Simon as if daring the man to sever the grip he had.

"Simon… this is madness…" Emily said, her voice thick with frightened horror as she abruptly understood what the two men were speaking of. "I cannot stand here and watch as the two men I adore to destroy one another for the sake of pride. Please do not do this."

Simon's gaze flickered to meet Emily's, his fury barely leashed as he said between clenched teeth, "If he loves you as he claims, then he will fight for you."

Wylder calmly regarded Simon, his lips pressed into a thin, grim line. "Demand that my blood be spilled for the sake of her honor, and I will not refuse you. But I will not raise a pistol against you, Simon. And if I fall, I fall loving Emily. Nothing you do will ever change that for me."

"I will not live without Wylder," Emily said quietly. "Simon, do you understand what I am saying to you? If you succeed with your intentions, you will also destroy me. Put aside your objections and open your eyes to this truth. I love Wylder. He loves me. We intend to spend the rest of our lives together and you may be part of that as either beloved family or bitter enemy. But you will not come between myself and this man. I won't allow it."

Silence stretched between the three of them, broken only by the soft strains of music drifting through the open doors, interspersed with the chatter and laughter of guests. Simon's chest rose and fell, his fists still clenched, but there was a spark of something else in his eyes. A sliver of pain and comprehension that was slowly eating away at his rage.

At last, he let out a sharp exhale, dragging a hand across his face. "Damn you both," he muttered. "You've left me little choice. I cannot condone your actions, nor will I give my blessing. But neither will I spill your blood for it when it would obviously destroy my sister. She loves you... even if it is foolish of her." He fixed Wylder with a dark, unwavering stare. "I expect you to take care of her. But I still think you are unworthy of her."

Relief washed through Emily in dizzying waves so overwhelming that it nearly buckled her knees. She clung to Wylder, unable to utter a word as her prayers were answered.

"You are right, Simon," Wylder agreed with a solemn nod. "I am unworthy. I shall never be deserving of her or her love. But I will spend the rest of my days worshipping her. I swear this to you, not only as your closest friend, but also as the man your sister has chosen to spend her life with. It's an honor that I do not take lightly. And perhaps one day, you will see that I never betrayed you. My crime is that I love her more than anything else in this world."

Simon gave Wylder a tight nod. "Lucien will be pleased by this outcome. He's tried his damnedest all afternoon to dissuade me from killing you."

"I shall thank him later if it was his counsel that changed your mind just now," Wylder drawled. Emily could see he still regarded Simon as though he were a stick of dynamite ready to blow up at any moment.

Simon's mouth curved with a sad smile, his gaze meeting Emily's. "It was the reality of my sister's unhappiness more than anything else."

"Now that we have reached an unsteady truce and will not be pointing pistols at one another, I must insist that you excuse us, Simon. I've ridden to London and back, and now there is a matter of the greatest urgency that I must attend to." Wylder murmured.

Simon bowed at the waist, and his gaze narrowed on Wylder. "If you ever harm her in any way, or break her heart, I will finish you, you know."

A sharp laugh escaped Wylder. "I would expect no less. If it ever came to pass, I would deserve the most painful and horrific of deaths at your hands." Sliding his arm around Emily's waist, he bowed to Simon. "Now, I must dance with my soon-to-be wife."

"Dance?" Emily squeaked in alarm. "But, Wylder… we cannot."

Wylder smiled at her hesitancy. His expression was so tenderly fierce that Emily nearly melted in his arms when he declared, "We most certainly can. And we will. This very moment, actually. Everyone has joined in Lucien and Charlotte's waltz, and so shall we." Then he kissed her forehead, murmuring, "I will not hide my love for you any longer. I want everyone to know that you are mine as surely as I am yours."

Emily nearly burst into tears while behind them Simon snorted out an exasperated groan. "Dear God, save me from ever sounding like a lovesick swain." Throwing his hands up in the air, he whirled away from Emily and Wylder and stalked back toward the ballroom without a backward glance.

"Don't worry about your brother." Wylder grinned at Emily, drawing her attention back to him. "I am convinced Simon will be the worst of us when he finally falls in love. And he will fight it until he is bloody and screaming, but he *will* succumb." Pulling Emily closer, his breath hitched as if he were overwhelmed by the feel of her in his arms. "Will you dance with me, Emily? Will you allow me to publicly claim you as mine?"

A thread of disbelief and shy acceptance wrapped around Emily's heart. Was this truly happening? It was like a dream, and she finally nodded in speechless agreement. The next instant, Wylder was sweeping her into the ballroom, whirling her into a kaleidoscope of color and beauty.

The shock of their sudden appearance caused more than a few couples to falter in their steps. In the swirling motions of the dance, Emily caught sight of Charlotte as Lucien twirled her close by. Her new friend beamed at her, a twinkle of triumph in her eyes, while Lucien gave them both a wink. On the edges of the ballroom, Emily's parents stood arm in arm as they watched. Their faces were aglow with smiles of approval even as Lady Blackthorne dabbed the corners of her eyes with a silk handkerchief that her father handed to her.

A roar of whispers and conversations swirled around the room as the waltz continued, and soon, Emily realized every pair of eyes in the ballroom was now trained on herself and Wylder. Even Lucien and Charlotte graciously retreated until finally, it was simply Emily and Wylder dancing alone, the sole couple waltzing around the glittering ballroom to the lilting music.

When the song finally faded, Wylder surprised Emily by bending low at the waist, gallantly bowing to her as she dipped into a deep curtsey. While a thunderous applause rang out, Wylder swiftly pulled Emily back into his arms. Raising her hand, he pressed an ardent kiss to her gloved fingers, and for a moment, the world blurred until there was nothing other than Wylder and his love for her.

"Come with me now, Emily," he whispered, his silver-gray eyes holding her gaze until she could see no one else other than him.

"I will go anywhere with you, Wylder," she breathed.

"For the moment, just to the gardens," Wylder murmured in quiet amusement. "I must speak with you privately now that we've given the ton something to chew on."

They quickly made their way toward the terrace, ignoring the chatter of excited guests and the many hands attempting to halt their progress. The ballroom was alive with curious eyes and quick tongues, a hum escalating like bees escaping a hive. Emily had never felt so exposed to the gossip of society but Wylder was determined. His stride was purposeful, and in a few moments, they were descending a set of stone steps that led into the south rose garden.

"Where are we going, Wylder?" Emily asked breathlessly, trotting to keep up with his longer strides. All of her questions now rushed to the surface, and she was thirsty for answers to so many things. "How is it that you returned from London so quickly? Were you able to obtain the license? Perhaps we should go back to the ballroom?"

Wylder paused, stopping to tweak Emily's nose with an indulgent smile. "So many questions, minx. I can see that you shall be a very inquisitive little wife. Sure to get into mischief on a regular basis." Moonlight illuminated the way as he directed her to sit on a marble bench beneath a bower of white and pink roses. Their fragrance, soft and sweet, surrounded them as the breeze gently ruffled the branches.

Wylder sat beside her and gently lifted her injured hand. "Does it hurt?"

She barely even felt the inconvenient ache in her wrist when Wylder smiled at her. "No, my lord."

Wylder's eyes darkened. "Good. I want no distraction when I kiss you. It feels as though I've been away from you for an eternity."

Emily tenderly brushed a lock of thick, dark hair back from his brow and out of his eyes. Everything inside her body tightened with anticipation, her heart still racing from the waltz. Her blood pounded through her veins like a runaway river as the yearning crashed through her. "I feel the same." Curling a hand around Wylder's neck, she arched toward him until their lips nearly touched. "And I'm waiting with desperate longing for you to kiss me, my lord."

A groan rumbled from deep within Wylder's chest as he gently set her back away from him. "I shall kiss you until you cannot breathe, minx. God above, I've thought of nothing else since I left you this morning, all sleepy and warm in your bed. But first, my darling love, I must ask you a crucial question."

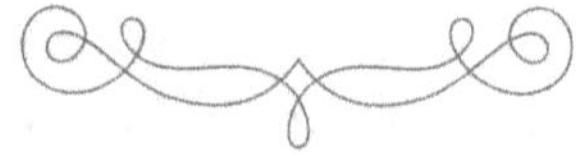

CHAPTER THIRTY-TWO

Emily

S HE GAZED UP at him, puzzled by his statement but eager to please him.

"You may ask me anything, Wylder," she replied softly.

"Do you desire a ceremony with our families and acquaintances in attendance?" Using his forefinger, Wylder tilted her chin higher. "Waiting will satisfy the gossip and the scandal that is sure to erupt now that our relationship is no longer a secret."

"Or?" Emily breathed, her tongue darted out to lick her upper lip nervously.

"Or would you marry me as soon as I can make the arrangements?" He sounded curious as to what her answer might be. Did he wonder if she would choose the safer option? Because any proper young lady of the ton would seek to avoid scandal at all costs.

But Emily was no ordinary, proper young lady. She was a woman in love with a scandalous rakehell. And she wanted Lord Wylder St. Clair of Wyldewood as much as he wanted her.

"Oh, Wylder…" Her breath caught in her throat, tears pricking her eyes as her world narrowed to the man before her. She witnessed in his face not just desire, but a desperate devotion. It was a longing so fierce and powerful that it made her heart tremble. "Do you believe that I would wait a moment longer when I've spent an eternity hoping for this moment? I care nothing for wagging tongues. I only care that I am with you."

"Then marry me now, Emily." His voice was harsh with emotion, and as Emily watched in dazed amazement, he slid to one knee before her. "Marry me not in months, nor weeks, but now. Any scandal our wedding creates will dissolve beneath the certainty of my devotion to you. If this is your choice, then let us bind ourselves to one another tonight." From his coat pocket, Wylder withdrew a ring. The large diamond glittered with such brilliance that it appeared to have been crafted from rays of moonlight and fire.

Emily's body trembled with wild excitement as Wylder carefully stripped her gloves away, taking care of her injured wrist. The ring was slid onto her finger, where it sparkled as brightly as any star in the ebony dark sky above them.

"This is just one piece of the St. Clair jewels. My father, even with his mountain of debts, did not dare gamble these away. When I informed them today that you'd agreed to marry me, my mother wept with joy. She insisted I take this ring to give to you. Her exact words were that the future Duchess of Claymore and mother of her grandchildren deserved the very best from the St. Clair coffers. As for my father, he puffed out his chest and claimed victory in the fact that I will settle down at last and save our bloodline and estates. I let him bluster since I hold all the power when it comes to his excesses. However, I must give the man credit. Once the Archbishop realized I was the son of the Duke of Claymore, my application for a special license was granted within the hour." Wylder kissed the tips of Emily's bare fingers, gazing up at her with dark intensity as his breath warmed her skin. "And so, it comes to this. Will you become my wife tonight, Emily?"

"Yes," Emily breathed. She was decidedly lightheaded as reality crashed over her. This was truly happening. She would be Wylder's bride—his *wife*. "Oh, yes, Wylder."

Wylder's face lit with unabashed relief as he grinned. "Then let's not keep Thorne Park's vicar waiting in vain. Come with me now, my love. The arrangements have been made for us to exchange our vows tonight. I hoped you would say yes, so I've instructed your maid to begin packing your belongings and ready them for delivery within the next few days."

"My belongings?" Emily repeated, so overwhelmed by the turn of events that her brain could not keep up with the conversation.

"As soon as we are wed, we shall leave for Wyldewood Lodge, my country estate in Kent. And if you are worried about what you will wear before then, then you must know I intend for you to spend that time naked and in my bed."

"But, the ball, Wylder! And all of the guests... my parents... Lord and Lady Ashcroft... whatever will they think when they learn I've stolen away with you? And Simon. Oh, Simon will likely be furious that you did not tell him of your plans."

"It might be the most shocking headline for tomorrow's gossip sheets, but the moment I arrived this evening, I sought out your parents. They gave their permission for us to wed tonight, provided you said yes. They will announce our wedding not as a disgrace, but as a victory. They will say that our love for one another could not wait another day, and everyone will secretly envy our boldness in doing what *we* want rather than what society deems proper." Wylder pulled Emily up from the bench, his strong, muscled arms wrapping about her waist. Bending his head, he nuzzled his nose alongside hers.

"Are we truly doing this, Wylder?" Emily laughed in disbelief. Surely this was a dream. A wild, vivid dream where joy fluttered around her insides and left her giddy with love for this man. "Are you certain that we should?"

Wylder took a deep breath and kissed the tip of Emily's nose as he confessed softly, "I've never been more certain of anything in my life, Emily Blackthorne. I love you and I want to spend the rest of my life with you."

THE COACH RUMBLED through the evening mist, the hooves of the matched bays setting a rhythmic beat on the dirt road. The countryside rushed past in shadows and moonlight, unfurling toward the dawn with every mile that passed. Emily pressed her cheek to her husband's shoulder, closing her eyes as exhaustion threatened to overtake her. She still wore her ballgown, the pale-violet silk with its expensive beadwork shimmering in the coach's lamplight and only partially covered by Wylder's cloak.

She'd never done anything so reckless before in her life. Her body vibrated with the thrill of it.

Come morning, the truth of what she and Wylder had done would blaze across London like an errant comet. But she felt no regret. No shame. Just anticipation of what it would mean to be Wylder's wife in truth.

"You should sleep, my love," Wylder murmured, wedging himself in the corner of the coach and pulling her so that she half reclined against his chest, her cheek pressed to the spot over his heart. Emily smiled drowsily. It was impossible to heed his suggestion when she was so excited.

"If you will follow your own advice, my lord, I will try as well. I know you must be exhausted."

"It's not the first time I've gone almost twenty-four hours without sleep. I can hold on just a bit longer if it means providing you a small measure of comfort." He chuckled against the top of her head. "Close your eyes now, minx."

Emily tilted her head back, staring up at Wylder. He was being so sweet. So tender and considerate. Would he always be so indulgent when it came to her? A needlelike twinge of worry assailed her. Would he agree to help Penelope when it became necessary? "I believe I need a kiss before I consider obeying you, husband."

"Shall I kiss you as I did when the vicar declared us man and wife?"

A blush heated Emily's cheeks. Mister Collins, Thorne Park's vicar, had laughed softly at Wylder's enthusiasm when it came to kissing his bride. "I think you scandalized the man. But yes, kiss me like that, lord husband."

"Very well, Lady Wyldewood." Wylder smiled, notching his hand under Emily's chin so she could not escape the burning heat of his mouth.

He kissed her with slow, precise thoroughness, sweeping his tongue over hers, tangling and teasing until she was breathless and squirming against him. When he finally drew back, his eyes were hot, silver coals, and his breath was ragged, as if he were holding himself back from ravishing her right there.

"Were you not suffering from a sprained wrist, and if you were not so tired, little minx, I would consider making you mine on this coach seat." He traced the upper bow of her lip with the tip of his tongue, kissing her softly again as if he could not get enough of her taste. "But I will exercise restraint for now so that I may take you at my leisure later. I shall spend hours learning your body and your responses to the things I do to you. I will savor the shocked gasp you make when our bodies finally join together as one. I will memorize the whimpers and little cries of passion that escape you as I bring you to climax on my tongue, on the tips of my fingers, and with my cock buried deep inside you." Although her body trembled at his words, Wylder gently coaxed her into lying her head back down against his chest. "Now, go to sleep, brat," he said, his voice husky with affection. "You will certainly need your strength once I finally have you in my bed."

Emily grumbled, but her eyes were already closing when she said, "I shall not always obey you, my lord. My obstinate nature will not allow it."

She sensed Wylder's smile in his lighthearted reply.

"I know. But you've no idea how much I will enjoy those instances of disobedience, my darling wife." Raising her hand to his lips, he pressed a kiss to the ring she wore that proclaimed her as his as she drifted away. "And I promise you will as well."

CHAPTER THIRTY-THREE

Wylder

WYLDEWOOD LODGE HAD undergone extensive renovations in the last year, and Wylder was now glad he'd sunk the funds into it. It was an amazing sense of fulfillment to bring his new bride to his home, knowing that it was a space to be proud of.

Emily slept for most of the journey while Wylder occasionally dozed as the coach bumped along the uneven country roads. When they finally arrived late the next afternoon, she drowsily stood beside him as he introduced her to the staff and his housekeeper, Miss Dawson. After arranging to have a light meal prepared as well as a bath for two, Wylder guided Emily up the curved staircase.

"Your home is so beautiful," Emily said, her fingers trailing along the polished mahogany banister. Plaster walls painted in a soft, sky-blue shade were enhanced by several works of art set in gilded frames. Above the large, airy foyer, an enormous gilt and crystal chandelier hung from an ornately carved medallion of carved acanthus leaves set high in the soaring ceiling. Highly polished wood floors gleamed, the aroma of wax mingling with the scent of fresh flowers arranged in a vase on a rosewood circular table set in the middle of the gently curved room.

"Our home," Wylder corrected her, his arm slipping around

her waist as they continued ascending the stairs. "Everything I have is now yours, Emily."

"I only care that I have possession of your heart," she replied with a smile.

"That is the one thing of mine that has been yours from the moment I laid eyes on you, although I was far too immature and selfish to understand it." Wylder led the way down a long corridor, watching as Emily took in the quiet grandeur of Wyldewood Lodge. Turning down a secondary hallway, they finally came to a stop before the doors to his suite of rooms. He swung the heavy oak panels open. Allowing her to enter ahead of him, Wylder heard her soft intake of breath and curiosity.

"How masculine it is," she murmured, pulling away from him to step farther into the space. Her gaze darted around the room, taking in the heavy, dark wood of the furniture and the massive four-poster bed that occupied one wall. The bed was truly a piece of artwork, the post heavily carved with trailing vines and leaves. Tiny foxes peeked out amongst the carvings, and a tester canopy of dark hunter green brocade topped the bed as if it were icing on a cake.

"Am I to sleep here? With you?" Emily asked quietly, her gaze returning to Wylder's. Her blue eyes glowed as she waited for his answer, and Wylder felt his body clench with sudden, overwhelming possessiveness.

"You shall sleep nowhere else," he declared, stalking toward her. Taking her hands, he stripped off her gloves and tossed them aside. For a moment, he admired the diamond ring sparkling on her finger before wrapping his arms around her tiny waist. Bending his head, he brushed his mouth over hers, delighting in her contented sigh.

"I am glad to hear it. I know it is fashionable for the lady of the house to have her own set of rooms, but I do not want to be away from your side, Wylder," Emily said, melting in his embrace.

"Nor shall you be if I can help it."

A knock on the door interrupted what he might have done then, and Wylder reluctantly stepped back as a chattering parade of excited servants began carrying in covered trays of food and a decanter of wine. Everything was quickly set up on a small table flanked by two carved chairs of matching rosewood in the alcove of a set of floor-to-ceiling windows. In another section of the large room, an enormous brass tub sat behind a paneled screen of the same hunter green brocade as the bed's canopy. Four footmen carried in steaming pails of water, dumping them into the tub as a maid efficiently stacked towels and soaps on a stool beside the tub under Miss Dawson's watchful eye.

Emily watched quietly as all this was done, but Wylder noticed how she twisted the ring she wore in a subconsciously nervous gesture. Once they were alone, he took her in his arms again. How slowly must he move when it came to making love to her for the first time? He prayed his patience would hold out… that he would not frighten her with the burning force of his desire.

"That bath looks heavenly. I am torn between it and satisfying my hunger." Emily met his gaze, her eyes twinkling with a mischievous glint.

"We should enjoy the bath first while the water is hot. We can eat afterward," Wylder breathed, his thumbs moving upward until they rested just beneath the undercurve of her breasts. His body hardened to a painful degree as his hands framed those luscious swells.

"But my hunger is for you, my lord." The corners of Emily's pouty lips curved upward when Wylder sucked in a deep breath.

"Dammit, Emily. You cannot say such things and not expect me to tear every stitch of your clothing away from your body. I'm barely holding onto my restraint as it is."

Emily did not look away, her blue eyes growing heated as she licked her upper lip and her hands came up to grip the lapels of his suit coat. "But I do not wish for your restraint. I prefer you to be as wild with longing as I am." Standing on tiptoes, she kissed him, her mouth growing more bold as the seconds passed. "Help me remove my gown, husband," she whispered. "And remove your clothing as well."

"With the greatest of pleasure, wife," Wylder muttered.

When they were both finally divested of their clothing, Wylder helped Emily into the tub, then followed behind her. Their legs tangled together as they sat facing one another, the steam of the water rising between them in little tendrils. Emily's breasts bobbed in the water, full and creamy pink from the heat. She was as beautiful as a water nymph and just as tempting.

With a shy smile, she reached for one of the sponges and lathered it up with one of the bars of soap. Then, as if she'd done so a thousand times before, she leaned forward and began washing Wylder's chest, her fingers following the path of suds and rivulets.

Wylder choked back a groan when Emily's fingernails raked over his nipples. Her expression was intent as she explored, satisfying her curiosity and becoming bolder as her hands dipped beneath the water. He held his breath as she encircled his shaft with one hand. She dropped the sponge but did not bother to retrieve it as her full attention centered on Wylder.

"You are so hard, Wylder. So strong and beautiful." Emily's voice was full of wonderment, her teeth catching her bottom lip in awe as she caressed the muscled planes of his chest. The ridges of his abdomen. The aching stiffness of his cock.

"Fuck, Emily." The words came out in a grunt, full of need and lust. "Let us be done with this so I can take you to bed. I need to be inside you more than I need air to breathe."

"Is it not possible to do such things here?" she asked innocently, the hand wrapped about his cock slowly working his flesh as she stared up at him.

"You are driving me mad, brat." His hips involuntarily bucked toward her, his cock swelling within the small circle of her hand. Emily's smile was one of satisfaction, and she leaned forward to kiss him, her lips teasing his.

"It's only fair that you suffer, too. I've waited so very long to become your wife in every sense of the word, Wylder. I ache for you. I want you. I love you. Will you show me everything that you desire? Will you teach me to please you?"

In response, Wylder suddenly lifted her so that her curved bottom rested on the top of his thighs, her warm, wet cunny achingly close to his erection. His body strained toward hers, throbbing to be embedded within her. He stopped just short of surging into her, however, worried that he might hurt her if he took her like this for her first time. Now that her breasts were even with his mouth, he lazily kissed the glistening globes. "Place your arms around my neck, Emily," he instructed in a husky voice. When she obeyed, he sucked one of her pink nipples into his mouth with a low growl. "Good girl."

The praise wrung a whimper from her throat, and Wylder's free hand slid up to her throat. Wrapping his fingers around the slim column, he forced her head to tilt back. When she shifted against him, seeking the friction of his body, he tightened his grip. "Be still, else I fuck you right here in this tub, Emily." He tongued the erect bud of her nipple, then moved onto the other, sucking and licking as her moans grew more desperate. When her hips rocked against his, the soft curls of her pussy brushing against his cock, he nearly combusted with lust.

Water sloshed over the sides of the tub, puddling on the polished wood floor. Wylder's teeth nipped Emily in warning, catching the tip of her breast and worrying the sensitive flesh. "Is this what you want, little minx? For your husband to take your virginity like this?"

"Yes," she breathed helplessly, her chin still pointed upward by the force of his hand around her throat. "P-please, Wylder. Please... take me now. Here. Like this. I'm begging you."

The untamed side of Wylder thrilled to her impassioned plea but still, he hesitated. "It will hurt you more than is necessary, minx."

"It hurts now..." she said in a breathy complaint. "It hurts that you are not inside me, making me your own. If I have any say in my own deflowering, then this is how I choose it to happen. Later, you may punish me for my impertinence, my lord."

"You can be certain that I will. When you are tied to my bed and I'm spanking that gorgeous arse of yours, you may be sorry you goaded me into this." Sliding his hand to the nape of her neck, Wylder forced her to look at him. His fingers tangled in her damp hair, his gaze roaming over her beautiful face. Emily's eyes were half-lidded with desire, her lips full and trembling. A rosy flush pinkened her damp skin.

"I won't be sorry, Wylder. I'll never be sorry that I am your wife," she said with a fierceness that took his breath away. "I *chose* you. A rakehell. A scoundrel. A rogue. A man who captured my heart long ago. So, I won't ever be sorry."

Wylder groaned out loud, his hand tightening on the back of her neck. He'd married a wild temptress that he would never tire of.

Shifting his free hand, he used the buoyancy of the water to aid in lifting her hips so that she was poised over his shaft. His fingers dug into the fleshy part of her buttocks, holding her at bay as he made sure one more time that this was what she wanted. And while he somehow managed to show the barest hint of restraint, in reality, he wanted to violently thrust up into her softness and explode inside her.

"Be very certain of this, Emily. I won't be able to stop once I'm inside you."

"I am." Her arms locked even more tightly around his neck, her eyes fluttering shut with the force of her desire. "And I won't allow you to stop."

"Then look at me, Emily," he commanded harshly. "Look at me, and don't you dare close your eyes as I make you mine."

"Yes, my lord," she whispered, her arms winding around his neck even more.

Then she was crying out as Wylder notched himself against

the opening of her body. His hips surged upward, breaching her slowly but surely until he reached the barrier of her innocence. He held her gaze as he conquered her, shoving past the flimsy bit of tissue until he was seated deep inside the warm silkiness of her pussy. She was so tight around him… impossibly so. Her virginal channel was pulsating in a strange rhythm of frantic rejection and helpless, melting acceptance.

"I'm hurting you…" Wylder grunted. The size of his cock was likely splitting her in two, and the sudden realization made his heart leap with irrational panic. His fingers gripped her buttocks in preparation of dragging her off of him.

"It hurts but it also feels amazing," Emily breathed in wonder. Her body ground against him, and a gasp flew past her lips when her clitoris made contact with his pubic area. "Oh! Oh… my God…" Her gaze met his, her pupils so dilated with pleasure they were now dark pools of blue. "You are so big and I feel so… full of you. As if I might burst apart… but I never want it to end."

"Fucking hell, Emily. Keep talking and I will erupt inside you," he swore between clenched teeth.

Emily smiled at that, a slow, sensuous smile that was at odds with the pinch of pain that still furrowed her brow. "Show me what that means, Wylder."

Wylder caught her hand, drawing it to his mouth and pressing a burning kiss to her palm. The diamond ring glittered in the dim light of the room, catching the flames of the fire in the hearth.

"My wife," he murmured, kissing her hand again and putting all of his emotion and love and desire and possessiveness into the simple, powerful words.

"My lord husband," she whispered as he began rocking up into her. More water splashed over the edge of the brass tub as he claimed her in earnest, watching closely as the pain still evident in her face faded into pleasure.

Emily met every thrust, her features softening with a magical glow that Wylder could not tear his eyes away from. The entire universe seemed to center on this one patch of Earth, narrowing until nothing mattered other than this woman who had claimed his heart and soul. A woman who was now the entirety of his universe. When she reached her orgasm, there was such a look of dazed wonderment on her features that Wylder could not contain his own reaction. His cock jerked and pulsed as she quivered around him, the helpless shuddering of her body demanding that he join her in bliss.

With a muffled shout of conquest, Wylder exploded inside her, both of his hands now gripping her buttocks to hold her in place as his seed poured inside her body.

Emily buried her hands into the thick waves of his hair, tugging his head back so that she could breathlessly kiss him. Their tongues tangled and fought as the spasms from their orgasms faded into pleasant waves of aftershocks. Finally stilling, Emily leaned away, gazing deep into Wylder's eyes.

"I love you, Wylder St. Clair," she murmured, her gorgeous blue eyes brimming with tears of happiness and adoration. "I love you."

"And I love you with all that I am," Wylder replied, pushing the curls of her hair off her forehead as he confessed with a chuckle, "Oh, my sweet, little minx. This rakehell has met his match, and I could not be more content." He kissed her again, his tone filled with humor as he said, "Now, let us move to the bed. I want to make love to you again with no danger of flooding the house."

EPILOGUE

SIMON SANK AGAINST the seat of the coach. His head ached from too much whisky the night before. All attempts to fill the emptiness inside him, to somehow deal with the fact he was now the sole rakehell left standing, were for naught.

By now, every guest attending the ball the night before knew that Wylder and Emily had been wed in a secret ceremony. The scandalous event was the highlight of the afternoon, and his parents were busy fielding questions and proclaiming how excited and pleased they were. There was sure to be some minor gossip, but it would be tempered by breathy sighs of the utter romanticism of a rakehell stealing away with his love and marrying her underneath everyone's noses. The new couple was sure to be celebrated, and the ton would absolutely adore their boldness.

Simon rubbed his forehead, willing the ache there to subside, but knowing it would not. While he'd been furious over Wylder's actions in seducing his sister, now, in the bright, unforgiving light of day, he admitted to a tiny twinge of happiness for the couple. And while he acknowledged that, he was also dealing with the unusual sense of being alone in the world.

Both of his closest friends had fallen in love. They were married. They had willingly given up the moniker of "rakehell" for the title of "devoted husband." Speculation was sure to follow. Would Simon be the next to fall from the pedestal the trio had placed themselves upon?

Simon's jaw tightened. "I will not find myself trapped into compliance. I will continue seeking pleasure and freedom as I see fit. No matter how disappointed Mother and Father may be with my actions."

It was why he'd left Thorne Park that very afternoon. He needed to submerge himself back into the hazy world of gambling and wicked women. That world where he did as he pleased with none to answer to. Of course, he would now travel that path alone, but he was perfectly fine with that. Indulging his vices would take precedence over anything else. And now that he was purchasing his own townhome, he would gain the freedom to come and go as he wished without the frowning censure of his own father.

Once he'd checked in with his solicitor regarding the Curzon Street property, he would make a much-needed visit to The Grinning Cockerel for an evening of blissful forgetfulness and fulfillment of illicit vices.

Simon's body tightened with anticipation... it had been too long since he'd enjoyed the attentions of a submissive woman kneeling at his feet. His fingers twitched with the need to possess and command a lovely, willing female who would obey and fulfill his every wish. Such encounters never failed to make him feel as though control, elusive and seductive, was back in his grasp. After all, this was who he truly was. A man floundering in a world of strict duty and expectations... a man who craved those moments of power... of dominance... and needed them to feel somewhat whole.

So, he would do what he did best as a young, handsome, entitled lord of one of the most powerful families in all of England. He would sin with the best of them and laugh while doing so. As the last Rakehell of Mayfair, he would show all of London just how much he enjoyed that nefarious title.

And all the pleasures that came with it.

The End

About the Author

April enjoys writing both historical and contemporary/dark romance with a generous splash of heat. When not penning tales of passion, she enjoys traveling with her husband, attending rock concerts with friends, and time spent with family. Brainstorming new storylines is best done while riding her horse or during long walks with her German Shepherd. A tumbler of good whiskey helps tie all the details together and brings her characters to life.

VISIT APRIL'S WEBSITE
www.aprilmoranbooks.com

SIGN UP FOR NEWSLETTER AND UPDATES
http://bit.ly/AprilMoran_BookUpdates
April Moran Book Updates

FOLLOW APRIL EVERYWHERE
facebook.com/AuthorAprilMoran
facebook.com/groups/aprilshoneybees
bookbub.com/profile/april-moran
instagram.com/aprilmoranbooks
goodreads.com/Author-AprilMoran
pinterest.com/aprilmoranbooks
tiktok.com/@authoraprilmoran